THE SEVENTH SHOT

THE SEVENTH SHOT

Harry Coverdale

WILDSIDE PRESS

Originally published in 1924.

Published by Wildside Press for release in countries where it is in the public domain.
Visit us online at wildsidepress.com.

CHAPTER I
"BROOK TROUT FOR TWO"

IT WAS TWELVE O'CLOCK—A hot, sunny noon in the latter part of August. Broadway blazed with the last fiery effort of the passing summer; there was a steady stream of humanity pouring up and down on either side of the clanging cars, and occasionally swirling between them. In spite of the temperature, New York was as fervently busy as usual, especially here on what is affectionately known as the Rialto. For in nearly every theater in the Forties rehearsals had begun, and those actors who were not already employed were frantically hunting jobs. Gone the brief weeks in which they had forgotten calcium and make-up boxes; it was nearly September—time to work.

Chorus girls, half dead from three hours of ceaseless dancing, came hurrying from stage doors, wiping their dripping faces and talking shrilly of new steps, tired legs, and the brutalities of their stage managers. "Principals," in scarcely less haste, repaired to one of the big restaurants for a cold buffet lunch, wearing the blank, concentrated expression that is born of trying to memorize lines or to estimate the cost of new costumes. Clean-shaven young men, all dressed precisely alike, forgathered on street corners or plunged pallidly into cafés. Shabby little actresses, out of work and wearing their best clothes of last year, scurried anxiously from agent to agent.

A few stars sank wearily into touring cars or limousines and flew homeward for an hour and a half of rest and refreshment before the long, grinding, sweltering afternoon. Stage managers, with scripts sticking out of their pockets and a grim and absent glare in their eyes, strode along, mentally blue-penciling the prompt book and cursing the company. Authors crept miserably away to eat without appetite and wonder if there would be any play at all left by the date of the opening. In short, theatrical Broadway was at one of its most vigorous seasons of activity, and to walk along it was like turning the pages of a dramatic newspaper.

At the side door of one of the big, cool, luxurious hotels extensively patronized by the profession when it has enough money in its pockets, two young women nearly ran into each other, laughed, and exchanged greetings:

"Miss Legaye! How nice to see you again!"

"It has been ages, hasn't it? Are you lunching here, too, Miss Merivale?"

"I hardly know," returned the younger and taller girl, adding, with a frank laugh: "I was wondering whether it would be too sinfully extravagant to blow myself to a gilt-edged meal all alone. However, I believe I had about succumbed to temptation; I have a manager to see this afternoon, and I really think I should fortify myself."

"Lunch with me," suggested Kitty Legaye. "I hate my own society, and I am all alone."

"For a wonder!" laughed the other. "Yes, I'd love to, if you'll let it be Dutch. I've been up and down a thousand pairs of stairs this morning, and I'm nearly dead."

They went together into one of the most comfortable dining rooms in the city. They chose a little table so placed that an electric fan, artificially hidden behind flowering plants, swept it with a very fair imitation of aromatic summer winds.

Miss Legaye, who always knew exactly what she wanted, waved aside the menu proffered by the waiter and rapidly ordered: "Brook trout in aspic for two. I'll tell you the rest later."

Then she tossed off her fur neckpiece and turned to the other girl.

"I never asked you if you liked trout!" she exclaimed, in a sweet, rather high voice which her admirers called "larklike." "Now, that's so like me! Do you?"

"Very much," said her companion, smiling. "I don't often get it, though. You are looking awfully well, Miss Legaye!"

"I am always well," replied Kitty Legaye.

She was an exceedingly pretty woman, already in her early thirties, but even by daylight she did not look more than twenty-five. On the stage, with the glamour of rouge and footlights to enhance her naturally youthful appearance, she passed easily for a girl in her teens. Very small, very dainty, with the clear, ivory-white skin which keeps its freshness so well, big dark eyes, brown curls, and a very red, tiny, full mouth, she still made an enchanting ingénue and captivated every one who saw her.

To-day she was entirely charming in one of the innocently sophisticated frocks she particularly loved to wear—a creation of black and white, most daring in effect, though demurely simple in cut. Always pale by nature, she was doubly so now from fatigue and heat, yet she still looked young and lovely, and her smile had the irresistible and infectious quality of a child's.

If at times her eye grew a bit cynical or her pretty mouth a trifle hard, such slips in self-control occurred seldom. As a rule she kept a rigid guard upon herself and her expressions, not only because an obviously ugly mood or reflection made her look older, but because, if permitted to become a habit, it would be perilously and permanently aging.

Kitty Legaye was too truly clever not to know that her one valuable asset, both as an actress and a woman, was her quality—or illusion—of youth. When she lost that, she shrewdly judged, she would lose everything. She was not a sufficiently brilliant actress to continue successfully in character work after her looks had gone. And so far as her personal and private life was concerned she had lived too selfishly to have made a very cozy human place for herself in the world.

Not that she was a disagreeable or an unkind woman; she could even be generous on occasion, and she was almost always pleasant to her associates; but the spirit of calculation which she strove so hard to keep out of her face had left its mark upon her life. She had few close friends, though she liked many persons and many persons liked her. She had long since drifted away from her own people, and she had never been willing to give up her independence for the sake of any man. So, in spite of a great number of admirers and a remarkably handsome salary, her existence seemed just a little barren and chilly sometimes.

We have said that she never had been willing to give up her independence. That had been true all her life until now. To-day she was considering just that proposition. Did she care enough, at last, to marry? Love—she had had no small measure of that all her life, for Kitty was by way of being temperamental; but marriage! That was another and a vastly more serious matter.

She looked almost wistfully across the table at Sibyl Merivale. For a moment she had an unaccountable impulse to confide in her. She wished she knew her well enough. She looked, Kitty thought, like the sort of girl who would understand about this sort of thing—loving enough to get married, and—and all that.

Sybil was as unlike Miss Legaye as she well could be. She was tall, and built strongly though slenderly, like a young Artemis, and her eyes were very clear and starry and blue. Her hair was of that rare and delicious shade known as *blonde cendrée*, and the silvery, ashen nimbus about her face made her brown eyebrows and lashes effective. Her skin was very fair, and her color came and went sensitively. She was not a beauty; her nose was decidedly *retroussé*, and her mouth too large. But she was unquestionably sweet and wholesome and attractive, and her lovely forehead and the splendid breadth between her eyes suggested both character and intelligence.

Kitty looked disapprovingly at the dust-colored linen dress she wore; it was far too close to the tint of her hair to be becoming. Blondes, thought Kitty, could wear almost any color on the face of the earth except—just that!

However, she felt rather pleased than otherwise that Miss Merivale was not looking her best. When she appeared in public with another woman, she was well satisfied to have the other woman badly dressed. She herself never was.

Both women were honestly and healthily hungry, and talked very little until they were half through the trout. Then they met each other's eyes and laughed a little.

"Thank goodness you don't pretend not to have an appetite, like most girls!" said Miss Legaye. "I'm starved, and not a bit ashamed of it! Boned squab, after this, waiter, and romaine salad."

"If you let me eat so much I shall be dull and stupid," declared Sybil. "And I want to be extra brilliant to talk to my manager. I simply have to hypnotize him into engaging me!"

"Who is he?"

"Altheimer."

"Altheimer! You aren't going into musical comedy, surely?"

Sybil flushed a bit and bent over her plate to hide her discomfort.

"I—I'm going into anything I can get," she answered in a low voice. Then she smiled and went on more bravely: "I've been out of work since March, Miss Legaye. Beggars can't be choosers."

"Oh, dear—how horrid!" Miss Legaye felt sincerely sympathetic—for the moment. "It's a thousand pities that you have to go into one of the Altheimer shows. You can really act, and there—well, of course, he doesn't care about whether you can act or not; he'll take you for your figure." And she looked the other girl over candidly.

Sybil flushed again, but answered promptly: "I think he has some sort of part for me—a real part. He knows I don't sing or dance. You are rehearsing, aren't you, Miss Legaye?"

"Yes; with Alan Mortimer."

"I wish you'd tell me what you think of him!" said Sybil, with interest. "He's such a mystery to every one. His first play, isn't it? As a star, I mean."

"Yes; Dukane is trying an experiment—starring an unknown actor in a Broadway production. Pretty daring, isn't it? But Dukane doesn't make many mistakes. He knows Alan Mortimer will make good. He's got a lot of personality, and he's extremely attractive, I think. I—saw a good deal of him down at Nantucket during the summer."

Kitty Legaye never blushed, but there was a certain soft hesitancy about the way in which she uttered the simple words that was, for her, the equivalent of a blush. Sybil, noting it, privately concluded that there had been something like a romance "down at Nantucket during the summer."

Being a nice girl, and a tactful one, she said gently:

"Is it a good play, do you think?"

Miss Legaye shrugged her shoulders carelessly; the moment of sentiment had passed.

"It's melodrama," she rejoined; "the wildest sort. 'Boots and Saddles' is the name, and it's by Carlton; now you know."

They both laughed. Carlton was a playwright of fluent and flexible talent, who made it his business always to know the public pulse.

"What time is your appointment with Altheimer?"

"Quarter past one."

"What an ungodly hour! Doesn't the man ever eat? But finish your lunch comfortably; if you're late he'll appreciate you all the more. Besides——"

She paused, regarding the girl cautiously and critically; and that evanescently calculating look drifted across her face for the space of a breath.

"Besides what?" demanded Sybil. "If I lose that part, I'll sue you for a job! Besides what?"

Kitty, for all her pretty, impulsive ways, rarely did things without consideration; so it was with quite slow deliberation that she answered Sybil's question with another:

"Would you like to come with Alan Mortimer?"

"Mercy!" The girl put down her knife and fork and stared with huge blue eyes. "Do you mean to say that there's a part open—after rehearsing ten days?"

"How do you know how long we've been rehearsing?" queried the older woman.

Sybil grew delicately pink. "I know a man in the company," she confessed, laughing shyly. "Norman Crane—oh, he's only got a little bit of a part; perhaps you haven't noticed him, even. It's a big company, isn't it? But he's quite keen about your play."

"Norman Crane?" repeated the other thoughtfully. "Why, yes, I know him. A tall, clean-looking fellow with reddish hair and a nice laugh?"

"That's Norman! He isn't a great actor, but—he's quite a dear."

Miss Legaye nodded slowly, still regarding her. The notion which had come to her a minute before seemed to her more and more markedly a good notion, a wise notion—nay, even possibly an inspired notion! Mortimer's leading woman, Grace Templeton, was a brilliant blonde with Isoldelike emotions, and Kitty had loathed and feared her from the first, for the new star swung in an orbit that was somewhat willful and eccentric, to say the very least of it, and his taste in feminine beauty was unprejudiced by a bias toward any special type.

For a long time Kitty had yearned to get rid of Miss Templeton. If the thing could possibly be managed, here was a girl of undoubted talent—she had seen her act and knew that she had twice the ability of the average young player—presentable, but not too radiantly pretty, and proper and conventional and all that—not at all the sort of girl who would be likely to have an affair with the star. And then, if she was interested in young Crane, why, it would be altogether perfect!

"So you know Norman Crane," she said. "Then if you did come into the company, that would make it particularly nice for you, wouldn't it?"

"Why, yes," the girl returned, frankly enough. "We're quite good friends, though I don't see much of him these days. We used to play together in stock out West two years ago; we were both most awful duffers at acting."

Kitty Legaye nodded as though fairly well satisfied. It was on the tip of her tongue to say that she would try to get Sybil a small part in the play, with the chance to understudy Miss Templeton—it was all she could even partially promise until she had conferred with Dukane and Mortimer—when her attention was sharply distracted by the sight of two men who had just entered the room and who were looking about them in choice of a table. She uttered a quick exclamation, as quickly suppressed.

"Look at those two men standing near the door!" she said. "There, close to the buffet. What do you think of them? Do tell me: I've a reason for asking."

Sybil's eyes followed hers.

The two men were both noticeable, but one of them was so striking in appearance that one hardly had eyes for any one else near by. He was a very tall, very broad, very conspicuous type of man. Everything about him was superlative—even the air of brooding ill temper which for the moment he seemed to wear. He was exceedingly dark, with swarthy coloring, coal-black hair, thick and tumbled, and deeply set black eyes. His features were strong and heavy, but well shaped. Indeed, he was in his general effect unquestionably handsome, and the impression which he made was one not lightly to be felt nor quickly to be forgotten.

"Well?" insisted Miss Legaye impatiently, as Sybil did not immediately speak. "I asked you what you thought of him." This time she did not say "them," but Sybil did not notice the altered word.

The girl continued to look at the tall, dark man as though she were mesmerized, and when she spoke it was in a curious, detached tone, as she might have spoken if she were thinking aloud.

"He is a very strange man," she said. "He does not belong here in a Broadway restaurant. He should be somewhere where things are wild and wonderful and free—and perhaps rather terrible. I think he belongs in—is it

Egypt? He would be quite splendid in Egypt. Or—the prairies——" She spoke dreamily as she stared at him.

"You look as though he were a ghost, not a man!" exclaimed Kitty, with a laugh. "I must tell him what you said——"

"Tell him?" repeated Sybil, rousing herself. "You know him, then?"

"My dear child," said Kitty Legaye, "that is Alan Mortimer!"

At the same moment Mortimer caught sight of her and strode toward her, passing between the fragile little luncheon tables with the energy of a whirlwind.

"Guess what has happened now!" he exclaimed in a deep but singularly clear and beautifully pitched voice. "Dukane has fired Templeton, and apparently I open little more than two weeks from to-night without a leading woman! What do you know about that!"

"Without a leading woman? No, you don't, either," promptly rejoined Kitty, the inspired. She always liked a neat climax for a scene, especially when she could supply it herself. "I've just picked out Miss Merivale to play *Lucille*."

Breathless and amazed, Sybil looked up to meet his eyes. They were dark and piercing. At first she thought only of that, and of their fire and beauty. Then something obscurely evil seemed for a transient second to look out of them. "What an awful man!" she said to herself. But he was holding out his hand.

"Did you think of that all by yourself, Kit?" he said. A faint but rather attractive smile lightening his moody eyes. "How do you do—Lucille? You may consider the engagement—ah—confirmed."

But Sybil, as she drew her hand away, felt vaguely frightened—she could not have told why.

CHAPTER II
THE WOMAN IN PURPLE

MORTIMER HAD BEEN DRINKING, else he would never have assumed the entire responsibility of engaging Sybil Merivale for the leading part in his play. When sober, he had a very wholesome respect for Dukane, the producing manager who had discovered him and who was "backing him blind" to the tune of many thousands of dollars. But when he had even a little too much to drink, the man's whole personality and viewpoint underwent a metamorphosis. He became arrogant, self-assertive, unmanageable. Eventually it was this, as even his friends and adherents were wont to prophesy, which would be the means of his downfall.

Now, though Dukane himself stood at his elbow, the actor, with a swagger which he had too much sense to use on the stage or when he was entirely himself, cried:

"Let us sit down here with you, Kitty, and we'll drink the health of the new *Lucille*." Kitty smiled indulgently as she watched him seat himself and give a whispered order to the waiter which presently resulted in the party being served with high balls. Meanwhile, as Dukane also sat down, Kitty introduced him to Sybil.

Dukane was short and squarely built, with gray hair and steely eyes, a face as smooth and bland as a baby's, and an air so gentle and unassuming that his occasional bursts of biting sarcasm came upon his victims as a shock. His gaze, clear yet inscrutable, swept Sybil Merivale in the moment taken up by his introduction to her. He was used to thus rapidly appraising the material presented him.

He was inclined to approve of her appearance. She was not startlingly beautiful, but the hair was unusual and would light up well. She carried her head properly, too, and her low-voiced "How do you do, Mr. Dukane!" was quite nicely pitched. It would be worth while hearing her read the part, at any rate. For once Mortimer had not too crassly put his foot in it, as he was apt to do after four or five high balls.

That the actor had taken a good deal too much upon himself in practically engaging Miss Merivale without even consulting his superior troubled

Dukane not a whit. He was not a little man, and he did not have to bluster in order to assert his authority. His actors and actresses were to him so many indifferently controlled children. When they said or did absurd things, he usually let them rave. If they really became troublesome or impertinent—as Miss Templeton had been that morning—he discharged them with the utmost urbanity and firmness.

He sat down and quietly told the waiter to bring him cold meat and coffee, while Mortimer ordered more high balls. "Miss Merivale can come back with us and read the part in the last act," Dukane said, sipping his coffee. "I shan't ask the company to go through the early part of the play again to-day. In any case"—and he smiled at the girl pleasantly—"in any case, Miss Merivale will look the part."

"That's more than Templeton ever did!" exclaimed Kitty Legaye, with open spite.

Dukane smiled once more. "Miss Templeton," he said, "is rather too—er—sophisticated to play *Lucille*. She is growing out of those very girlish leading parts."

"Why don't you say," interposed Kitty sharply, "that she's too old? She is—and, what's more, she looks it!"

"She's a ripping handsome woman, all the same," declared Alan Mortimer, scowling into his half-emptied glass.

Kitty bit her lip. "Of course *you* would be sorry to see her go!" she began.

"Who said I was sorry?" demanded the actor rather rudely. "I am not; I'm glad. She was getting to be a nuisance——" He checked himself, a glimmer of something like shame saving him in time. He turned to Sybil Merivale, and there was a warm light in his black eyes as he added: "I'm growing more glad every minute."

Sybil was uncomfortable. She hated this man and feared him; she hated the tone of the talk, the atmosphere of the table. She had a violent instinct of repugnance when she thought of joining the company. And yet—and yet a leading part, and on Broadway, and under Dukane! She could not, she dared not lose so wonderful a chance. Her big blue eyes were eager and troubled both at once.

Dukane watched the play of expression in her sensitive face. "Mobile mouth—quick emotions—excellent eyes." He went over these assets mentally. Aloud he said, in the nice, impersonally friendly tone with which he won people whenever he had the fancy: "You need only read the part, you know, Miss Merivale. You're not committed to anything."

Sybil looked at him gratefully; he seemed to read her thoughts. All at once, with a surge back of her usual gay courage, she cried, laughing:

"Committed! I only wish I were—or, rather, that *you* were, Mr. Dukane!"

"What's that?" exclaimed Mortimer, a little thickly. "'Course he's committed! You're under contract, Miss—Miss M-Merivale. Word as good as his bond—eh, Dukane?"

He was deeply flushed and his eyes glittered. In his excitement Sybil found him detestable. Fancy having to play opposite that!

"Suppose you eat something," suggested Dukane, pushing a plate with a piece of cold beef on it in his direction. "Oh, yes, you do want it; you've had a hard morning. Eat it, there's a good fellow."

"A-all right," muttered Mortimer, attacking the beef somewhat unsteadily. "Must keep up m' strength, I s'pose."

A waiter leaned down to him and murmured something in French.

"Eh?" said Mortimer. "Come again, George. Try Spanish; I know the greaser lingo a bit."

The waiter spoke again in halting English. The others could hardly help hearing part of what he said. It concerned a "lady in mauve—table by the window—just a minute, monsieur."

"Oh, damn!" ejaculated Alan Mortimer, and immediately directed an apologetic murmur toward Sybil. He got up, and walking with surprising steadiness and that lithe, animal grace so characteristic of him, made his way toward a table where a woman sat waiting with an expectant face.

"Grace Templeton!" exclaimed Kitty under her breath. Her brown eyes snapped angrily. "I didn't see her before—did you, Mr. Dukane?"

"I saw her when I first came in," answered the manager quietly. "That hair is so conspicuous. Really I think she should begin to confine herself to adventuress parts. She is no longer the romantic type."

"*And* the dress!" Kitty shivered with a delicate suggestion of jarred nerves or outraged taste.

Dukane dropped his eyes to hide the twinkle in them. It was true that even in that lunch-time Broadway assemblage, in which brilliant color combinations in the way both of hair and of garments proclaimed right and left the daring and the resourcefulness of womankind, Miss Templeton was a unique figure. Her hair was of a magnificent metallic gold, and a certain smoldering fire in her black-fringed gray eyes and a general impression she gave of violent and but half-controlled emotions saved her beauty from being merely cheap and artificial and made it vivid and compelling. A passionate, unforgettable woman, and her gown, sensational as it was, somehow expressed her.

The French waiter had drawn upon his fund of native tact in calling it mauve. It was, as a matter of fact, a sharp and thunderous purple—the sort of color which is only permissible in stained glass or an illuminated tenth century missal. It was a superb shade, but utterly impossible for any sort of modern clothes. It blazed insolently against the massed greenery of the restaurant window. A persistent ray of yellow August sunshine, pushing its way past the cunningly contrived leafy screen, fell full upon it and upon the burnished golden hair above it. In that celestial spotlight Miss Templeton was almost too dazzling for unshaded mortal eyes.

Now, as she sat looking up at Mortimer, who stood beside her table, her expression was in keeping with the gown and the hair. It was violent, conspicuous, crudely intense. Alan Mortimer's expression, in its way, was as violent as hers. They looked, the two of them, as though they could have torn each other's eyes out with fierce and complete satisfaction.

"Am I very late, Mr. Dukane?" said an agreeably pitched voice just behind Sybil.

Dukane started and raised his eyes. His face brightened.

"Barrison, my dear fellow, I am glad you came! Do you know, you were so late that I had almost forgotten you! Miss Legaye, let me present Mr. Barrison; Miss Merivale, Mr. Barrison."

The newcomer smiled and sat down at the already crowded little table.

"If you say you had forgotten me," he protested, "I shall think you did not really need me at all, and that would be a hard blow to my vanity."

"Nonsense!" said Dukane. "Nothing could touch the vanity of a dyed-in-the-wool detective. What are you going to have, Barrison?"

"I have lunched, thanks. If that is coffee—yes, I will have a demi-tasse. I thought Mr. Mortimer was to be with you, Mr. Dukane."

"He is talking to Miss Templeton over there."

Barrison's eyes darted quickly to the other table. "Your leading woman, is she not?"

"She was," said Dukane calmly. "At present we are not sure whether we have any leading woman or not—are we, Miss Merivale?" And he looked at her kindly.

"And, what is more," said Kitty Legaye irritably, "we shall never find out at this rate. Do you people realize"—she glanced at a tiny gold wrist watch—"that it is nearly two, and that our rehearsal——"

"Nearly two!" Sybil's exclamation was one of real dismay. "And my engagement with Mr. Altheimer——Oh!"

"Altheimer, eh?" Dukane looked at her with fresh interest. Whether a manager wants an actress or not, it always makes him prick up his ears to hear of another who may want her. "Telephone him that you have been asked to rehearse for me to-day, and that"—he paused, considering—"that you personally look upon your contract as very nearly signed."

"Oh, Mr. Dukane!" Sybil flushed brilliantly. At that moment she forgot her dread of being in Mortimer's company; she was conscious of pure joy and of nothing else.

"There—run along and phone him. You understand," he added cautiously, "I'm not really dependable. If you are very bad, I shall say I never thought of engaging you."

"I won't be," she laughed valiantly, and sped away in the direction of the telephone booths.

Dukane turned to watch the way she walked. In a second he nodded. "Can hurry without scampering," he murmured critically, "and doesn't swing her arms about. H'm! Yes, yes; very good."

"What do you really think of her?" asked Kitty, leaning forward. "You know she is my discovery."

"My dear girl, who am I, a mere worm of a manager, to say? I haven't seen her work yet. She has carriage and a voice, but she may lose her head on the stage and she may read *Lucille* as though she were reciting the multiplication table. I should say she was intelligent, but one never knows. I engaged a woman once who was all dignity and fine forehead and bumps of perception and the manner born and all the rest of it; and when it came to her big scene, she chewed gum and giggled. I am too old ever to know anything definitely. We must wait and see."

"She is charming to look at," Barrison ventured.

"Ah, you think so?" said the manager quickly. "I am inclined to like her looks myself. And she has youth—youth!" He shook his head half wistfully. "Here comes Mortimer back again, and in a worse temper, by the powers, than when he went!"

The actor was evidently in a black mood. He made no reference to the woman he had just left, but stood like an incarnate thundercloud beside his empty chair and addressed the others in a voice that was distinctly surly in spite of its naturally melodious inflections:

"What are we waiting for, anyway? Hello, Barrison! Let's get back to rehearsal."

"My own idea exactly," said Dukane. "As soon as Miss Merivale returns——Ah, here she comes! Waiter——"

"This is my party," remonstrated Kitty.

"Rubbish! I feed my flock. Barrison, you are of the flock, too, for the occasion. How do you like being associated with the profession?"

The young detective laughed. Dukane looked at him with friendliness. The manager was a man who liked excellence of all kinds, even when it was out of his line. Barrison's connection with the forthcoming play, "Boots and Saddles," was a purely technical one. A vital point in the drama was the identification of a young soldier by his finger prints. Dukane never permitted the critics, professional or amateur, to catch him at a disadvantage in details of this kind. He knew Barrison slightly, having met him at the Lambs' Club, and found him an agreeable fellow and a gentleman, as well as an acknowledged expert in his profession. So he had asked him to show the exact Bertillon procedure, that there might be no awkwardness or crudity in the development of the stage situation.

Barrison himself was much entertained by this fleeting association with the seductive and mysterious world "behind the scenes." His busy life left him small time for amusement, and for that reason he was the more interested when he came upon a bit of professional work which was two thirds play.

He was a quiet-seeming chap, with innocent blue eyes, a lazy, pleasant manner, and a very disconcerting speed of action on occasion. His superiors said that half of his undoubted success came from his unexpectedness. It is certain that no one, on meeting him casually and socially, would ever have suspected that he was one of the most redoubtable, keen-brained, and steel-nerved detectives in all New York.

The bill was paid, and every one was standing as Sybil came back. She was a little breathless and flushed, and Dukane, with a new note of approbation on his mental tablets, got a very good idea of what she would look like with a bit of make-up.

"I told Mr. Altheimer," she cried eagerly. "And he was quite cross—yes, really *quite* cross! I was ever so flattered. I don't believe he wanted me one bit till he thought there was a chance of Mr. Dukane's wanting me." She laughed joyously.

"Very likely, very likely," Dukane murmured. "Why—what is the matter, Miss Merivale?"

For the pretty color had faded from Sybil's sensitive face. Her big blue eyes looked suddenly dark and distressed. "What is the matter?" the manager repeated, watching her closely.

She pulled herself together and managed a tremulous smile.

"Some one is walking over my grave," she said lightly.

But as she turned to leave the dining room with the rest, she could not help another backward glance at the brilliant figure in purple with the golden sunbeam across her golden hair, and the odd look which had just terrified her.

Barrison, accustomed to noticing everything, followed her gaze, and, seeing the expression on Miss Templeton's face, drew his lips into a noiseless whistle. For there was murder in that look; Jim Barrison had seen it before on other faces, and he knew it by sight.

As for Sybil, the memory of the woman in purple haunted her all the way to the theater—the woman in purple with the black-fringed eyes full of living, blazing, elemental hate.

CHAPTER III
THE "TAG"

THE STAGE ENTRANCE OF the Mirror Theater was on a sort of court or alley which ran at right angles from one of the side streets near Times Square. A high iron gateway which barred it except during theatrical working hours stood half open, and the little party made their way over the stone flags in the cool gloom cast by the shadow of the theater itself and the neighboring buildings—restaurants, offices, and shops. It looked really mysterious in its sudden dusk, after the midday glare of the open street.

"Do you know," said Jim Barrison, "this is the first time I have ever gone into a theater by the stage door!"

"What a record!" laughed Miss Legaye. She was in excellent spirits, and inclined to flirt discreetly with the good-looking and well-mannered detective. "And so you never had a stage-door craze in all your properly conducted life! Don't you think it's high time you re—no, it isn't reformed I mean, but the reverse of reformed. Anyway, you should make up for lost time, Mr. Barrison. Ah, Roberts! I suppose you thought we were never coming. Every one else here?"

She was speaking to the stage doorkeeper, a thickset man of middle age, with a stolid face that lighted up somewhat as she addressed him. He did not answer, but beamed vacuously at her. She was always charming to him, and he adored her.

They went on into the theater. Barrison was taken in tow by Dukane. "Hello, Willie! Mr. Barrison, this is Mr. Coster, my stage manager, and I am inclined to dislike him, he knows so much more than I do. Mr. Barrison is a detective, and has come to help us with those finger-print scenes, Willie."

"Pleased to meet you," said Willie, absently offering a limp, damp hand. "Gov'nor, is it true you've canned G. T.?"

"Quite true," said Dukane cheerfully. "Let me present you to Miss Merivale. She will rehearse *Lucille*."

"Lord!" groaned Willie, who was hot and tired and disposed to waste no time on tact. "About two weeks before——"

Mortimer lurched forward. "Say!" he began belligerently. "She's my lead-ing lady—see? Any one who doesn't like——"

"Oh, go 'way and take a nap!" interrupted Willie, without heat. He was no respecter of persons. "So *that's* it! All right, gov'nor. I'm glad to see any sort of a *Lucille* show up, anyhow. Even if she's bad, she'll be better than nothing. No offense, Miss Merivale."

"I quite understand," said Sybil, so sweetly that Willie turned all the way round to look her over once more with his pale, anxious eyes.

"Come on, folks; they're all waiting," he said, and led the way onto the big, bare stage.

Willie Coster was a small, nervous man with a cynical pose and the heart of a child. His scant hair was sandy, and his features unbeautiful, but he was a good, clever, and hard-working little chap, and even the companies he trained were fond of him. He constantly and loudly proclaimed his disgust with all humanity, especially the humanity of the theaters; but he was usually broke because he hated to refuse a "touch," and every one on earth called him Willie.

He was a remarkable stage manager. He was a true artist, was Willie Coster, and he poured his soul into his work. After every first night he got profoundly drunk and stayed so for a week. Otherwise, he explained quite seriously—and as every one, including Dukane, could quite believe—he would have col-lapsed from nervous strain.

Only a few electric lights had been turned on. The stage looked dim and dingy, and the auditorium was a vast abyss of unfathomable blackness. Close to the edge of the stage, where the unlighted electric footlights made a dully beaded curve, stood a small table littered with the four acts of the play and some loose sheets of manuscript, presided over by a slim little youth who was Coster's assistant. This was the prompt table, whence rehearsals were, tech-nically speaking, conducted. As a matter of fact, Willie Coster never stayed there more than two minutes at a time.

The company had already assembled. They looked hot, resentful, and ap-prehensive. They stood around in small groups, fanning themselves with newspapers and handkerchiefs, and making pessimistic conjectures as to what was going to happen next.

Every one knew that something had gone wrong between Templeton and the management, and collectively they could not make up their minds whether they were glad or sorry. She had been the leading woman of the show, and every one felt a trifle nervous until reassured that another lead would be forthcoming.

It was Claire McAllister, one of the "extra ladies," who first recognized Sybil.

"Gee, ain't that the Merivale girl?" she exclaimed to the young man who played a junior officer in one very small scene. "I saw her in a real part once, and she got away with it in good shape, too."

The young man to whom she spoke looked up, startled, and then sprang forward eagerly, his eyes glowing.

"Sybil!" he cried gladly.

She turned quickly, and, laughing and flushing in her beautiful frank way, held out both her hands to him.

"Isn't it luck, Norman?" she exclaimed gleefully. "I'm to have a chance at *Lucille!*"

Alan Mortimer had scarcely opened his lips since leaving the restaurant. Now, with a very lowering look, he swung his tall figure forward, confronting Norman Crane.

"I don't think I remember you," he remarked, with an insulting inflection. "Not in the cast, are you?"

Norman, flushing scarlet, started to retort angrily, but Dukane stopped him with a calm hand upon his arm.

"All right, all right, my boy," he said evenly. "You're in the cast, all right; but—come, come! We are rehearsing a play to-day, and not discussing personalities."

In some occult fashion he contrived to convey his meaning to young Crane. It was not the smallest of Dukane's undoubted and unique talents; he knew how to appeal directly and forcibly to a human consciousness without putting the thing into words. Crane, who was extraordinarily sensitive, understood instantly that the manager wished to excuse Mortimer on the grounds of his condition, and that he put it up to the younger man to drop the issue. Wherefore, Crane nodded quietly and stepped back without a word.

It is proverbial that red hair goes with a peppery disposition. Norman Crane's short, crisply waving locks were not precisely red, and his temper was not too savage, but there was a generous touch of fire in both. His hair was a ruddy auburn, and there was in his personality a warmth and glow which could be genial or fierce, according to provocation or occasion. He was a lovable lad, young even for his twenty-three years, with a clean ardor about him that was very attractive, especially to older and more sophisticated persons. Norman Crane was in all ways a fine fellow, as fine for a man as Sybil Merivale was for a woman. They were the same age, buoyant, clear-eyed young people, touched both alike with the spark of pure passion and the distinction of honest bravery.

Dukane was too truly artistic not to appreciate sentiment; in his business he had both to appraise and exploit it. And as he saw the two standing together he experienced a distinct sensation of pleasure. They were so obviously made for each other, and were both such splendid specimens of youth, spirit, and wholesome charm. He determined mentally to cast them opposite each other some day, for they made a delightful picture. Not yet; but in a few years——

The managerial calculations came to an abrupt end as he chanced to catch sight of Alan Mortimer's face.

Intense emotion is not generally to be despised by a manager when he beholds it mirrored in an actor's face, but this passion was a bit too naked and brutal, and it was decidedly out of place at a rehearsal. The man could be charming when he liked, but to-day the strings of his self-restraint were un-keyed. His face had become loose in line; his eyes smoldered beneath lowered lids. Dukane saw clearly revealed in that look what he had already begun to suspect—a sudden, fierce passion for Sybil Merivale.

This sort of thing was nothing new for Mortimer. He was a man who attracted many types of women—some of them inexplicably, as it seemed to male onlookers—and whose loves were as fiery and as fleeting as falling stars. He had made love both to Kitty Legaye and Grace Templeton, playing them against each other not so much with skill as with a cavalier and amused mercilessness which might well have passed for skill. Now he was tired of the game, and, in a temporarily demoralized condition, was as so much tinder awaiting a new match.

Then the youth and freshness of the girl unquestionably attracted him. Alan Mortimer was in his late thirties and had lived hard and fast. Like most men of his kind, he was willing enough to dally by the wayside with the more sophisticated women; but it was youth that pulled him hardest—girlhood, unspoiled and delicate. Dukane, more than a bit of a philosopher, speculated for a passing minute as to whether it was the inextinguishable urge toward purity and decency even in a rotten temperament, or merely the brutish wish that that which he intended to corrupt should be as nearly incorruptible as possible.

But the manager permitted himself little meditation on the subject. He had no wish that others should surprise that expression upon the countenance of his new star.

"Last act!" he called sharply.

Willie Coster glanced at him in surprise. It was unusual for the "governor" to take an active hand in conducting rehearsals.

"How about Miss Merivale?" he said. "Isn't she to read *Lucille*?"

"Here is the part." Dukane took it from his pocket and dropped it on the prompt table. "Miss Templeton—er—turned it in this noon." He suppressed a smile as he recalled the vigor with which Grace Templeton had thrown the little blue-bound booklet at him across his desk. He added: "Let Miss Merivale take the complete script home with her to-night; that will give her the best idea of the character." For Dukane, unlike most of his trade, believed in letting his people use as much brain as God had given them in studying their rôles.

"Then we start at the beginning of Act Four," said Coster. "Here's the part, Miss Merivale. Just read it through for this rehearsal, and get a line on the business and where you stand. Everybody, please! Miss Merivale, you're not on till Mr. Mortimer's line, 'The girl I would give my life for.' Then you enter up stage, right. Ready, Mr. Mortimer?"

The company breathed one deep, unanimous sigh of relief. They had feared that the advent of a new *Lucille* would mean going back and doing the whole morning's work over again. But Dukane was—yes, he really *was* almost human—for a manager!

There were three other persons who had seen Mortimer's self-betraying look as his eyes rested on Sybil Merivale's eager young beauty. One was Norman Crane, one was Kitty Legaye, and one was the detective, Jim Barrison.

Barrison's eyes met those of Dukane for a moment, and he had a shrewd idea that the manager was telegraphing him a sort of message. He resolved to hang around as long as he could and get a word alone with Dukane after rehearsal was over.

At this point John Carlton, the author, arrived. He was a dark, haggard young man, but, though looking thoroughly subdued after a fortnight under the managerial blue pencil, he quite brightened up on being introduced to Barrison.

"Thankful, no end," he muttered in a hasty aside. "Was afraid they'd cut out the whole finger-print business."

"Cut it! Why? No good?"

"Too good!" sighed the discouraged playwright. He had, however, hauled a lagging sense of humor out of the ordeal, for shortly after, he went with Barrison to sit in a box in the dark auditorium, and evolved epigrams of cynic derision as he watched the rehearsal of his play. Barrison found him not half a bad fellow, and before the hot afternoon wore itself out, they had grown quite friendly.

Barrison's own part in the rehearsal was soon disposed of. After he had explained the way the police detect finger prints upon objects that seem innocent of the smallest impression, and illustrated on a page of paper, a tumbler, and the surface of the table, his work was over for the day. Mortimer promised to practice a bit, that the effect might be quite technical and expert-looking. Barrison was to come to another rehearsal in a few days and see how it looked.

Then the detective found himself free to enjoy the rest of the rehearsal, such as it was.

"Which won't be much," Carlton warned him. "This is just a running over of lines for the company, and to start Miss Merivale off. Nobody will do any acting."

"The last act ought to be the most important, I should think," said Barrison.

"Oh, well, so far as action and hullabaloo goes—shots and soldiers and that sort of thing. But it's a one-man play, anyway, and I've had to make that last act a regular monologue. It's all Mortimer. He's A1, too, when he cares to take the trouble. Drunk now, of course, but he's no fool. He'll keep sober for the opening, and if the women don't go dippy over his looks and his voice and his love-making, I miss my guess. Now, watch—this is going to be one of the exciting scenes in the play, so far as action goes. Pure melodrama, but the real thing, if I say it as shouldn't—girl in the power of a gang of ruffians, spies and so forth. Night—dark scene, you know—a really dark scene, with all the lights out, front and back. Pitch black. Just a bit of a wait to get people jumpy, and then the shots."

Willie Coster cried out: "Hold the suspense, folks! No one move. Lights are out now." He waited while ten could be counted; then deliberately began to strike the table with his fist. "One—two——"

"Those are supposed to be shots," explained Carlton.

"Three—four—five—six——"

"That's enough!" interposed Dukane. "The women don't like shooting, anyway."

"All right. Six shots, Mortimer. Now you're coming on, carrying *Lucille*—never mind the business. Miss Merivale, read your line: 'Thank God, it's you—in time!' Right! All the rest of you—*hurry up*! You're carrying torches, you boobs; don't you know by this time what you do during the rescue? Oh; for the love of——"

He began to tell the company what he thought of it collectively and individually, and Carlton turned to Barrison.

"All over but the shouting—and the love scene. Mortimer can do that in great form, but you'll get no idea of it to-day, of course. He isn't even trying."

"He's a good bit soberer than he was, though," said Barrison, who was watching the star carefully.

"Well, I'm inclined to think he is. Maybe he'll wake up and do his tricks, but you never can tell with him. There go the extras off; it's the love scene now."

The last scene in the play was a short, sentimental dialogue between *Tarrant*, the hero, and *Lucille*. Sybil read her lines from the part; Mortimer knew his, but recited them without interest or expression, giving her her cues almost mechanically, though his eyes never left her face, and as they played on toward the "curtain," he began to move nearer to her.

"A little more down front, *Lucille*" said Coster from the prompt table. "*Tarrant* is watching you, and we want his full face. All right; that's it. Go on, *Tarrant*———"

"'What do you suppose all this counts for with me,'" said Mortimer, speaking slowly and with more feeling than he had used that afternoon. "'What does it all amount to, if I have not the greatest reward of all—*Lucille*?'"

Barrison, listening to the sudden passion vibrating in the genuinely splendid voice, thought he could begin to understand something of the man's magnetism. If he really tried, he could make a tremendous effect.

"'But the honors that have been heaped upon you!'" read Sybil, her eyes bent earnestly upon the page before her. "'Your success, your achievements, your———'" She stopped.

"Catch her up quicker, Mortimer!" exclaimed Coster. "We don't want a wait here, for Heaven's sake! Speak on 'your success, your'—speak on 'your.' Now, once more, Miss Merivale!"

"'Your success,'" read Sybil again, "'your achievements, your———'"

"'Honors! Success! Achievements!'" Mortimer's tone was ringing and heartfelt. "'What do they mean to me, *Lucille*—without you? They are so many empty cups; only you can fill them with the wine of life and love———'"

"Noah's-ark stuff," murmured Carlton. "Likewise Third Avenue melodrama. But it'll all go if he does it like that!"

"'Lucille—speak to me———'"

"'You are one who has much to be thankful for, much to be proud of! Your medal of honor—surely that means something to you?'"

"'Ah, yes! I am proud of it—the gift of my country! But it is given to the soldier. The man still waits for his prize! There is only one decoration which I want in all this life, *Lucille*, only one———'"

"*And* so forth—all right!" said Willie, closing the manuscript; for the final line of the play, the "tag," as it is called, is never given at rehearsals.

But Mortimer appeared to have forgotten this ancient superstition of the theater—seemed, indeed, to have forgotten everything and everybody save Sybil and the opportunity given him by the situation.

He caught the girl in his arms and delivered the closing line in a voice that was broken with passion:

"'The decoration that I want is your love, *Lucille*—your kiss!'"

And he pressed his lips upon hers.

Sybil wrenched herself free, flaming with indignation. Crane, very white, started forward. Mortimer, white also, but with a very slight, very insolent smile, wheeled to meet him. But Dukane, moving with incredible swiftness, stood between them. His face was rather stern, but his voice was as level and equable as ever as he said quietly:

"All right, all right—it is the business of the piece. But just a bit premature, Mortimer, don't you think? Suppose we let Miss Merivale get her lines first? There will be plenty of time to work up the action later. Rehearsal dismissed, Willie. Have every one here at nine sharp to-morrow. What's the matter with *you*?"

For Willie Coster was sitting, pale and furious, by the prompt table, swearing under his breath with a lurid eloquence which would have astonished any one who did not know him of old.

"Damn him!" he ended up, after he had exhausted his more picturesque and spectacular vocabulary. "He's said the tag, gov'nor—he's spoken the tag—and queered our show!"

"Oh, rot, Willie!" said Dukane impatiently. "You're too old a bird to believe in fairy tales of that sort!"

But Willie shook his sandy, half-bald head and swore a little more, though more sorrowfully now.

"You mark my words, there'll never be any luck for this show," he declared solemnly. "Never any luck! And when we open, gov'nor, you just remember what I said to-day!"

CHAPTER IV
THE LETTER OF WARNING

"BUT ISN'T IT VERY early to stop rehearsal?" asked Barrison of John Carlton.

"Of course it is. They ought to have gone over the whole act again, and lots of the scenes several times. That rescue stuff was rotten! But it's an off day. Something's wrong; I'm not sure what, though I *think* I know. Oh, well, it's all in the day's work. Wait till you've seen as many of your plays produced as I have!"

"It's as mysterious to me as one of the lost arts of Egypt. I couldn't think out a scene to save my neck."

"And yet," said John Carlton reflectively, "a detective gets an immense amount of raw dramatic material in his business. He must. Now, right here in our own little happy family circle"—he waved an arm toward the stage—"there's drama to burn! Can't you see it—or are you fellows trained only to detect crime?"

"How do you mean—drama?" queried Barrison, seeking safety in vagueness.

"Well," said Carlton, reaching for his hat and stick, "it strikes me that your well-beloved and highly valuable central planet draws drama as molasses draws flies. Pardon the homely simile, but, like most geniuses, I was reared in Indiana."

"He's a queer sort of chap," said Jim, looking at the tall actor as he stood talking to Dukane, his heavy, handsome profile clearly outlined against an electric light.

"Queer? He's a first-class mystery. 'He came like water, and like wind he goes'—though I hope he'll prove a bit more stable as a dramatic investment. Seriously, no one knows anything about him. He's Western, I believe, and I suppose Dukane fell over him some dark night when he was out prospecting for obscure and undiscovered genius."

"He's good looking."

"My son," said Carlton, whose familiarity and colloquialism were in striking contrast to the grandiloquent lines he gave his characters to speak, "wait till you see him in khaki, with the foots half up and a little incidental music on the violins going on! Manly beauty is not a hobby of mine, but I've had experience with matinée idols, and I bet that Mortimer is there with the goods. What are you laughing at?"

"The difference between your stage dialogue and your ordinary conversation."

"Oh, well, I can't help talking slang, and I don't know how to write it so that it sounds like anything but the talk of a tough bunch in a corner joint." He stopped abruptly at the entrance to the box and said, as though acting on impulse:

"See here, speaking of Mortimer, did you ever see a three-ring circus?"

"Yes. I always found it very confusing."

"Me, too. Mortimer doesn't. He likes it. Takes three at least to make him feel homelike and jolly. He's been—between ourselves—the temperamental lover with Grace Templeton, and the prospective fiancé with Miss Legaye; at least, that's how I dope it out; and now it looks as though he was going to be the bold, bad kidnaper with this charming child just arrived in our midst. What do you think, from what you've seen to-day?"

"He hasn't been himself to-day," answered Barrison. "And, anyhow, there can't be a three-ring circus with one of the three features absent. Miss Templeton, I understand, is not to be counted any longer."

He spoke with rather forced lightness. He disliked bringing women into conversation. He did Carlton the justice, however, to see that it was not a vulgar predilection for gossip which centralized his interest in the three who had received Mortimer's attention. Obviously he looked upon them as cold-bloodedly as did Dukane; they were part of his stock in trade, his "shop."

"Not to be counted any longer! Isn't she just? If you'd ever seen the lady you'd know that you couldn't lose her just by dismissing her."

Barrison had seen her, but he said nothing.

"However," went on the author, leading the way out of the box and through the communicating door between the front and back of the house, "it's none of my business—though I'll admit it entertains me, intrigues me, if you like. I *can* talk something besides slang. I'm nothing but a poor rat of an author, but if I were a grand and glorious detective with an idle hour or so to put in, I'd watch that combination. I'm too poor and too honest to afford hunches, as a rule, but I've got one now, and it's to the effect that there'll be more melodrama behind the scenes in 'Boots and Saddles' than there ever will be in the show itself!"

Though Barrison said nothing in reply, he privately agreed with the playwright. Nothing very startling had happened, to be sure, yet he was acutely conscious of something threatening or at least electric in the air—a tension made up of a dozen small trifles which might or might not be important. It would be difficult to analyze the impression made upon him, but he would have had to be much less susceptible to atmosphere than he was not to have felt that the actors in this new production were playing parts other than those given them by Carlton, and that they stood in rather singular and interesting relation to each other.

Mortimer infatuated with Sybil Merivale; Kitty Legaye, he strongly suspected, in love with Mortimer; Crane wildly and youthfully jealous; Miss Templeton in the dangerous mood of a woman scorned and an actress supplanted! It looked like the makings of a very neat little drama, as John Carlton had had the wit to see.

Barrison, however, was still inclined to look upon the whole affair as something of a farce; it was diverting, but not absorbing. There was nothing about it, as yet, to quicken his professional interest. He did, to be sure, recall Grace Templeton's wicked look in the restaurant, and had a passing doubt as to what she was likely to do next; but he brushed it away lightly enough, reminding himself that players were emotional creatures and that they probably took it out in intensity of temperament—and temper! They were not nearly so likely actually to commit any desperate deeds as those who outwardly or habitually were more calm and conservative.

But something happened at the stage door which disturbed this viewpoint.

When they crossed the stage the company was scattering right and left. Miss Legaye was just departing, looking manifestly out of sorts; Sybil and young Crane were talking together with radiant faces and evident oblivion of their whereabouts; Mortimer was nowhere to be seen. Carlton had stopped to speak to Willie Coster, so Barrison made his way out alone.

He found Dukane standing by the "cage" occupied by the doorkeeper, with an envelope in his hand.

"When did this come, Roberts?" he said.

"About twenty minutes ago, sir. You told me not to interrupt rehearsals, and the boy said there was no answer."

"A messenger boy?"

"No, sir—just a ragamuffin. Looked like he might be a newsboy, sir."

Dukane stood looking at the envelope a moment in silence; then he turned to Barrison with a smile.

"Funny thing, psychology!" he said. "I haven't a reason on earth for supposing this to be any more important than any of the rest of Alan Mortimer's notes—the saints know he gets enough of them!—and yet I have a feeling in my bones that there's something quite unpleasant inside this envelope. Here, Mortimer, a note for you."

The actor came around the corner from a corridor leading past a row of dressing rooms, and they could see him thrust something into his coat pocket.

"Went to his dressing room for a drink," said Barrison to himself. Indeed, he thought he could see the silver top of a protruding flask.

"Note for me? Let's have it."

He took it, stared at the superscription with a growing frown, and then crumpled it up without opening it.

"Wrenn!" he exclaimed in a tone of ungoverned rage. "Where's Wrenn? Did he bring me this?"

"Wrenn?" repeated Dukane, surprised. "You mean your valet? Why, no; he isn't here. A boy brought it. Why don't you read it? You don't seem to like the handwriting."

With a muttered oath, the actor tore open the envelope and read what was written on the inclosed sheet of paper. Then, with a face convulsed and distorted with fury, he flung it from him as he might have flung a scorpion that had tried to bite him.

"Threats!" he exclaimed savagely. "Threats! May Heaven curse any one who threatens me! Threats!"

He seemed incapable of further articulation, and strode past them out of the stage door. Barrison could see that he was the type of man who can become literally blind and dazed with anger. Mentally the detective decided that such uncontrolled and elemental temperaments belonged properly behind bars; certainly they had no place in a world of convention and self-restraint.

Quietly Dukane picked up both letter and envelope, and, after reading what was written on them, passed them to Barrison.

"When I have a lunatic to dry nurse," he observed grimly, "I have no scruples in examining the stuff that is put in his feeding bottles. Take a look at this communication, Barrison. I'll admit I'm glad that I don't get such things myself."

Jim glanced down the page of letter paper. On it, in scrawling handwriting, was written:

> You cannot always escape the consequences of your wickedness and cruelty—don't think it! Just now your future looks bright and successful, but you cannot be sure. You are about to open in a new play, and you expect to win fame and riches. But God does not forget, though He seems to. God does punish people, even at the last moment. I should think you would be afraid that lightning would strike the theater, or that a worse

fate would overtake you. Remember, Alan, the wages of sin; remember what they are. Who are you to hope to escape? I bid you farewell, *until the opening night!*

The last four words were heavily underlined. There was no signature.

"What do you make of it?" asked Dukane.

"It's from a woman, of course. Quite an ordinary threatening letter. We handle hundreds of them, and most of them come to nothing at all."

"Possibly," said Dukane thoughtfully. "And yet I don't feel like ignoring it entirely. Not on Mortimer's own account, you understand. He's not the type of fellow I admire, and I don't doubt he richly deserves any punishment that may be in store for him. But he's my star, and if anything happens to him I stand to lose more money than I feel like affording in these hard times."

"I can have a couple of men detailed to keep an eye on him," suggested Barrison.

Dukane shook his head. "He'd find it out and be furious," he returned. "Whatever else he is, he's no coward, and he detests having his personal affairs interfered with. Hello! What is it you want?"

The thin, gaunt, white-haired man whom he addressed was standing, hat in hand, in the alley just outside the stage door, and he was evidently waiting to speak to the manager.

"If you please, sir," he began, half apologetically, "Mr. Mortimer told me to——"

"You're Mortimer's man, aren't you?"

"Yes, sir; I'm Wrenn. I came down in the car for Mr. Mortimer, sir. He—he seemed a bit upset-like this morning." His faded old eyes looked appealingly at the manager.

"He did," assented that gentleman dryly. "You take very good care of Mr. Mortimer, Wrenn," he added, in a kinder tone. "I've often noticed it."

"Thank you, sir. I try——"

"He sent you back for something?"

"Yes, sir." The old servant was clearly anxious and ill at ease, and the answer came falteringly: "A—a letter, sir, that he forgot——"

Barrison had already thrust that letter into his own pocket. He knew that Dukane would prefer him not to produce it. As a specimen of handwriting it was worth keeping, in case of possible emergencies in the future.

Dukane affected to hunt about on the floor.

"Here is the envelope," he said, giving it to the valet. "I don't see any letter. Mr. Mortimer must have put it in his pocket; indeed, I think I saw him do so. He seemed a good deal excited, and probably doesn't remember."

"Yes, sir, but——" Wrenn still hesitated.

"That's all. Go back to your master and say the letter is nowhere to be found. Tell him I said so."

"Yes, sir."

Unwillingly Wrenn walked away.

"A decent old chap," commented Dukane, looking after him. "I can't understand why he sticks to that ill-tempered rake, but he seems devoted to him."

They went out together, and saw Wrenn say something at the window of the great purring limousine that was waiting in the street at the end of the court. After a minute he got in, and the car moved off immediately.

"No," said the manager, as though there had been no interruption to his talk with Barrison, "I hardly think that we'd better have him shadowed, even for his own protection. I think that the writer of that note means to save her—er—sensational effect for the first night, don't you?"

"Well," admitted the detective, "it would be like a revengeful woman to wait until a spectacular occasion of that sort if she meant to start something. Particularly"—he spoke more slowly—"if she happened to be a theatrical woman herself."

"Ah, yes," said Dukane calmly. "Especially if she happened to be a theatrical woman herself."

He was silent for a long minute as they walked toward Broadway. Then, as he stopped to light a cigar, he said:

"Every woman is a theatrical woman in that sense. My dear fellow, women are the real dramatists of this world. If a man wants to do a thing—rob a bank, or elope with his friend's wife, or commit a murder, or anything like that—he goes ahead and does it as expeditiously and as inconspicuously as possible. But a woman invariably wants to set the stage. A woman must have invented rope ladders, suicide pacts, poisoned wine cups, and the farewell letter to the husband. Next to staging a love scene, a woman loves to stage a death scene—whether it's murder, suicide, tuberculosis, or a broken heart. Would any man in *Mimi's* situation have let himself be *dragged* back to die in the arms of his lost love? Hardly! He'd crawl into a hole or go to a hospital."

"It was a man who wrote the story of *Mimi*," Barrison reminded him.

"A man who, being French, knew all about women. Yes, I think we can safely leave our precautions until September the fifteenth. Just the same, Barrison, I shall be just as well pleased if you'll manage to drop in at rehearsals fairly often during the next fortnight. There might be developments. I'll leave word with Roberts in the morning that you are to come in when you like."

Barrison promised, and left him at the corner of Broadway.

As he walked back to his own rooms, Dukane's words lingered in his memory:

"Women are the real dramatists of this world!"

He thought of the same phrase that evening when, while he was in the middle of his after-dinner brandy and cigar, his Japanese servant announced:

"A lady on business. Very important."

Barrison started up, hardly able to believe his eyes. The woman who stood at his door was Miss Templeton!

CHAPTER V
MISS TEMPLETON

SHE WAS IN FULL evening dress, with her splendid shoulders and arms bare, and her brilliant hair uncovered and elaborately dressed. Her tightly clinging gown was black, embroidered in an orchid design of rose color and gold. A long black lace scarf, thrown over one arm, was her only apology for a wrap. She was just then, as Barrison was obliged to confess to himself, one of the handsomest women he had ever seen in his life. He realized now that she was younger than he had thought.

Also she looked far less artificial and flamboyant than she had looked at luncheon. Jim's orange-shaded reading lamp was kinder to her than that intrusively glaring sunbeam had been. There was even a softness and a dignity about her, he thought. Perhaps, though, it was merely a pose, put on for the occasion as she had put on her dinner dress.

Moving slowly and with a very real grace, she came a few steps into the room and inclined her handsome head very slightly.

"Mr. Barrison?"

He bowed and drew a high-backed, brocaded chair into a more inviting position. "Won't you sit down?"

"Thank you. I am Grace Templeton."

"I know," he said, smiling courteously. "I feel enormously honored."

"Ah, yes. You saw me at lunch to-day."

"I have seen you before."

"Really!" Her eyes lit up with genuine pleasure. She was inordinately vain of her stage reputation. She thrilled to the admiration of her anonymous audiences. Jim, looking at her, marveled at that imperishable thirst for adulation which, gratified, could bring a woman joy at such a moment. For he felt sure that it was no ordinary crisis which had brought Miss Templeton to consult him that night.

She sank into the chair he proffered, and the high, square back made a fine frame for the gilded perfection of her hair. He thought, quite coolly, that no one ever had a whiter throat or more exquisitely formed arms and wrists. Her manner was admirable; not a trace now of that primitive and untamed ferocity of mood which had blazed in her whole face and figure not so many hours before.

She was very beautiful, very sedate, very self-contained. Barrison was able to admire her frankly—but never for a second did he lift the vigilance of the watch he had determined to keep upon her. In his own mind he marked her "dangerous"—and not the less so because just at present she was behaving so extremely, so unbelievably well.

"You are surprised to see me here, Mr. Barrison," she said, making it a statement rather than a question.

"I confess that I am."

"I wanted your help, and—when I want a thing I ask for it."

She paused a moment, looking at him steadily. "Won't you please sit down yourself?" she said. "And move your lamp. I like to see the face of the person I am talking to."

Barrison did what she wished silently. In half a minute more they confronted each other across the library table, with the reading light set somewhat aside. Miss Templeton drew a deep breath and leaned forward with her lovely arms upon the table.

"When I heard that you were to be called in as an expert to help in—our—play"—she paused, with a faint smile that was rather touching—"you see, it *was* 'our play' then—I made up my mind to consult you. For I was troubled even then. But the best laid schemes——" She broke off, with a little gesture that somehow made her look younger. "Oh, well—I found myself, in an hour, in a minute, in a position I was not used to: I was dismissed!" She made him feel the outrageousness of this.

"My mind was naturally disturbed," she went on. "It is a shocking thing, Mr. Barrison, to find yourself cast adrift when you have been counting on a thing, believing in it——"

"I should scarcely have thought that it would be so awful," Jim ventured, "for you, who surely need not remain in such a predicament any longer than you care to."

She flashed him a grateful glance. "That is nice of you. But I truly think that it is worse in a case like mine. One grows accustomed to things. It is somewhat appalling to find oneself without them, to find them snatched away before one's eyes. You see, I have never been 'fired' before." She uttered the last words with a surprisingly nice laugh. "It was rather terrible, truly. I asked Alan Mortimer to-day who you were," she said quietly. "When I knew, I determined that I would come to see you."

"And so——" he suggested encouragingly.

She was, if this were cleverness, much too clever to change her gentle, rather grave attitude. "And so," she said, as she leaned upon the table, "I have come to speak to you of the things which a woman does not speak of as a rule."

Jim Barrison was slightly alarmed. "But why come to me?" he protested, though not too discourteously. "We are strangers, and—surely you do not need a detective in your trouble, whatever it is?"

"Why not?" she demanded swiftly. "In your career, Mr. Barrison, have you never found yourself close to the big issues of life, the deep and tragic things? Does not the detective's profession show him the most emotional and terrible and human conditions in all the world? It is as a detective that I want you to help me, Mr. Barrison."

"I—I shall be only too glad," stammered Barrison, with a full-grown premonition of trouble. He wished the woman had been less subtle; he had no mind to have his sympathies involved.

She seemed to guess at something of his worry, for she lifted her black-fringed eyes to his and laughed—not gayly, but sadly. "It's all said very quickly," she told him. "Alan Mortimer used to be in love with me; he is not now."

Barrison found himself dumb. What on earth could a man say to a woman under such circumstances? He was no ladies' man, and such homely sympathy as he had sometimes had to proffer to women in distress seemed highly out of place here. Miss Templeton, in her beauty and her strangeness, struck him as belonging to a class in herself. Resourceful as he was, he had not the right word just then. She did not appear to miss it, though. She went on, almost at once, with the kind of mournful calmness which nearly always wins masculine approbation:

"Understand, there was no question of marriage. I do not claim anything at all except that—he did care for me." She put her hand to her throat as if she found it difficult to continue, and added proudly: "I am the sort of woman, Mr. Barrison, who demands nothing of a man—except love. I believed that he gave me that. There were other women; there was one woman especially. She wanted him to marry her. She did not love him, as I understand love, but she did want to marry him. She had lived a selfish, restless life for a good many years—she is as old as I, though no one knows it—but she had never settled down. She is the type that eventually settles down; I am not. She wants to be protected and supported; I don't. She is a born parasite—what we call a grafter; I am *not*. Perhaps you can guess whom I mean."

"Perhaps I can," conceded Barrison, remembering what Carlton had said about Kitty Legaye and Alan Mortimer.

"Ah!" She smiled faintly. "Very well. Here am I, flung aside from my part—and from him. She is left in possession, so to speak. That is almost enough to send a woman's small world into chaos, is it not? But there was something more left for me to endure. Another woman came into the little play that I thought was fully—too fully—cast. I don't mean Mr. Carlton's play; I mean the one that goes on night and day as long as men and women have red blood in their veins and say what they feel instead of what is written in their parts! Another woman was engaged—or practically engaged—to take my place."

"Yes, I know. Miss Merivale."

"Miss Merivale." She repeated the name slowly and without heat. "She is fresh and young and charming. I do not hate her as I do the other, but I am more afraid of her. She is just what he cannot find in the rest of us. She will win him. Yes, I know quite well that she will win him."

"But I don't think she wants to win him," said Barrison, recollecting the scene in which the "tag" had been prematurely spoken. He had a mental picture of Sybil, scarlet of cheek and indignant of eyes, shrinking from Mortimer's kiss.

But Miss Templeton looked at him almost scornfully.

"He can make her want to," she declared positively. "Don't contradict me, because I know!" Miss Templeton paused a moment and then continued: "Mr. Barrison, do not detectives occasionally undertake the sort of work that necessitates their following a person and—reporting on what he does—that sort of thing?"

"Yes, Miss Templeton."

"And would you undertake work of that kind?" Her fine eyes pleaded eloquently.

"No, Miss Templeton; I'm afraid not."

"But why not? You've said detectives do it."

"Plenty of them."

"Do you mind telling me, then, why not?"

Jim hesitated; then he decided to be frank. "You see," he said gently, "I don't do this entirely as a means of livelihood."

"You mean you're an amateur, not a professional?"

"I am a professional. But, since I can pick and choose to a certain extent, I usually choose such cases as strike me as most useful and most interesting."

"And my case doesn't strike you as either?"

"I don't see yet that you have a case, Miss Templeton. I don't see what there is for a detective to do."

"Then I'll explain. I want you to follow—shadow, do you call it?—Mr. Mortimer every day and every night. I want to know what he does, whom he sees, where he goes. I will pay—anything——"

Barrison put up his hand to check her. "Yes, I know," he said quietly. "I quite understood what you wanted me to do. But your determination, or whim, or whatever we may call it, does not constitute a case."

"I can make you see why. I can tell you the reasons——"

"I'm afraid that I don't want to hear them, Miss Templeton. I simply can't do what you ask me to. I'm sorry. There are detectives who will; you'd better go to them. I don't like cases of that sort, and I don't take them. Again—I'm sorry. Try not to think me too rude and ungracious."

She sat with down-bent head, and he could not see her face. He felt unaccountably sorry, as he had told her he felt. He could not have felt more grieved if he had hurt some one who had trusted him.

Suddenly she flung up her head, and there was another look on her face—a harder, older look.

"All right," she said, in a metallic tone, "you won't help me. I'm sure I don't know why I should help you. But—if you won't shadow Alan Mortimer these next two weeks, you take a tip from me: Shadow Kitty Legaye."

CHAPTER VI
THE DIVIDED DANGER

AS SHE SWEPT TO the door, her golden head held high, her black scarf floating from one round white arm, she encountered a newcomer, one Tony Clay.

"Beg pardon!" he gasped, standing aside.

He was a cherubic, round-faced cub detective whom Barrison liked and helped along when he could—a nice lad, though a bit callow as yet.

Miss Templeton's trailing scarf caught in a chair and Tony hastened to extricate it. Feeling profoundly but unreasonably reluctant, Barrison made the introductions:

"Miss Templeton, may I present Mr. Clay? He will put you in a taxi—won't you, Tony?"

"Rather!" breathed the patently enraptured Tony.

"My car is waiting," Miss Templeton said sweetly. "I shall be so glad if Mr. Clay will see me safely as far as that."

Five minutes later Tony Clay returned, with sparkling eyes and a delirious flow of language:

"I say, Jim, where did you—how did she happen to——Oh, gee! Some people have all the luck! Isn't she a peach? Isn't she a wonder? Isn't she just the——"

"Have a brandy and soda, Tony, and shut up," said Barrison, rather wearily. He was feeling a bit let down, for Miss Templeton was not a restful person to talk to, nor yet to hear talk for any long period.

But Tony raved on. "She reminds me," he babbled happily, "of some glorious, golden lioness——"

"Fine for you!" murmured Barrison, burying himself in a particularly potent drink.

Long after Tony Clay had gone, Jim sat scowling at the cigarettes which he lighted from one another with scarcely an interval, and at the brandy and soda of which he consumed more than what he usually considered a fair allowance. Both as a man and a detective he admired Miss Templeton.

He wished he had seen her handwriting and could compare it with the note which he still kept put away in a locked cabinet where he cached his special treasures. He wondered if——

But her suggestion as to Kitty Legaye, inspired by jealousy as it was, was not without value. On the face of it, it seemed far-fetched, or would have to a less seasoned experience; but Jim Barrison had forgotten what it was to feel surprise at anything. Stranger things—much, much stranger things—had turned out to be quite ordinary and natural occurrences.

There are, as Barrison knew, many varieties of the female of the species; he had come up against a goodly number of them, and could guess what the different sorts would do in given extremities. And he knew that in the whole wild lot there is none wilder, none more secret, none more relentless, none more unexpected and inexplicable, than she who has counted on snatching respectability and domesticity at the eleventh hour and been disappointed. If Kitty Legaye had really expected to marry Alan Mortimer, and if he was getting ready to throw her over for a perfectly new, strange young girl, then one need not be astonished at anything.

Yet, little Miss Legaye seemed a steady bit of humanity, not emotional or hysterical in the least.

"Oh, hang it all!" he muttered resentfully, as he turned out his light at least two hours later than was his habit. "I wish women had never learned to write—or to talk! It would simplify life greatly."

Then he fell asleep and dreamed queer dreams in which Grace Templeton, Kitty Legaye and Sybil Merivale chased each other round and round, quarreling for possession of the anonymous note which for some reason the old man Wrenn was holding high above his head in the center of the group. As the three women chased each other in the dream, Jim grew dizzier and dizzier, and finally woke up abruptly, feeling breathless and bewildered, with Tara, the Jap, standing beside him.

"Honorable sir did having extreme bad dreams!" explained Tara, with some severity of manner.

Barrison answered meekly and lay down again to fall only half asleep this time and toss restlessly until morning.

He kept his word to Dukane and attended rehearsals with religious regularity, though what technical use he had was exhausted after a few days. He found himself becoming more and more interested in the play—or, rather, in the actors who were appearing in it. Their personalities became more and more vivid to him; their relations more and more complex.

Not the least curious of the conditions which he began to note as he grew to feel more at home behind the scenes was the strange, almost psychic influence which Mortimer appeared to have over Sybil Merivale. Almost one might have believed that he hypnotized her; only there was nothing about him that suggested abnormal spiritual powers, and the girl herself was neither morbid nor weak.

Barrison, now at liberty to roam about "behind" as he willed, overheard Miss Merivale one day talking to Claire McAllister, the extra woman.

"Say, I heard him ordering you about to-day as if he had a mortgage on you," said Claire, who was practical and pugnacious. "What do you let him play the grand mogul with you for?"

"I don't believe I can make you understand," said Sybil, breathing quickly, "but I don't seem able to disobey him. When he looks at me I—it sometimes seems as if I couldn't think quite straight."

"D'you mean," demanded Claire McAllister sharply, "that you're in love with him?"

Sybil flushed indignantly. "That's just what I do not mean!" she exclaimed. "Can't you see the difference? I—I hate him, I tell you! It's something outside that, but—but it frightens me. Sometimes it seems, when I meet his eyes, that I can't move—that he can make me do what he likes." She shivered and hid her face in her hands. "It's *that* which makes me so frightened," she whispered in a broken way.

The extra girl regarded her curiously, then hunched her shoulders in the way of extra girls when they wish to indicate a shrug of indifference.

"Well," she remarked cheerily, "when little Morty takes the last high fall, we'll look round to see if there wasn't a certain lady handy to give him the extra shove."

Sybil turned on her quickly. "What do you mean?" she cried. "What do you mean by that?"

Miss McAllister stared in surprise. "Sa-ay!" she remonstrated. "I was just kiddin'! Say, you didn't suppose I thought you were goin' to murder the guy, did you?"

Sybil was rather white. "Awfully silly of me!" she apologized. "Only—sometimes I've felt as though——And it sounded awful, coming from some one else like that."

"Sometimes felt—what?"

"As though—I almost—could!" She turned abruptly and walked away.

Barrison, standing leaning against a piece of scenery, felt a hand upon his arm. He looked around into the agitated face of Norman Crane.

The boy had heard just what he himself had heard, and the effect thereof was written large upon his handsome, honest young countenance.

"Think of her—think of Sybil up against that!" he whispered huskily. "And me able to do nothing! Oh, it's too unspeakably rotten, that's what it is! If I could just wring that bounder's neck, and be done with it——"

"Look here!" said Jim Barrison, losing his cast-iron, chain-held patience at last. "There are about a dozen people already who want to murder Alan Mortimer. I'm getting to want to myself! For the love of Heaven, give a poor detective a rest and don't suggest any one else; I'm getting dizzy!"

Norman stared at him and edged away.

"Does that fellow drink?" he asked Carlton, a few minutes later.

"I hope so," said the author absently, rumpling his hair with one hand while he wrote on a scrap of copy paper. "Mortimer has waited until now to have the last scene lengthened. Maledictions upon him! May his next reincarnation be that of a humpbacked goat!"

Crane left him still murmuring strange imprecations.

Barrison went home, divided between annoyance and amusement at the promiscuous hate Mortimer had aroused. He was unquestionably the most unpopular man he had ever heard of; yet he was sometimes charming, as Barrison had already seen. Several times at rehearsal, when he deliberately had chosen to exert his power of magnetism, the detective, critical observer as he was, could not fail to note how successful he was. His charm was something radiant and irresistible, and he could project it at will, just as some women can. A singular and a dangerous man, Jim decided. Such individuals always made trouble for themselves and for others. The theater was becoming rather electric in atmosphere, and Barrison was glad to get home. But his troubles were not over yet—even for that day!

Just as he was sitting down to dinner Tony Clay appeared, looking hot and unhappy.

"Hello, Tony! Have you eaten?"

Tony nodded in a most dispirited fashion. His friend watched him a moment, and then said kindly:

"Go ahead; what's the trouble?"

The young fellow looked uncomfortable. "Nothing," he began; "that is——Oh, hang it all! I can't lie to you. I'm upset, Jim!"

"No!" said Barrison, with a smile.

"Jim," Tony went on, rather desperately, "do you believe that there ever are occasions when it is permissible to give a client away? To a colleague, I mean. Do you?"

"You just bet your life I do!" said Jim emphatically. He put down his knife and fork and eyed his young friend with kindling interest. "Go on, kid, and tell me all about it."

"Well"—poor Tony looked profoundly miserable—"you know—that is of course you don't know—but—Miss Templeton engaged me to shadow Alan Mortimer."

"I knew that as soon as you did," remarked Jim.

Tony opened his round eyes till each of them made a complete O.

"The devil you did!" he ejaculated, somewhat chagrined. "Well, she did engage me, and I shadowed away to the best of my ability. But now—Jim, I'm up against something too big for me, and I've brought it to you."

He looked pale and shaken, and Barrison said good-humoredly:

"Go to it, Tony. I'll help you if I can."

"Jim!" Tony Clay faced him desperately. "I think you ought to know that Miss Templeton has it in for Mortimer——"

"I do know it, lad."

"And that—she bought a revolver to-day at the pawnshop near Thirty-ninth Street. I saw her. I suppose she got a permit somehow. But I hope I'll never again see any one look the way she did when she came out with the parcel!"

CHAPTER VII
THE DARK SCENE

IT WAS A LITTLE after eight in the evening of September the fifteenth—the opening night of "Boots and Saddles" at the Mirror Theater.

Already the house was filling up. From his seat on the aisle half a dozen rows back, Jim Barrison saw that it was going to be a typical first-night audience. As this was a comparatively early opening, there were a goodly number of theatrical people present, and practically every one in the social world who had already returned to town was to be seen. Max Dukane's productions were justly celebrated all over the country, and Carlton was a popular playwright. Then there was much well-stimulated curiosity in regard to Alan Mortimer. Dukane's press agent had done his work admirably, and the mystery surrounding the handsome new light in the dramatic heavens had been so artistically exploited as to pique the interest even of jaded theatergoers.

It was an oppressively hot evening, though September was so far advanced. All the electric fans in the world could not keep the theater cool and airy. To Barrison the air was suffocating. The gayly dressed people crowded down into neat rows; the hurrying, perspiring ushers in overheavy livery; the big asbestos curtain that shut them all into a simmering inclosure—these things in combination were strangely oppressive, even in a sense imprisoning. Moreover, he was not free from a half-sincere, half-humorous sense of apprehension. Hardly anything so definite, so full-fledged, or so grave; but undoubtedly a mental tension of sorts which would not readily conform to a perfunctory festal spirit.

Dukane, for all his coolness and poise, had insisted on taking the warning letter seriously—at least to the extent of taking every conceivable precaution against danger, of arranging every possible protection for Mortimer. It was understood that, while Jim Barrison had his allotted seat in the front of the house, he would spend most of the evening back of the scenes. Tony Clay was also on duty. There was a husky young guard on the communicating door which was back of the right-hand boxes and opened on the world behind. No one was to be allowed to pass through that door that night but Dukane, Barrison, and his assistant. Roberts, at the stage door, had been similarly cautioned to let no one enter the theater on any pretext whatsoever after the members of the company had come for the performance.

Barrison thought Dukane's precautions rather exaggerated. He did not really think personally that any peril threatened Alan Mortimer that night. Murderers did not, as a rule, send word in advance what they mean to do. Still, such things had happened in his experience, and it was no harm to make sure. As for Miss Templeton and the revolver—well, that looked a bit more serious. He had not told Dukane of Tony's confidential information, but he raked the many-hued audience with his sharp gaze, trying to see if the erstwhile leading woman was present. So far there was no sign of her. He was even inclined to treat Tony's fears as somewhat hysterical. It will be recalled that Miss Templeton had made rather a good impression upon the detective, who was only human, after all, and prone to err like other mortals.

The truth was that the whole situation struck him as a little too melodramatic to be plausible. He was suffering from the disadvantages of being a bit too cool and superior in view, a bit too well-balanced, a bit too much the practical sleuth regarding theatrical heroics with a pleasantly skeptical eye. Nevertheless, cavalierly as he was disposed to treat them, he thought that it was possible that these many concessions to a possible gravity of situation, a more or less apocryphal danger, did add to the feeling of oppression which held him. It really seemed hard to breathe, and it was difficult even for his trained judgment to determine just how much of the sensation was physical and how much psychological.

At all events it was a very close, sultry night. As people came in and took their seats there were constant comments on the weather.

"Humidity—just humidity!" pompously declared a man next Jim, one of those most trying wiseacres who know everything. "You'll see it will rain before the evening is over."

"There's not a breath stirring outside," said the girl who was with him, fanning herself. "I wish we were sitting near an electric fan."

The asbestos drop had gone up, and the orchestra began to play music specially written for the piece. It drowned the chatter of the well-dressed, expectant crowd. But the overture was short, and the lights all over the house soon began to go down in the almost imperceptibly gradual fashion affected by Max Dukane in his big productions. When the other instruments had dwindled to a mere mist of retreating sound, one high, silver-clear bugle played the regimental call, "Boots and Saddles," as a cue for the rise of the curtain upon the first act.

But Barrison was not looking at the stage. Before the last lights had gone out in the front of the house he had caught sight of a woman who had just entered the right-hand stage box. She stood for a moment looking out over the audience before she slipped out of her gorgeous gold-embroidered evening cloak and took her seat.

"Look!" exclaimed the girl to the pompous man—and, though she spoke in an undertone, it was an undertone pregnant with sharp interest, almost excitement. "Look! There's Gracie Templeton, who started rehearsing with this show and got fired. They say she had quite an affair with Mortimer."

"Not much distinction in that," remarked the man. "He's crazy about women."

"Not much distinction either way," said the woman lightly and heartlessly. "Grace has played about with ever so many men. But she isn't altogether a bad sort, you know, and this Mortimer man seems to have the power to make women care for him awfully."

"Do you know him?" demanded her escort jealously.

"Not I!" She laughed. "But seriously, Dicky, I shouldn't think she'd want to come to-night and see him playing with another woman."

"Maybe she means to pull a Booth-and-Lincoln stunt," suggested the pompous man. "She's fixed just right for it if she does."

"Oh, don't! It's horrible just to think of! You're so cold-blooded, Dicky! Hush! The play's beginning. I do like military shows, don't you?"

Barrison did not wait to see the opening of the piece. He had seen it once at dress rehearsal, and, anyway, he had other fish to fry. He slid out of his seat swiftly and almost unnoticeably and made his way without waste of time up the aisle and around in discreetly tempered darkness to the stage box which held Miss Grace Templeton.

As he passed between the box curtains and came up behind her, she did not hear him, and he stood still for a moment before making any move which would reveal his presence. In that moment he had noticed that she was dressed entirely in black, that melancholy rather than passion was the mood which held her, and that she was watching the stage less with eagerness than with a wistful, weary sort of attention. She leaned back in her chair, and her hands lay loosely folded in her lap. There was about her none of the tension, none of the excitement, either manifest or suppressed, that accompanies a desperate resolve.

Barrison felt the momentary chill of foreboding, which certainly had crept up his spine, pass into a warmer and more peaceful sentiment of pity. He slipped into a chair just behind her without her having detected him. This, too, was reassuring. People with guilt, even prospective guilt, upon their consciences were always alert to interruption and possible suspicion. She was looking fixedly at the stage where Mortimer was now making his first entrance.

He was a splendid-looking creature behind the footlights. Barrison had been obliged to admit it at dress rehearsal; he admitted it once more unreservedly now. Whatever there was in his composition of coarseness or ugliness, of cruelty, unscrupulousness, or violence, was somehow softened—no, softened was not quite the word, since his stage presence was consistently and notably virile; but certainly uplifted and tinged with glamour and colorful charm. Every one else in the company paled and thinned before him.

"A great performance, is it not?"

Jim spoke the words very gently into her ear, and then waited for the inevitable start. Strangely enough, in spite of the suddenness of the remark, she barely stirred from the still pose she had adopted. Dreamily she answered him, though without pause:

"There is no one like him."

Then all at once she seemed to wake, to grow alive again, and to realize that she was actually talking to a real person and not to a visionary companion. She turned, with a startled face.

"Mr. Barrison! I thought I was quite alone, and—what did I say, I wonder? I felt as though I were half asleep!"

"You voiced my thoughts; Mortimer is in splendid form, isn't he?"

She nodded. "I never saw him to better advantage," she said, speaking slowly and evidently weighing each word. "Watch him now, Mr. Barrison, in his scene with *Lucille*. So much restraint, yet so much feeling! Yes, a superb impersonation!"

Barrison looked curiously at the woman who spoke with so much discrimination. Was she really capable of being impersonal, disinterested? Yes, he believed that she was. A certain glow of returning confidence swept his heart; it was surely not she whom he had to fear—if, indeed, there were any one. He made up his mind to take a look at what was taking place behind the scenes, and rose to his feet, resting his hand lightly, almost caressingly, on the back of Miss Templeton's chair.

"Good-by, until later," he murmured. "I am going back to pay my respects to Dukane."

And as he spoke, his fingers closed upon the beaded satin bag which she had hung upon the back of her chair. Something uncompromisingly hard met his sensitive and intelligent touch. Instantly he withdrew his hand as though it had met with fire. There was a pistol in that pretty reticule; so much he was sure of.

A moment later he tapped lightly on the communicating door, and, meeting the eyes of the suspicious young giant on guard there, and speedily satisfying him as to his reliability, passed through into the strange, bizarre world of scenery and grease paint and spotlights with which he had lately become so familiar.

"Remember," he said to the blue-capped lad with the six inches of muscle and the truculent tendency, who stood as sentinel at that most critical passageway, "no one—no one, Lynch—is to go through this door to-night. Understand?"

"Right, sir!"

Barrison made his way through a labyrinth of sets to where Dukane, against all precedent, was standing watching the performance from the wings.

"You ought to be in front," the detective told him reprovingly.

"Indeed!" Dukane looked at him with tired scorn. Then he fished a paper out of his waistcoat pocket. "Read this. It came this afternoon."

The new letter of warning ran:

No man can run more than a certain course. When you look with love at the woman who claims your attention to-night, do you not think what might happen if a ghost appeared at your feast? You have called me wild and visionary in the past. Will you call me that when this night is over?

Having read it and noted that the writing was the same as the previous one, Jim asked: "Have you shown this to Mortimer?"

"Am I an idiot?" demanded Dukane pertinently. "No, my prince of detectives, I have not. I have troubles enough without putting my star on the rampage. Just the same, I think it is as well to be prepared for anything and everything. What do you think?"

Unwillingly Barrison told him that he was not entirely happy in his mind concerning Miss Templeton. He asked minutely as to where Mortimer was going to stand during various parts of the play, notably during the dark scene in the last act. That, to his mind, offered rather too tempting a field for uncontrolled temperaments.

"Ah!" said Dukane once more, looking at him. "You have found out something, eh? Well, no matter. Whether you suspect something or not, you are going to help, you are going to be on guard. Miss Templeton, now—do you think it would be a good thing for you to go and spend the evening with her in her box?"

Barrison did not think quite that, but he consented to retire to Miss Templeton's box for at least two acts. The which he did, feeling most nervous all the time, as though he ought to be somewhere else. Miss Templeton was most agreeable as a companion, and most calm. Once in a while his eyes would become glued to the beaded bag hanging on the back of her chair. Just before the last act he fled, and sent Tony Clay to take his place on a pretext. He did not think he could stand it any longer.

Behind, he found a curious excitement prevailing. No one had been told anything or warned in any way, yet a subtle undercurrent of suspense was strongly to be felt. There is no stranger phenomenon than this psychic transmission of emotion without speech. To-night, behind the scenes at the Mirror Theater, the whole company seemed waiting for something.

Sybil Merivale seemed particularly nervous.

"I can't think what has got into me!" she said with rather a shaky little laugh. "I wasn't nearly so upset at the beginning of the play, and usually one gets steadier toward the end of a first night. I'm doing all right, am I not?"

"You're splendid!" Kitty Legaye said cordially. "I'm proud of you! You have no change here, have you?"

"No; I'm supposed to be still in this white frock, locked up in the power of the border desperadoes."

"And I, praise Heaven, am through!"

Kitty did sound profoundly grateful for the fact. Barrison thought she looked very tired and that her eyes were rather unhappy. She had played her part brilliantly and gayly, appearing, as usual, a fresh and adorable young girl. Now, seen at close range, she looked both weary and dispirited under the powder and grease paint.

"I'm awfully fagged!" she confessed. "And my head is splitting. I think I'll just sneak home."

"Oh, but Mr. Dukane will be wild!" exclaimed Sybil in protest. "Isn't it a fad of his always to have the principals wait for the curtain calls, no matter when they've finished?"

"Oh, stuff! We're through with the regulation business, all of us bowing prettily after the third act, and Jack Carlton trying to make a speech that isn't unintelligible with slang! That's enough and to spare for one night. And I really feel wretched. Like the Snark, I shall slowly and silently vanish away! I call upon you, good people, to cover my exit."

She slipped into her dressing room, and a moment later the dresser, Parry, whose services were shared by her and Sybil, came out. She was a fat, pasty woman whose long life spent in the wardrobe rooms and dressing rooms of theaters seemed to have made her pallid with a cellarlike pallor.

She disappeared around the corner that led to the stage door, and in a minute or so returned. As she opened Kitty's door and entered, Barrison heard her say:

"All right, Miss Legaye; Roberts is sending for a taxi."

Of the dressing rooms Kitty's was the farthest back, Sybil's next, and Mortimer's—the star room—so far down as to be adjoining the property room, which was close to what is professionally known as "the first entrance." There Willie Coster and his assistant ruled, supreme gods, over the electric switchboard. The passage to the stage door ran at right angles to the row of dressing rooms, so that any one coming in or out at the former would not be visible to any one standing near one of the rooms, unless he or she turned the corner made by the star dressing room. This particular point—the turning near Mortimer's door—was further masked by the iron skeleton staircase which started near Sybil's room and ran upward in a sharp slant to the second tier of dressing rooms where the small fry of the company and the extras dressed.

It is rather important to understand this general plan. Make a note, also, that Mortimer's big entrance in the "dark scene," or, rather, at the close of it, must be made up a short flight of steps; that the scene was what is called a "box set"—a solid, four-walled inclosure; that it was but a step from the door of his own dressing room, and that the spot where he had to stand waiting for his entrance cue was in direct line, from one angle, with the stage door, and from another with the door communicating with the front of the house. This wait would be a fairly long one, since, when the dark scene was on, no lights of any sort would be permitted save perhaps the merest glimmer to avoid accidents. The actors were all expected to leave their lighted dressing rooms and have their doors closed before the melodramatic crash upon the stage told them that the property lantern had been duly smashed and that blackness must henceforth prevail until the "rescue."

"All ready?" came Willie Coster's anxious voice. "The act is on. Miss Merivale, don't stumble on those steps when you are trying to escape. You nearly twisted your ankle the other night. This is a rotten thing to stage. Lucky Carlton made it about as short as he possibly could. Playing a whole act practically in the dark! Fred, put that light out over there; it might cast a shadow."

"'Tain't the dark scene yet!" growled the harassed sceneshifter addressed. He put it out, however.

"My cue in a moment!" whispered Sybil. "I must run! Where are my two deep-dyed ruffians who drag me on?"

"Present!" said one of them, Norman Crane, laughing under his breath.

They hurried down to their entrance, where the other "deep-dyed ruffian" awaited them.

Kitty Legaye, in a vivid scarlet satin evening coat, stole cautiously out of her dressing room.

"Shut that door!" commanded Willie in a sharp undertone. "No lights, Miss Legaye!"

Parry closed it immediately.

"And now, Mortimer!" added the stage manager in an exasperated mutter. "Of course he'll let it go until the last moment, and then breeze out like a hurricane with his dressing-room door wide open and enough light to——What is it?" And he turned to hear a hasty question from his assistant.

Kitty came close to Barrison and whispered beseechingly:

"Do, please, tell Mr. Dukane that I only went home because I really did feel ill. It's—it's been quite a hard evening for me." Her brown eyes looked large and rather piteous.

Barrison was sorry for her. She seemed such a plucky little creature, and so glitteringly, valiantly gay. Her red wrap all at once struck him as symbolic of the little woman herself. She was defiantly bright, like the coat. If her heart ached as well as her head, if she really was disappointed, hurt, unhappy—why, neither she nor the scarlet coat proposed to be anything but gay!

She waved her hand and tiptoed lightly away in the direction of the stage door. Barrison turned to look through a crack onto the stage. They were almost—yes, they were actually ready for the dark scene.

In another moment the lantern crashed upon the floor. There were shouts from the performers, and audible gasps from the audience. For a full half minute not a light showed anywhere in the house.

Barrison felt oddly uncomfortable. The confusion, the noises from the stage, the inky blackness, all combined to arouse and increase that troubled, suffocating feeling of which he had been conscious earlier in the evening. The dark seemed full of curious sounds that were not all associated with the play. He almost felt his hair rise.

A single one-candle electric bulb was turned on somewhere. Its rays only made the darkness more visible, rendered it more ghostly.

A hand grasped his arm.

"I thought—I saw a woman pass!" murmured Dukane's voice. "Hello! There goes Mortimer to his entrance. He's all right so far, anyway." The actor's huge bulk and characteristic swagger were just visible in the dimness as he left his room, closing the door behind him at once. "Barrison, like a good fellow, go out to Roberts and find out if any one has tried to come in to-night."

Dukane's tone was strangely urgent, and Barrison groped his way to the stage door.

The old doorkeeper, when questioned, shook his head.

"No one's passed here since seven o'clock," he declared emphatically. "No one except Miss Legaye, just a minute ago."

"You're sure?"

"Sure!" exclaimed the man, misunderstanding him. "I guess there ain't any two ladies with a coat the color of that one! I see it at dress rehearsal, and it sure woke me up. I like lively things, I does; pity there ain't more ladies wears 'em."

Barrison laughed.

"I didn't mean that," he said. "I know Miss Legaye went out; but you're sure no one came in?"

"I tell you, no one's gone by here since——"

Barrison did not wait for a repetition of his asseverations, but went back toward the stage. The "rescue scene" was just beginning. Willie Coster, a faint silhouette against the one dim bulb, was conducting the shots like the leader of an orchestra:

"One! Two! Three! Four! Five! Six!"

The six shots rang out with precision and thrilling resonance. And then Jim Barrison grew icy cold from head to foot.

For there came a seventh shot.

And it was followed by the wild and terrifying sound of a woman's scream.

CHAPTER VIII
AWAITING THE POLICE

THAT SCREAM ECHOED ACROSS the blackness. There was a smell of gunpowder in the air. It seemed an interminably long time before the lights flared up, and the big curtain was rung down. At last it formed a wall between the people on the stage and the people in the audience, all about equally excited by this time.

"What is it—oh, what is it that's happened?" gasped Claire McAllister.

Other women in the company echoed the bewildered and frightened cry. Panic was loose among them—panic and that horror of the unknown and uncomprehended which is the worst of all horrors. "What is it?" ran the quivering question from mouth to mouth like wind in the grass.

Barrison and Dukane knew what had happened even before, with one accord, they dashed to the little flight of steps where Mortimer must have been waiting for his entrance cue. One look was enough. Then the manager's voice, clear and authoritative, rang out:

"Quiet there, every one. Mr. Mortimer has been shot."

And swiftly upon the startling statement came Barrison's command, given with professional sharpness:

"Nobody is to leave the theater, please, until the police have been here!"

Shuddering and silent now, the men and women drew back as though the quiet figure upon the floor were a living menace, instead of something which never again could commit an action of help or of harm.

Alan Mortimer must have died instantly.

He lay at the foot of the steps, with his painted face upturned to the blaze of the glaring electric lights, and an ugly crimson patch of moisture upon the front of his khaki uniform. There was something indescribably ghastly in the sight of the make-up upon that dead countenance.

Old Wrenn, the valet, was kneeling at the side of his dead master, trying to close the eyes with his shaking, wrinkled fingers, and making no attempt to hide the tears that rolled silently down his cheeks. But, after one look into the stony, painted face of the murdered man, Jim Barrison turned his attention elsewhere.

At the head of the four little steps stood Sybil Merivale, in the white cos-tume of *Lucille*, as motionless as if she were frozen, with her hands locked together. No ice maiden could have been more still, and there was a chill horror in her look.

"Miss Merivale," said Barrison quickly, "you were standing there when he was shot?"

Slowly she bent her head in assent, and seemed to be trying to speak, but no sound came from her ashen lips.

"Was it you who screamed?"

"I—think so." She spoke with obvious difficulty. "I was frightened. I think—I screamed. I don't know."

Then every one who was watching started and suppressed the shock they felt; for she had moved her hands at last—the hands which had been so convulsively clasped before her. And on her white frock was a long splash of scarlet. One of the slim hands, as every one could see, was dyed the same sinister hue.

She raised it, and looked at it, with her eyes dilating strangely.

"His blood!" she murmured, in a barely audible voice.

Dukane had sent Willie Coster out before the curtain to disperse the audi-ence. The police had been sent for; the doors were guarded. Some of the girls in the company were sobbing. Only Sybil Merivale preserved that attitude of awful calm. She seemed unable to move of her own volition, and remained blind and deaf to every effort to help her down the four steps.

It was young Norman Crane, finally, who took her hand in both his, and gently made her descend. Then, as she stood there, looking like a pale ghost in her white dress with the rather dull make-up that the scene had demanded, the boy put his arm gently around her.

"It's all right, dear," he said tenderly. "Don't look so wild, Sybil. Of course, it was a shock to you, but you must rouse yourself now." He looked at Barrison as he spoke, and the detective thought that there was a touch of defiance in his tone as he emphasized the words, "Of course it was a shock to you." He seemed anxious to establish definitely this fact.

Jim quite understood and sympathized with him. That Sybil had had any-thing to do with Mortimer's death the detective did not for a moment believe, but her position was certainly an equivocal one. This young actor was clearly in love with her, and the situation must be an agonizing one for him.

In confirmation of his conclusions, Barrison heard Crane say to Dukane:

"Miss Merivale and I are engaged to be married, sir. She is very much upset, as you see. Will you let me take her to her dressing room?"

Dukane looked doubtfully at Barrison, who shook his head.

"I shall be very grateful if Miss Merivale will stay where she is until the police come," he said courteously, but firmly. "You might see if you can't find her a chair." For he had no desire to let a witness out of his sight at this stage of the game.

Norman Crane flushed under his make-up. "I think you are going rather far!" he exclaimed hotly. "Surely you don't think——"

"I think," said Barrison, deliberately cutting him short, "that you had better get the chair, and—has any one any brandy? Miss Merivale looks very bad indeed."

Old Wrenn spoke in a tremulous voice. "There is some in his—in the dressing room, sir."

He went off and brought it, then stood once more beside the body, wiping his shriveled old cheeks. Barrison, seeing his evident and genuine grief, made a mental chalk mark to the credit of Alan Mortimer. There must have been some good in the man, some element of the kind and the lovable, to have won the devotion of this old servant.

Crane held the brandy to Sybil's lips, and she drank a little mechanically. After a moment or so, her eyes became less strained, her whole expression more natural, and instead of the frozen blankness which had been in her face before, there now dawned a more living and at the same time an inexplicable fear. She looked up at the face of her young lover with a sort of sharp question in her blue eyes, a look which puzzled Jim Barrison as he caught it. What was it that she was mutely asking him? What was it that she was afraid of?

It had been scarcely five minutes since Mortimer's murder, yet already it seemed a long time. They all felt as though that still figure on the floor had been there for hours. Dukane would have had the dead man moved to his dressing room, but Barrison insisted that everything should be left as it was. It was just then that he espied a small object glittering on the floor just beyond the steps. He stooped, picked it up, and put it in his pocket. As he turned he saw, to his surprise, Tony Clay approaching.

The older detective stared and frowned.

"Where is Miss Templeton?" he demanded sharply. "I told you to stay with her whatever happened. Where is she?"

"That's what I want to know," said Tony. "She's gone!"

"Gone! When did she go?"

"Just before the dark scene. She felt faint and sent me for a glass of water. Before I got back, all that row on the stage started, and when the lights were turned on again, she'd gone; that's all."

"All!" groaned Barrison despairingly. "Tony, you fool! You fool! Well, it's too late to mend matters now."

"Did anything happen, after all?" asked Tony, with round eyes.

Barrison stood aside and let him see Mortimer's dead body, which had been hidden from his view by the little group around Sybil.

"Oh, Heaven!" gasped Tony, horror-stricken. "Then you don't think she—Miss Templeton—did it? Why, Jim, she couldn't—there wasn't time!"

"I don't think so myself. But it's not our business to do any thinking at all—just yet. This can be a lesson to you, Tony. When you're watching a person, *watch 'em!*"

"Well, I think it can be a lesson to you, too!" said Tony unexpectedly. "You've been acting all along as though this affair were a movie scenario, that you thought was entertaining, but not a bit serious, and——"

Jim Barrison flushed deeply and miserably. "I know it, Tony," he said, in a very grave voice. "Don't make any mistake about it; I'm getting mine! I'll never forgive myself as long as I live."

Willie Coster came up to them. He was paler and wilder-eyed than ever, and his scant red hair stood stiffly erect. Poor Willie! In all his long years of nightmarish first nights, this was the worst. Any one who knew him could read in his eyes the agonized determination to go and get drunk as soon as he possibly could.

"The police inspector has come," he said, in a low tone. "And, say, when you get to sifting things down, I've something to say myself."

"You have! You know who fired the seventh shot?"

"I didn't say that. But if you'll ask me some questions by and by, I may have something to tell you."

CHAPTER IX
RECONSTRUCTING THE CRIME

INSPECTOR LOWRY WAS AN old friend of Barrison's, though, like most of the regular force, inclined to treat the younger man as a dilettante rather than an astute professional. However, he was quite ready to include Jim in the investigation which he set about making without loss of time.

Lowry was a big, raw-boned man of middle age, with a peculiarly soft, amiable voice, and a habit of looking at almost any point on earth save the face of the person to whom he was speaking. This seemingly indifferent manner gave him an enormous advantage over any luckless soul whom he chanced to be examining, for when he shot the question which was of all questions the most vital and the most important, he would suddenly open his eyes and turn their piercing gaze full upon his victim. That unfortunate, having by that time relaxed his self-guard, would be apt to betray his innermost emotions under the unexpected gaze.

Naturally, the first thing to do was to get Sybil Merivale's story.

His manner to the girl was not unkindly. She was a piteous figure enough, as she sat drooping in the chair they had brought her, trying to keep her eyes from turning, with a dreadful fascination, to the spatter of red upon the steps so near her. Norman Crane stood at her side, with the air of defying the universe, if it were necessary, for her protection. Once in a while she would look up at him, and always with that subtle expression of apprehension and uncertainty which Barrison found so hard to read.

"Miss—ah—Merivale? Quite so, quite so. Miss Merivale, if you feel strong enough, I should be glad if you would tell us what you know about the shooting." The inspector's voice was mild as honey, and his glance wandered about this queer, shadowy world behind the scenes. It is doubtful if he had ever made an investigation in such surroundings. To see him, one would have said that he was interested in everything except in Sybil Merivale and what she had to tell.

"I don't know anything about it," she answered simply.

"But you were quite close to him when he was shot, were you not?"

"Yes." She shuddered, and looked down at the stain of blood upon her dress. "He was just taking me up in his arms to carry me on——"

"That was in the—ah—action of the play?"

"Yes. After the six shots, I heard another, and felt him stagger. I slipped to the floor, and he fell at once. He put out his hand to catch at the scenery." She pointed to the canvas door of the stage set which still stood open. "I felt something warm on my hand." She closed her eyes as though the remembrance made her faint. "Then he—he fell backward down the steps. That's all."

"Ah, yes." The inspector thought for a moment, and then he said to Dukane: "Would it be possible for every one to go to the places they occupied at the moment of the shooting? I am assuming that every one is here who was here then?"

"Every one; so far as I know, no one has been allowed to leave the theater. Willie, tell them to take their places."

Willie caused a rather ghastly sensation when he called out: "Everybody, please! On the stage, every one who is in the last act!"

There was a murmur among the actors.

"Good Lord!" muttered Claire McAllister. "They ain't goin' to rehearse us *now*, are they?"

Dukane explained, and with all the lights blazing, the players took the positions they had occupied at the beginning of the dark scene. Stage carpenters and sceneshifters did the same; also Willie and his assistant, even Dukane and Barrison. The woman Parry and old Wrenn went into the dressing rooms, where they had been, and closed the doors. Sybil Merivale mounted the little flight of steps and stood at the top, looking through the open door onto the stage.

"Is that just the way you stood?"

Every one answered "yes" to this question.

One or two things became apparent by this plan, which rather surprised Barrison. He had not, for one thing, realized how close Willie Coster stood to the place where Mortimer fell. Yet, of course, he should have expected it. It was, as a matter of fact, Willie who directed the six shots, which were supposed to come from the point back of *Tarrant's* entrance. There were, as it turned out, at least three persons who were so close as to have been material witnesses had there been any light: Willie, the man who fired the shots and had charge of other off-stage effects, and—Norman Crane.

Crane took up his position immediately inside the box set, close to the doorway.

"Is that where you stood?" asked Lowry.

"Yes. I played the part of a Mexican desperado, and was supposed to be on guard at the door leading down into the cellar, which was the stage."

"The door was open, as it is now?"

"Yes."

"Then you could have seen through it anything that happened on the steps off stage?"

"I could have if there had been light enough."

"As it was, you didn't see anything?"

"No."

"Didn't hear anything?"

The young man seemed to pause for just a moment before he said "No," to this question also. If the inspector noticed his hesitation, he did not appear to do so. He began to talk in an undertone to one of the men who had come with him.

John Carlton had been sending in frantic messages ever since the tragedy, begging to be permitted to come behind, but the allied powers there agreed that there were enough people marooned as it was. There was nothing to be gained by adding another, and one whom it would probably be unnecessary either to hold or to bind with nervousness and disappointment.

In an undertone, Dukane said to Jim Barrison: "I thought they always sent for a doctor first of all? Why isn't there one here?"

"There is," returned Jim, in the same tone. "He's over there with the two policemen and the plain-clothes man who came in with Lowry—the little, old fellow with spectacles. Lowry'll call on him again in a moment; he examined the body and pronounced life extinct. That was all that was absolutely necessary. Lowry has his own way of doing things, and he's supreme in his department. He's 'reconstructing the crime' just now."

Barrison, indeed, was listening with gradually increasing interest. This method which was being employed by Inspector Lowry, sometimes known as the "reconstruction-of-the-crime" method, was rather old-fashioned, and many younger and more modern men preferred the more scientific, analytical, and deductive ways of solving mysteries. Yet there was something distinctly fascinating, even illuminating, about the inspector's simple, sure-fire fashion of setting his stage and perhaps his trap at one and the same time. Barrison felt his own veins tingle with the leap of his roused blood.

"Barrison," said Lowry pleasantly, "just go up there on those steps, and be Mortimer for a minute. So!" The younger man obeyed with alacrity. "Miss Merivale, was that about where he stood?"

"Yes."

"And you are sure that you yourself were just where you are now?"

"Yes."

"Just there, you know. Not more to the right?"

She glanced at him with faint wonder.

"I think I may have been a little more to the right," she said. "That is, to your right, and my left. But I don't see why you thought so—and it doesn't matter, does it?"

"And you, Mr. Crane," pursued the inspector, paying no attention to her last words, "you are absolutely certain of where you stood?"

"Absolutely."

"Ah, yes, quite so; quite so!" murmured Lowry, looking dreamily into space. Suddenly he faced about and said sharply: "Mr. Crane, will you kindly lift your right hand and point it at Mr. Barrison? Just so; exactly! At that range, you could hardly have missed him."

Norman Crane clenched his fists in a white heat of indignation. "You dare to imply——"

"Only what your fiancée has already been fearing," said the inspector calmly, "that your position in this matter is, to say the least, not less unpleasant than hers. You were, as is evident, only a few feet away from the man."

Crane started to speak, but checked himself. Barrison thought he knew what he would have said; or, if he was not going to say it, he should have, for the direction of the bullet was a thing which ought to be easily determined. But something prevented the young actor from uttering anything resembling a protest; it was simple to see what it was.

Sybil Merivale, however unwillingly or unconsciously, had given color to suspicion against him by the low, heart-broken sobbing into which she had broken at the bare suggestion.

After one quick look at the obvious distress of the young girl whom he loved so well, Norman Crane suddenly changed his antagonistic attitude. He faced the detectives quietly, and said to them, in a manner that was not without dignity:

"Very well. I admit that it looks bad for me. I suppose that is enough? If you feel that you have any case at all against me, I shall make no trouble. Do you mean to arrest me?"

The inspector looked at him rather more directly than was his wont, and also longer.

At last he allowed himself to smile, and though he was known to be a hard man with even possible criminals, the smile was singularly pleasant just then.

"Bless you," he remarked tranquilly, "that's all a matter for our medical friends to settle! If the bullet entered the body at a certain angle and a certain range, it will let you out."

"Then all this," exclaimed Crane angrily—it was so like a boy to be most enraged when most relieved—"all this is waste of time—pure theatrics?"

But at this point Willie Coster interfered. "Say, Mr. Inspector," he said, awkwardly but determinedly, "I'm not crazy about a spotlight on myself, but just here there's something I ought to say. I was pretty close by, myself, you understand."

"Exactly where you are now?"

"Yes. And until the lantern was broken in the scrap scene, there was a little light shining through that door from the stage. See?"

"Yes!" It was not only the representatives of the law who listened eagerly now. "Go on, man, go on!"

"Well"—Willie hesitated, gulped, and plunged ahead—"I saw a woman's shadow on the wall, and she had something in her hand. That's all I wanted to say."

"Something in her——A revolver?"

"I don't know."

"Would you be prepared to—ah—say that you recognized the shadow?"

"I would not. One woman's shadow's much like another, so far as I can see; and the women, too, for that matter! I never troubled to tell 'em apart!"

"And you won't even express a—ah—an impression as to whether what this shadow woman held was a weapon or not?"

"No!" snapped Willie impatiently. "Why should I? I didn't think about it at the time. I was waiting to time those shots. All I know is that it was a woman, and that she was holding something. She had something in her hand."

"I'd give something if I had it in mine!" muttered the inspector fervently, more fervently than he usually permitted himself to speak when on a case.

Barrison put his hand in his pocket and drew out the thing which he had found in the shadow of the miniature stairway. He thought it the proper time to hand it over, and he said:

"I think you have it now, Lowry! The barrel was still warm when I picked it up a few minutes after the murder."

CHAPTER X
FACTS AND FANCIES

A SHORT WHILE LATER the inspector addressed them mildly:

"I very often get a great deal of blame because I won't do things in a regulation way. But, even while I get the blame, I also get the results—sometimes, not always." The inspector looked around him thoughtfully, and repeated: "Not always. As most people know, the first thing we must do in locating a crime is to find out who could have done it; next, who wanted to do it. The opportunity is valueless without the wish; the wish is not enough without the opportunity. But, of the two essential points, the opportunity is the big thing. For instance, some one standing in Miss Merivale's position—I mean, of course, her physical position—might have that opportunity. It also seems to me that some one standing on the stage level, on the right of the steps, and reaching upward, would have practically the same opportunity."

He took the little pistol and balanced it lightly in his big hand. Then he walked over to the point at which the weapon had been found at the side of the steps which was farthest from the front.

He raised his arm and pointed at Barrison, who still stood where Mortimer had been standing.

"You see," he said, "it could have been done this way. The bullet would have entered the body under the right arm as he picked Miss Merivale up, supposing her story to have been true."

"Then," exclaimed Norman Crane eagerly, "that eliminates both Miss Merivale and myself from the suspects!"

"It surely eliminates you," rejoined the police officer calmly, "because you couldn't have thrown this gun through the door so that it fell where it did fall, unless you were a particularly skillful baseball pitcher; and then you couldn't! But, as for Miss Merivale—Miss Merivale, we will suppose that you are going to shoot this man; please consider Mr. Barrison in that light. He is taller than you; the weapon you use may be held close to your side to avoid detection."

"I had no weapon!" she flashed.

"Naturally not, naturally not!" agreed the inspector, with a pacific wave of his hand. "But you might have had, you know——"

"How could——"

"Pouf, pouf, my dear Miss Merivale! How you carried it—or, rather, could have carried it, is a secondary matter. I never saw a woman's costume yet in which she could not secrete anything she wanted. Your dress is one of the very modern, extra loose coat affairs; there are a hundred ways in which you *could* have secreted anything you wished. I didn't say you had; I merely said that you were foolish to say it was impossible. As I was saying, if you did happen to have a pistol and did happen to shoot it off at Mr. Mortimer, the angle would be very much the same as that taken by the bullet of some one standing somewhat below and reaching upward as far as they could."

"Oh!" cried Sybil breathlessly. "You forget—he would have been shot squarely in front, if I had done it—or Norman!"

"Yes?" said Lowry, pleasantly attentive.

"Why, yes!" she reminded him. "He was facing me."

"We have only your word," said the officer gently.

"I——" began Norman Crane impulsively, then stopped in discomfort. He recalled that he had sworn not to have seen anything through the open door.

Lowry, on the other hand, restrained himself from reminding him that his testimony under the circumstances would be rather worse than nothing. To cover up any awkwardness, he went on: "Without any discourtesy to you, we are bound to consider any and all possibilities."

"But," protested Norman Crane, "you said all that would be settled by the doctors!"

"I said your part of it would be; not, necessarily, Miss Merivale's. Doctor Colton?"

The little man with spectacles stepped forward, and, after a brief interchange of words with the inspector, bent over the body of Mortimer.

Lowry turned to Dukane. "I should like to have the murdered man carried in somewhere, just as soon as the medical examiner arrives and sees it. The dressing room? Is that the closest? Quite so—quite so! That will do excellently. Very near, isn't it? Quite convenient." His eye measured the distance between the door of the room and the spot where the murder had taken place. "Just a moment first, though. I want to——Oh, here's the medical examiner now. In a minute I think you may dismiss your people, most of them, that is. We shall know where to reach them, if necessary, eh?"

"Of course—at any time."

"Then they may all go—except Miss Merivale, and—let me see—the man who was on guard at the door between the front and back. And your stage door keeper; I shall want to speak to him a bit later. But the rest—what do you call them—supers?"

"Extras. I may dismiss the extras?"

"I think so. They were all on the stage, or upstairs in the upper tier of rooms, weren't they?"

"Yes."

"Then I doubt if we want them———"

Barrison, though unwillingly, was obliged to whisper that Claire McAllister should be held. He knew that she was bound to talk sooner or later about Sybil's attitude toward the dead man, and he felt that it might as well be sooner as later. Barrison, looking toward the star dressing room, saw that the door was a little open, and that old Wrenn was standing in the aperture, with an expression of intense agitation upon his wrinkled face. Whether the look was horror, grief, or fear, it would be impossible at that juncture to say. Barrison rather believed it was the latter. Though of what could that old man be so acutely afraid?

There was another person who was taking an exceptional interest in the proceedings, the uniformed guard who had been placed on duty at the communicating door, the young man whom the inspector had said he wished to question later. Lowry suddenly turned upon him.

"Is that where you stood at the time of the shooting?" he demanded.

The young man started and flushed.

"N-no, sir," he stammered; "I was over there by the door."

"Then go back there over by the door, and stay there until you are told to move."

The man retreated hastily, looking crestfallen, and muttering something under his breath.

Somehow, although the extras had been dismissed, and the body was to be removed, Barrison felt that Lowry had not yet quite finished with his reconstruction work, so scornfully stigmatized by young Crane as "theatrics." His instinct was not at fault.

The inspector wheeled very suddenly toward Sybil Merivale. "Miss Merivale," he said, "you have already given us some testimony which doubtless was unpleasant to give. I am going to beg you to be even more generous. You have said that you stood there at the head of the steps, waiting for your cue. I should like you now to be more detailed. You are relating, remember, what occurred within the last two minutes of Alan Mortimer's life. There could scarcely be two minutes more important, and I must ask you as solemnly and urgently as I can to omit nothing that could possibly throw any light upon the problem of how he met his death. Will you repeat what you said before, with any additions that come to you as you strain your memory?"

"I don't understand," she faltered wearily. "What more is there to tell?"

"Try to remember!" said the inspector.

Barrison was convinced that he was bluffing, and that he had no idea of anything further that the girl could tell, but to his surprise Sybil flushed painfully and looked away. The younger detective shook his head in silent admiration. The inspector might be old-fashioned, but he had his inspirations.

"I was waiting for my cue," she began, in a low voice, "and looking at the stage through the open door. I have told you that."

"What was your cue, Miss Merivale?"

"But you know that—after the lantern was broken, there were to be six shots, and he"—she would not mention his name—"was to carry me on in his arms."

"Well, go on," said the inspector gently enough. "It is true that we have heard this before, Miss Merivale, but in my experience even the most honest witness—even the most honest witness"—he repeated the words with faint emphasis—"seldom tells a story precisely the same twice. You were standing there——"

"I was standing there, and I heard him come up behind me."

"How did you know it was Mr. Mortimer if you were not looking in his direction?"

"I heard him speak."

"What did he say?"

"I don't know. He was muttering to himself. He seemed horribly angry—upset. I thought——" She checked herself.

"What did you think?"

"That—he had been drinking. He—he was—very much excited. He kept muttering things under his breath, and once he stumbled."

Dukane interposed. "Mortimer—drank—occasionally; but he was cold sober to-night. I know."

"Ah!" The inspector nodded dreamily. "Then it was something else which had upset him; quite so. You see, one gets more from the second telling than the first. Go on, if you please, Miss Merivale. You knew from his voice that he was excited. Did he come up onto the steps at once?"

"I—I don't know." She looked at him appealingly; she seemed honestly confused. "When he spoke to me—I should think perhaps he had taken a step or so up—I don't know. I didn't turn round at once."

"Ah, he spoke to you. And said—what?"

"Do I have to tell that?" She flushed and then paled. "It hasn't—truly, it hasn't—anything to do with—all this!" she pleaded.

"I'm afraid we will have to be the judge of that," Lowry said, quite gently; Barrison had an idea that the old sleuth was truly sorry for the girl, but he never willingly left a trail. "What did he say?"

"He said—he said: 'If you knew the state of mind I'm in, you'd think I was showing great self-control toward you, this minute!' That's exactly what he said."

"What did he mean by that?" demanded the inspector, surprised and not taking the trouble, for once, to hide it.

She was silent.

"I asked you, Miss Merivale, if you have any idea what he meant by so peculiar a greeting? Can you think of anything in your acquaintance—in your relation with him—which might explain it?"

"Yes!" she said, lifting her head and answering boldly. "I know perfectly well what he meant. He was excited or probably he would not have said it then, for he cared awfully about his profession, his work on the stage, and he would ordinarily have been thinking most of that, just then. But he meant—I am sure he meant that—the darkness gave him—opportunities."

"Opportunities?"

"Opportunities—such as—such as—he had abused before."

There was the pause of a breath.

"You mean," said Inspector Lowry, "that he had forced his attentions upon you in the past?"

"Yes."

"Against your will? I asked you—against your will?"

"I had always refused his attentions," she answered, with hesitation.

The detectives noted the change of phrase as she answered, but the inspector made no comment.

"Very well," he said. "What did you answer then? I presume you turned round to face him?"

"Yes, I did."

"What did you answer?"

"I didn't say anything—then."

"Ah—not then! What did you do, Miss Merivale? Did you hear me?"

"Yes, I heard you. I did not do anything. I stood still. I was frightened."

"You stood still, facing him. Could you see him?"

"Yes. He was just below me. I could see him, and I thought I heard him laugh in a—a dreadful way. He came up two of the steps, and I could see his face."

"It was not the dark scene yet?"

"No; the lantern was not yet out. It was dark, but not pitch dark. His face frightened me. He had frightened me before."

"And did Mr. Mortimer speak to you again?"

"Yes."

The answer came in a gasping breath, and Norman Crane seemed to echo it unconsciously. He was following every syllable that she spoke with a terrible attentiveness, and at that last "yes" he shuddered and drew his breath quickly. Lowry fixed him with that disconcerting, unexpected look of his.

"So that was what you heard through the open door!" he said, making it a statement, not a query. "Well, Miss Merivale, he was coming up the steps toward you, and he said——"

"He said, 'When I pick you up to-night to carry you onto the stage—I shall kiss you!'"

The shudder that came with this admission shook her. Her eyes turned toward the body which, for some reason, had not yet been taken away, and in their gaze there was fear and loathing, and—it might be—contempt.

"Ah!" said Inspector Lowry, apparently unsurprised. "And what did you answer, Miss Merivale?"

She hardly seemed to hear. Her eyes were still fixed upon that dead face, awful in its paint and powder, such a handsome face, lately so full of compelling charm, even now a face that one could scarcely pass without a second look.

"What did you say, Miss Merivale?"

She paused for only a moment; then, looking straight at the inspector, she replied very deliberately indeed:

"I said: 'If you do that—I shall kill you!'"

CHAPTER XI
IN THE STAR DRESSING ROOM

A BRIEF PAUSE FOLLOWED Sybil's unexpectedly dramatic statement. Then Inspector Lowry bowed gravely.

"That is all, Miss Merivale," he said, without looking at her. "We shall not want you for a while, though I shall have to speak to you again later. I should advise you, as a friend, to go to your own dressing room to rest."

"May I—mayn't I—go home?" she asked piteously. But on such points as these no amount of courtesy or human sympathy could make Lowry less inexorable.

"Not just yet," he said calmly. "Later, we shall see. Go and rest, my dear young lady. Do go and rest!"

Norman Crane started forward to help her, but, to every one's surprise, Claire McAllister, the extra woman who had been kept for possibly relevant testimony, was before him.

"You come with me, you poor kid!" she exclaimed, as tenderly as she possibly could. "I'll see to you. Gee, but this is a bunch of boobs, not to see that you're about as apt to get in wrong as a two-months' one! Come on, deary!"

They vanished within the dressing room wherein Sybil had dressed for a possible triumph that selfsame evening—hard as it was for any of them to believe it. That evening? It might just as well have been a month earlier, and even Dukane, the imperturbable, was haggard with the strain already.

To him Lowry said something in a low voice, and the manager turned at once to Mortimer's valet, still standing at the door:

"Wrenn, clear the couch in there. We are——" He paused, respecting the man's feelings, and ended gently: "We are bringing him in."

They carried the big, splendidly made form into the room which he had left such a short time before, in such a high tide of life and strength. There was nothing of tragedy in this setting. Barrison looked about him curiously, as though he were in a queer sort of dream in which all manner of incongruities might be expected.

There were brilliant electric bulbs topping and framing the glass on the dressing table; Barrison knew that actors were obliged to test their make-up under various lighting effects, and there was something darkly strange in this array of lights still ready for a test that could not come again—for Mortimer. At that same table, under the same bulbs, other stars would put on paint and wigs and costumes. This one would do so no more.

In that vivid glare, the litter of the paraphernalia of make-up glowed with a somewhat gay, decorative effect. Rouge boxes and cold-cream jars and sticks of grease paint lay just as he had left them. Evidently Mortimer had been "touching up" for the last act, and the valet had not yet had time to clear up or put away anything.

Lowry's keen eyes ran over the room, in that seemingly cursory but actually minute inspection which characterized his methods. There was nothing about it unlike other theatrical dressing rooms. There was the usual long dresser with its rows of brilliant bulbs; there were the clothes hanging on the walls; there was the couch—now bearing that tragic burden, the magnificent body in khaki—the big trunk, the two chairs—the small one by the table, and the easy one for rest and visitors. Apparently, there was nothing in the room for a detective to note, save the dead man, and—here the inspector's glance became more vague, a sure sign that he was particularly interested, for he was looking at Wrenn.

The old man, in his decent black clothes, was standing near the couch; and he was watching the intruders with a sort of baleful combination of terror and resentment. The fear which he had shown in his face when he looked out of the dressing-room door a few minutes since, had not vanished from it; but to it was added another, and a not less violent emotion. He was angry, he was on the defensive. He might, for the moment, have been some cornered animal, frightened, but nevertheless about to spring upon his enemy.

It was against Lowry's principles to ask questions at such moments as might be considered obvious; so it was Dukane who said, with some asperity:

"What's the matter, Wrenn?"

The old man's face worked and his voice shook, as he returned:

"Mr. Dukane, sir—you—you aren't going to let all these people in here, to poke and pry about among my poor master's things? It's—it's a wicked shame, so it is! I'd never have thought it possible! It's an outrage——"

"You're crazy, Wrenn!" said Dukane, trying to remember the old fellow's bereavement, and doing his best to speak kindly instead of impatiently. "These are detectives, officers of the law. They are on this case, and they have a perfect right to do anything they want to."

"But, sir"—the old servant was working himself up more and more, and his cracked voice was growing shrill—"what are they doing here, sir? What can they have to do here? Can't his—his poor body rest in peace without a—a lot of policemen poking——"

The inspector interrupted him placidly. "Much obliged for the suggestion, Wrenn! We might not have thought of searching this dressing room, but, thanks to you, we certainly will now!"

"Of course," he said to Barrison later, "we'd have had to do it anyway, but I wanted to scare that old chap into thinking it was chiefly his doing!"

Wrenn gasped. "Oh, sir, oh, Mr. Dukane!" he implored. "Can't he—lie in peace—just for to-night? I—I'd like to sit with him to-night, sir. Surely there's no harm?"

"Was he so very kind to you?" said the inspector sympathetically.

Wrenn hesitated. "Mostly he was, sir," he said at last, quite simply. And then he added in a queer, forlorn way: "I—I've been with him a long time, you know, sir."

The detectives, despite Wrenn's protests, searched the room with methodical thoroughness. If there was one single thing, no bigger than a pin, which ought not, in the nature of things, to be in a dressing room of this kind, why, they were there to find it.

"But why?" Dukane whispered to Barrison. "Not that there is the slightest objection—but what is it Lowry expects to find?"

"He doesn't," replied Barrison. "He's from Missouri; he wants to be shown. We always search the premises, you know——"

"But it wasn't here he was killed."

"No; but it was so near here that——Hello! They've got something!"

He spoke in the tone of suppressed excitement that a fox hunter might have used.

The plain-clothes man with the inspector had opened the trunk, and was staring into it with a puzzled face. At the same moment, Wrenn emitted a low moan, as though, after a struggle, he found himself obliged to give up at last. He staggered a trifle, and caught at the back of a chair to steady himself.

"Well," said the inspector, softly jocose. "Haven't found the murderer in that trunk, have you, Sims?"

"No, sir," said the officer; but his voice was as puzzled as his eyes. "Only this."

He took something out of the trunk, and held it up in the unsparing glare of the dressing-room lights. It was assuredly an odd sort of article to be found in a man's theater trunk. For it was a piece of filmy white stuff, with lace upon it, badly torn.

"A sleeve," said the inspector, with an obvious accent of astonishment. "A woman's sleeve—let's have a look at it."

He took it into his own hands. Clearly, it was the sleeve and part of the shoulder of a woman's dress or blouse, trimmed with elaborate, but rather coarse and cheap lace. On the front, where it had evidently been ripped and torn away from the original garment, were finger prints, stamped in a brownish red.

The inspector's eyes strayed to the dressing table with its array of paints and powders.

"Anything there that will correspond? Barrison, take a look, while Sims goes through the rest of the trunk."

Barrison returned with a jar.

"It's bolamine," explained Dukane. "They use it for a dark make-up, to suggest tan or sunburn. Mortimer would naturally use it in an out-of-door part of this sort."

"On his hands, too?"

"Surely on his hands; only amateurs forget the hands."

"Ah!" said Lowry. "We'll have the finger prints examined and compared with Mortimer's, though it's scarcely necessary, I imagine. It's so evident that——"

Wrenn broke in, almost frantically:

"It's only a make-up rag, sir! Every one uses make-up rags, sir, to wipe the make-up off!"

"Ah!" said Lowry. "You provided yourself with these make-up rags, then?"

"Yes, sir!" Wrenn spoke eagerly. "I asked the chambermaid at the hotel for some old pieces for Mr. Mortimer, and——"

"Wrenn, don't be a fool," said Lowry, speaking sharply for the first time. "In the first place—unless I am much mistaken—make-up rags are used only when the make-up is taken off—right, Mr. Dukane?"

The manager nodded.

"And then—why, in that case, was this rag so precious that you had to shut it up in a trunk, before it had been used? For I take it that a make-up rag doesn't show just one or two complete sets of finger prints when a man gets through with it! It must look something like a rag that's used on brasses or an automobile! Also, I see that there are two or three cloths already on the dressing table."

He turned his back on Wrenn, and examined the bit of linen that he held, while the other detectives held their breath.

"This," he said at last, "was torn from the dress of some woman who was in the dressing room to-night, at some time after Mortimer was made up."

He turned to Dukane, with the faintest shrug, and said:

"You know, when I tried to reconstruct the crime by putting every one in their places—the places they had occupied at the time of the shooting—I was attempting the impossible. For there evidently was some one else here, some one who has gone; some one"—his eyes flew suddenly and piercingly to Wrenn—"whom this man wishes to shield."

CHAPTER XII
THE TWO DOORWAYS

WHETHER IT WAS STRICTLY correct or not, no one was in a position to question, but, anyway, Inspector Lowry told Sybil finally to go home after leaving her address. A lot of skeleton theories had come tumbling down with the discovery that another and unknown woman had been present in Mortimer's dressing room that night.

Even Claire McAllister's testimony—that Miss Merivale had told her she sometimes wished she could kill their star—fell flat after Sybil's own confession of not only what she had felt, but what she had threatened.

The whole business was, as Barrison could see, a sickening one for Inspector Lowry. He had fallen down right and left; practically speaking, he had nothing left now to work on, out of all his ingenious work of reconstruction.

Only his examination of the two men on guard at the doors had brought out anything clear cut, anything on which seriously to work.

First of all, he had questioned Joe Lynch, the young fellow whose job it had been to keep any one save the detective and the manager from passing either way through the communicating door.

"Your name is Joe Lynch, you say?"

"Yes, sir."

"You have already said that you stood there by the communicating door during the dark scene, Lynch?"

"Yes, sir."

"Just there?"

"As near as I can say, sir, yes. I was close up here by the door. My orders was to keep it shut except for the detectives or Mr. Dukane."

"And did you know why?"

"Why, how do you mean, sir?"

"Did you understand why the orders were so strict to-night of all nights?"

"Oh, that. Yes, sir; I knew there'd been some talk of Mr. Mortimer being in some sort of danger."

"Who told you?"

"Why, I couldn't say, sir. I don't rightly know. Them things gets about. Anyhow, I knew that; and I was, so to speak, sort o' set on taking care of Mr. Mortimer."

"Did you like him, then?"

The young man's dull eyes opened wide.

"Me, sir?" he said, in surprise. "I never see him to talk to. But I was wanting to do my part. Mr. Dukane and Mr. Barrison, too, told me I was to look sharp. So I did."

"Ah! You did, eh? You looked sharp, eh?"

"Yes, sir."

"Sure?"

"Why, yes, sir! Course I did! I—I was keen on showing I was as quick as the next."

"Ah! How were you going to show that?"

Young Lynch laughed frankly, yet with a sort of embarrassment, too.

"Well, sir, Mr. Dukane, he offered twenty-five dollars either to Mr. Roberts or me if we could spot any one trying anything suspicious, or anything."

"*Ah!*" The inspector's laconic monosyllable sounded a bit sharper than usual. "So that was it! Lynch, you were standing there when you heard the shot?"

"Yes, sir, as near as I can say now, in these very tracks."

The inspector stood beside him and let his eyes move slowly from the big door beside them to the little flight of steps where the star had met his death.

"Mighty narrow way to pass," he murmured, half to himself.

"Sir?" said Lynch respectfully.

The inspector continued to measure distances with his eye.

"You see," he said to Lynch, "if you will draw a straight line from here where we stand, past the angle of the property-room corner to the entrance where Mr. Mortimer was waiting, do you see what I mean?"

Lynch looked obediently where he was directed. "No, sir," he said, after he had looked.

Lowry sighed gently. "Not much space to pass any one, anyway," he murmured.

Lynch looked at him, still blankly.

"Lynch," said the inspector, "if I were in your place, and had a chance of making twenty-five dollars if I caught any one, and while I was on duty like this, and heard a shot——"

He paused, not seeming to look at Lynch, but really noting every shadow and light that passed over his face.

"If I were, in short, as you had been situated, I should have left my post when I heard that shot and run forward toward the man I was supposed to guard. I think I should have considered it my duty."

"Would you, indeed, sir?" cried young Lynch hopefully.

The inspector suddenly looked at him and said dryly. "So that's what you did? Suppose you tell me all about it. You heard the shot, and——"

"If you please, sir," protested the young man eagerly and rather unhappily, "it wasn't the shot; leastways, I didn't know about how many shots there'd be. It was the scream. I heard the shots, one after the other, and then the scream—a dreadful scream, if you please, sir. And, of course, I thought first of all of Mr. Mortimer, and there being danger, and—and all that. And I run forward, sir, a few steps, through the dark, wishing to be of some use, and——"

"And to get the twenty-five dollars?"

"Well, sir, that perhaps; of course, I'm not saying that wasn't in the back of my mind. But what I was thinking of first was that there was trouble, and that I might be needed."

"That's all right; I believe you." Lowry spoke shortly, but not at all unkindly. "The point is that, within half a second of the time of the shooting, you had left this particular point, and run in the direction of the shots. In other words, Lynch, this door was unguarded."

"Unguarded, sir!" Lynch was aghast, and truly so. "Unguarded, sir! But I had been at my post all the evening! No one had gone in or out——"

"No one had gone in or out during the evening, I am absolutely convinced. But, after the murder, any one who chanced to be there could have gone out. Isn't that so?"

"But——" The young guard's troubled eyes began to measure the distance between the door and the stage steps, just as the detectives had done before.

"Ah!" said Lowry. "You see why I spoke of the narrow passage which would have to be traversed. It would be very narrow, indeed. Any one who wanted to get from those steps to the communicating door would have to pass you at very close quarters, Lynch. And yet—the thing could be done. The thing could be done. I have not lived so long without learning that it is these unlikely, well-nigh impossible things that come off in the smoothest way of all. All right, Lynch, I'm obliged to you. It's not your fault. You were a bit overzealous, but I don't think we'll put you in jail for that. However you look at it, you've shown us one way in which the murderer might have escaped."

He turned and crooked his arm in that of Barrison.

"Now, we'll go and interview the stage doorkeeper," he said. Together he and Barrison attacked old Roberts, who confronted him at the entrance with a look of mingled apprehension and bravado. His round, flabby face was rather pale, and he gave the impression of a weak old child trying to act like a brave man.

"What do you want of me, gentlemen?" he demanded, in a tone that broke timidly in spite of himself.

They were both very nice to him. In this case, Lowry let Barrison do most of the talking, feeling that it was a case that required tact. He stood back in thoughtful silence while Jim got around the old doorkeeper in his very best and most diplomatic style with the result that within five minutes poor old Roberts was crumpling up in rather a piteous fashion, perfectly ready to tell them anything and everything he had ever done, said, or heard of.

"I didn't mean no harm," he protested at last, with such an attitude of abasement that neither Barrison nor, indeed, Lowry had the heart to rub it in. "I do hope—oh, I do hope, that you'll not let Mr. Dukane discharge me! I've been here a good many years, and no one can say as I've not been faithful. I don't believe there's been another night in all my life when I've left my post."

"It would have to be to-night!" murmured Lowry.

"It would!" agreed Barrison. "Go on, Roberts. No one wants to kill you, and I don't believe there's the least likelihood of your losing your job. Just tell us——"

"You don't know Mr. Dukane, sir!" Roberts almost wept. "He's strict, sir; very strict! He says a thing and you've got to do it, no matter what happens! *I* know—haven't I been working for him for twenty years? And now to be fired and out——"

"Who said you were going to be fired? Get along, Roberts! Tell us what it was that you did."

"I left the stage door, sir," said Roberts humbly.

"That we gathered. But why did you leave it, and when, and for how long?"

Roberts sniffed and answered in a small stifled voice:

"As to when I left it, sir—it was when Mrs. Parry came to ask me to get a taxi for Miss Legaye."

"Why didn't you get a taxi, then—telephone for one?"

"I did, sir. I telephoned two places, but there wasn't a single machine in. The starters all said the same thing: It looked like rain, and they couldn't guarantee a taxi for an hour yet. I—I like Miss Kitty, sir; she's always kind to me, and I didn't want her to have to wait, 'specially when she was sick, as Mrs. Parry said she was. So, when I found I couldn't get one over the wire, I went out into the alley to see if I could see one passing."

"Well, that doesn't seem very awful," said Barrison, smiling at him. "Did you get one?"

Poor old Roberts brightened a bit at the kindly inflection.

"I couldn't see one, sir, not from this door, so I went up to the gate at the end of the court, and looked up and down the street. And after a minute I saw one coming and hailed it, and it stopped. So I ran back again; and Miss Legaye was standing just outside the stage door, waiting. So I called to her 'All right, Miss Legaye, your taxi's here!' and went on back. She passed me, in her red coat, about halfway, and I told her I was sorry to have kept her waiting. Then I hurried back here."

"And you are sure you didn't pass any one but Miss Legaye in the alley, no one coming in?"

The old fellow shook his head. "So far as any one going out goes," he said, "how do I know? My eyes are not so young as they were. But coming in! Why, I was back here! How could any one pass me in the light without my seeing them?"

"But," suggested Barrison, "while you were down at the street signaling the taxi, some one who had been hiding in the alley might have slipped in, mightn't they?"

Old Roberts hung his head, and his whole heavy body expressed dejection.

"That's what I keep saying to myself, sir!" he whispered. "Not that I think it's likely—but—my eyes aren't what they once were, and suppose the murderer was hiding there, and just waiting for a chance to get in?"

"And how long, altogether, were you away?" Lowry spoke for the first time.

"That's easy, sir. I went out a few minutes after Mrs. Parry told me to send for the taxi, and I had just come back when Mr. Barrison here came out to ask me if I'd seen any one pass."

"That was just before the shooting," Barrison said.

"*Before* the shooting. And you're prepared to swear, Roberts, that no one came out of the theater after that?"

"I am, sir!" The old man's eyes, dim as they were, left no room for doubt; he was speaking the truth.

"All right, Roberts. I'm sure you've told the truth, and Mr. Dukane shall be told so. I don't believe you'll lose your job. Just the same, I wish you hadn't gone to hunt taxicabs at that particular moment."

As the two detectives walked away, Lowry said under his breath: "We've proved that no one left the theater by the stage door after the shooting, but we've proved that they might have done so by the communicating door. We've proved that Lynch was at his post for the whole evening up to the shooting, so that no one could have come in by that way before then; but, since he left it afterward, there is no reason to suppose that that some one could not have made their exit that way after the crime. In other words, my dear friend and colleague, while we can't prove it, we can find a perfectly possible way for the murderer to have entered and an equally possible way for him, or her, to have departed."

"You think that—whoever it was—came in while Roberts was blundering up or down the alley?"

"I see no other explanation. Barrison, you are not officially under me, but I respect your judgment, and I like your work. I should be obliged if you would take on such branches of this case as seem to lie in your way. You have been in it since—so to speak—its inception. You should have a line on many aspects of it that I couldn't possibly get, coming into it as I must, from a purely and coldly official standpoint. I'll expect you to do your darnedest on it, and help me in every way you can. Right?"

"Right, sir." The young detective's tone was full of ardor.

"Then good night to you. One moment. Did you notice the initial on this pistol, the one you picked up?"

He produced it as he spoke.

"No," said Jim. "I didn't want any one to see it, so tucked it away without a look."

"Take it along with you," said Lowry unexpectedly. "You may be able to spot the owner."

Barrison seized the tiny weapon with avidity; it was too dark where they stood for him to see clearly, and he said, with open eagerness:

"What is the initial? That of any of the principals in the case?"

"Of two of them," said the inspector, as he turned to round a corner. "It's M. Good night."

CHAPTER XIII
THE INITIAL

THE INSPECTOR'S ANNOUNCEMENT GAVE Jim Barrison food for thought.

Then why had Lowry let Sybil go with no further examination? They would have to establish next her possession of a weapon, and the fact that she was sufficiently practiced in the use of firearms to have hers marked with her initial, and——

But just then he discovered that it had begun to rain at last; big drops heralded the storm that had been threatening all the evening. Under the circumstances, his library at home would be a pleasanter place for speculation than the corner of a street. He turned up his coat collar and ran for a Sixth Avenue car. As he passed the clock outside a jeweler's shop, he saw that it was ten minutes past one o'clock, and suddenly he was conscious that he was tired. The evening had been a long one, and hard on the nerves.

He stood on the back platform, and let the rainy winds blow about him. His dinner coat was getting noticeably wet, but he wanted to think and breathe. How hot the theater had been! The smell of a singularly vile cigarette close beside him made him turn in a disgusted sort of curiosity to see what manner of man could smoke it. It turned out to be Willie Coster, who had boarded the car when he did.

"Hello!" said Jim. "Didn't see you before. I thought you left the theater before we did."

"I had," said Willie, puffing deeply on his rank weed. "I stopped at the corner to get this."

Unblushingly he indicated an object done up in brown paper, which he carried under his arm. There was not the slightest doubt that it was a bottle of quart dimensions. Barrison recalled the legend that Coster always got drunk after a first night. He could not help smiling at the serious deliberation with which he was going about it.

"I see!" he said. "Well, it's been a pretty trying time for you, a thing like this, coming on top of all your hard work on the piece. I dare say you feel the need of something to brace you."

Willie shook his head. "That's a nice way of putting it," he said soberly; "but it won't wash. No, sir; the fact is, I mean to get drunk to-night. I never touch anything while I'm working, and when my work's done, I consider I'm entitled to a little pleasure."

"I see," Barrison said again. "And does getting drunk give you a great deal of pleasure?"

"Oh, yes!" said Coster gravely. "I'm not a drunkard, understand. I don't go off on bats; *that* wouldn't give me pleasure. And I can always sober up in time for anything special. But I like to go quietly home like this and drink—well, say, about this bottle to-night, and another to-morrow. Then I'll taper off and quit again. See?"

"Perfectly. If you have to do it, it seems a very sensible method. Look here; is there any particular hurry about this systematic debauch of yours?"

"Hurry? Oh, no, there's no hurry. Any time will do. Why?"

"Then," said Barrison, who had an idea, "why not come over to my rooms—we're almost there—and have a couple of drinks with me and a bite to eat, first? You can go home and get drunk later, you know, just as well."

"Just as well," said Willie, with surprising acquiescence. "I don't want any drinks, thanks, for I only drink alone. But now you mention it, I'm hungry."

Barrison knew that he himself was far too tired already to lengthen out this night so preposterously, but that idea which had so suddenly come to him drove all consideration of fatigue from his mind. He was a detective, and thought that in the dim distance he could see a shadowy trail. In a weird case of this sort, anything was worth a chance.

At Barrison's rooms they found a cold supper waiting, and Tara asleep in a chair, contriving somehow to look dignified even in slumber. There is no dignity like that of a superior Japanese servant. He even woke up in a dignified manner, and prepared to serve supper. But Barrison sent him to bed, and sat down to talk to Willie over cold chicken and ham, and macedoine salad. The little stage manager ate hungrily, but stubbornly refused to drink. He also scorned his host's expensive smokes, preferring his own obnoxious brand.

"Coster," said Barrison at last, "I want you to tell me what you know of Alan Mortimer."

"What I know! He was the yellowest guy in some things that ever——"

"That isn't just what I meant. I mean—you've been with Dukane a long time, haven't you?"

"Sure thing. I've been with the gov'nor five—no, six—years."

"Then you must know how he came to take up Mortimer. Where did he discover him first? He's a stranger on Broadway."

"Why don't you ask the gov'nor about it?" demanded Willie shrewdly.

"Well," Jim was obliged to admit, rather uncomfortably, "he's not the sort of man you feel like pumping. Of course, Lowry will get it all out of him sooner or later, but I'm curious. And I can't see what objection he could have to your——"

"Being pumped," finished Willie. "Maybe not, but I don't really know much about it, anyway." His eyes strayed wistfully to his brown paper package. "See here," he said, "I'm much obliged for the eats, but I guess I'll be trotting along. I've got a very pressing engagement!"

"With John Barleycorn?" laughed Barrison. "Oh, see here, Willie, what's the difference? If you prefer your whisky to mine, I'll get you a corkscrew, and you can just as well start here. Eh? Make an exception and have a couple of drinks with me, like a good sport."

He felt slightly ashamed of himself, but he prodded his conscience out of the way by telling himself that as long as the man was going to get drunk anyway, he might just as well——

Willie hesitated and was lost. The first drink he poured out made his host gasp; it nearly filled the tumbler.

"Will you take it straight, man?" he asked, in a tone of awe.

"Certainly I will. I don't take it for the taste, I take it for the effect. The more you take at a time, the quicker you get results. What's the good of little dabs of drinks like yours, drowned in soda water? When I drink, I drink."

"I perceive that you do!" murmured Barrison, and watched him swallow the entire contents of the glass in three gulps. He choked a bit, and accepted a drink of water, then leaned back with an expression of pure bliss stealing over his face.

"Gee, that was good!" he whispered joyously. "Now I'll have one more in a minute; that will start me off comfortably. Then I'll go home. You know," he added, with that shrewd glance of his, "I'm on to your getting me to tank up here; you know I'll talk more. But I'm blessed if I can make out what it is you want to know. If there's any dark mystery going, I'm not in it. But you just pump ahead."

He poured out another enormous draft.

"Mortimer used to be in a sort of circus, a wild West show, didn't he?"

Willie grunted assent between swallows. "It was a sort of punk third-class show," he said. "Never played big time, just ordinary tanks and wood piles out West. They had a string of horses and a few cowboys who could do fancy riding; Mortimer was one of them. His real name was Morton. The gov'nor was waiting to make connections somewhere on his way to the coast, and dropped in to see one or two of the stunts. This chap was a sort of matinée idol wherever he went, and the gov'nor spotted him as a drawing card if he ever happened on the right part. You know the gov'nor never forgets anything, and never overlooks a bet. He took the guy's name and address, and put him away in the back of his head somewhere, the way he always does. When Carlton came to him with this war-play proposition, the gov'nor thought of Morton, and wrote him. That's all I know about it."

"Was Mortimer married?"

"Not that I know of. Not likely—or, rather, it's likely he had half a dozen wives!"

Barrison was disappointed; he had thought it just possible—there was the pistol, marked with M, and the unknown woman who had been in the dressing room that night. However, Willie was not proving much of a help. Barrison yawned and thought of bed.

"One more question," he asked suddenly. "What was the name of the show?"

"I don't remember. Blinkey's or Blankey's, or something like that. Blinkey's Daredevils, I think, but I'm not sure. Say, you'd better let me go home while I can walk."

"All right; you go, Willie. Were there any women in the show?"

"A couple, I think—yes, I'm sure there were, because I remember the gov'nor speaking about a sort of riding-and-shooting stunt Mortimer did with some girl, a crack shot."

Barrison started. Was that the trail, then?

"Much obliged to you, Willie," he said carelessly. "There wasn't much to tell, though, was there? Why did Dukane keep it all so dark, I wonder? I should have thought that would have been good advertising, all that cowboy stuff, and the traveling show, and the rest of it."

"I don't know why the gov'nor does some things; no one does," said Willie, getting to his feet with surprising steadiness, and carefully corking his precious bottle. "But he's never given any of that stuff to the press agent, and I've a notion he doesn't want it made public. I don't know why, but I'm pretty sure he has some reason for keeping it dark. Now you know as much about it as I do, and I'd never have told you as much as that if I hadn't started in here!"

While he was wrapping up his bottle, with a painstaking deliberation which was, as yet, almost the only sign of what he had drunk, Barrison drew the little pistol from his pocket and laid it on the table. It was almost a toy, and mounted in silver gilt, a foolish-looking thing to have done such deadly harm. The letter was in heavy raised gold, a thick, squarely printed M. In the rays of the student lamp it glittered merrily, like the decoration on some frivolous trinket.

"Hello!" said Willie Coster, looking dully at it from the other side of the table. "So that's the gun that did it? Let's see the letter." He swayed forward to look closer.

"It's an M," said Barrison.

"You're looking at it upside down," said Willie; "or else it's you that's drunk and not me. That's a W, man, a W! Good night!"

He ambled toward the door, bearing his package clasped to his breast, and disappeared.

Barrison seized the pistol and turned it around. Willie was right. The initial, seen so, was W!

CHAPTER XIV
A TIP—AND AN INVITATION

JIM BARRISON HAD SCARCELY grasped this fact when the telephone rang. In the dead silence of that hour, half after two in the morning, the shrill tinkle had a startling effect. Barrison, his fatigue forgotten, sprang to the instrument.

It was Tony Clay's voice that came to him. "I want to come up for a minute."

"Oh, confound you!" ejaculated the detective irritably. "What do you want at this hour? I'll have to come down and let you in; the place is closed."

"I know it is. That's why I'm calling up. I'm in the drug store at the corner, and I'll be there as soon as you can get downstairs. All right?"

"I suppose so. But I'd like to wring your neck!"

"Welcome to try, old man, just a bit later. So long!"

Barrison hung up, and tramped downstairs with suppressed profanity on his tongue, to let Tony in at the front door of the apartment house where he roomed. The younger man was already waiting on the steps, dripping wet, but whistling softly, rather off the key.

"Come in, you blamed night owl!" growled Barrison, under his breath. "Don't slam the door. And if you haven't something worth while to tell me, after routing me out like this, I'll wake Tara and give him full permission to jujutsu you into Bellevue! Come on, and stop whistling."

Upstairs, Tony demanded Scotch and cigarettes, and took off his wet coat.

"Heavens! Does that mean you're intending to *stay*?"

"Not permanently," Tony reassured him soothingly. "I do manage to arrive at inconvenient times, don't I?"

"You do, you do! Now what is it?"

"Well," said Tony, settling himself in the chair recently vacated by Willie Coster. "I've been calling on Miss Templeton."

Barrison was conscious of a queer little thrill, not entirely unpleasant. Truth to tell, he had not been able to dismiss a certain vision from his mind, through all his practice and professional occupations. He could see it now, all in a moment, gold hair, dark-fringed eyes, marble-white throat and arms, and a mouth that could soften and droop like a child's at the most unexpected moments.

"She's out of the case, I suppose you know," he said shortly. "Go ahead, though."

"You see," said Tony, "when you pitched into me like that about her giving me the slip, I was sort of sore, but I knew you were right, too. So I gave you the slip, in my turn, and chased over to her hotel. I wasn't at all sure she'd see me, but I thought I'd try it on anyhow, and she sent down word I was to come up. She wore a kimono thing, and looked like an angel——" He paused in fatuous reflection.

"Get on, you young fool!"

Barrison's tone was the sharper because he himself admired Miss Templeton rather more than was wholly consistent with the traditions of a cold-blooded detective.

So Tony went on: "She seemed to know that there had been something wrong at the theater; that impressed me at once. The moment I came into the room, she said: 'Something has happened to him?' I told her about it, and she just sat for a moment or two looking straight in front of her. She looked—strange, and awfully white and tired and—sort of young. After a while she said: 'Thank Heaven it wasn't I'—just that way. Then she asked some questions——"

"What sort of questions?" interrupted Barrison, who was looking at the floor, and had let his cigarette go out.

"Oh, the usual thing: Who was behind at the time, and whether any one was suspected, and—she made rather a point of this—where Miss Legaye was when it happened."

"I know; she's always harped on that." Barrison frowned impatiently, yet he was thinking as hard as he knew how to think. "Anything else, Tony?"

"Yes; she asked me to give you this."

Tony took a small unsealed envelope out of his waistcoat pocket and handed it over. "She said it was important," he added; "that's why I insisted on coming in to-night."

Barrison read his note, and then looked up. "Do you know what this is?" he said.

The boy flushed indignantly. "Good heavens, Jim!" he exclaimed. "You don't suppose I read other people's letters? She just gave it to me to bring, and I brought it, that's all."

Barrison smiled at him, with a warm feeling round his heart. "That's all right, Tony," he said kindly, "and you're all right, too! You'd better look at it." He held it out.

Tony shook his head. "If there's anything in it you want to tell me, fire ahead!" he said stoutly. "I—I haven't any particular reason for seeing it, you know."

Barrison understood him, and smiled again. "I'll read it to you, then," he said, and read:

"My Dear Mr. Barrison: I have just heard, though scarcely with surprise, I admit, of Mr. Mortimer's death. It has shocked me very much, I find, even though it was the sort of tragedy that was bound to come sooner or later. I cannot pretend complete indifference to it, nor yet indifference to the conviction of his murderer. I am going to assume that you really want any sort of help, from any source, in solving this mystery. Though you refused to help me once, I am ready to help you now in whatever way I can, and I believe that my help may be worth more than you are now prepared to see. I knew Alan Mortimer rather well; it is possible that I can throw light upon certain phases in his life of which you are still ignorant. I promise nothing, for I do not yet know how valuable my testimony may prove. But—will you lunch with me at one o'clock to-morrow—or, rather, to-day—at my hotel? And meanwhile, if you will forgive me for reiterating the suspicion I once suggested to you, you can hardly do better than look up Miss Kitty Legaye, and get her views on the murder. Far be it for me to suggest a course of action to an expert detective like yourself, but—if Miss Legaye left the theater early, she would hardly be likely to learn of the tragedy until she got the morning papers. Don't you think that it would be interesting to forestall them, and yourself be the one to break the news to her? Just suppose that you found it was not precisely 'news' after all!

"If I do not hear from you, I shall expect you for luncheon at one. Sincerely yours,

"Grace Templeton."

Jim Barrison automatically registered the fact that the writing was not that of the threatening letters, and sat still staring at the sheet after he had read it aloud. His brain was in a whirl of excitement. The words which he had just read seemed, in the very utterance of them, to have taken on a vitality, a meaning, that they had not had in the first place.

One could read such a communication in more ways than one; at present he could read it only as a curious and inscrutable message, or inspiration. He could not have said just why it seemed to him so important, so imperative. He only knew that the phrases of it, simple as they were, seemed to fill the room and echo from wall to wall. Miss Templeton herself might have stood before him; he might have been listening to her voice.

Tony Clay, poor lad, was looking troubled, huddled there in the big chair on the other side of the table. He had forgotten to finish his whisky and soda, and was staring at Barrison in a queer, uncomfortable way.

"I say, Jim!" he burst out at last, desperate through his shyness. "You're looking not a bit like yourself. What's the matter? That note doesn't sound so very important, now I hear it, and yet, to look at you, one would say you'd received a message from the tomb."

Barrison laughed. "I haven't!" he said lightly. "But I have received a tip. Just a plain, ordinary, every-day sort of tip! And I'm going to follow it, too! How much sleep do you need, Tony?"

Tony considered. "Four will do me," he said judicially.

"You'll get five. It's three o'clock now. At eight you'll be ready for business; at eight thirty we'll be at Miss Kitty Legaye's door. It may be a pipe dream, but I've taken kindly to the notion of announcing the news of Mortimer's death in person! Now tumble in on that couch there, and don't dare to speak again until eight in the morning!"

As he fell asleep, he was still repeating the pregnant words: "Just suppose that you found it was not precisely 'news' after all!"

CHAPTER XV
A MORNING CALL

MISS LEGAYE LIVED AT a very smart little hotel near Fifth Avenue. It was not one of the strictly "theatrical" hostelries, since Kitty had always had leanings toward social correctness. But the house was patronized by so many actresses of exactly the same predilections that it could not help being run with an indulgent and sagacious understanding of their tastes and peculiarities, and might almost as well have been one of the just-off-Broadway variety.

When Barrison and Tony Clay presented themselves at the "Golden Arms" at twenty minutes after eight in the morning, they found the hotel barely awake. The clerk who had just come on duty at the desk eyed them with surliness and distaste. The very electric lights, turned on perforce, because of the outrageous dinginess of the morning, seemed to glare at them with disfavor. Bell boys looked unrelentingly cross; a messenger boy was making his exit with as much dripping and mud as he could; and a departing patron appeared to be becoming quarrelsome over a fifteen-cent overcharge.

"Well?" demanded the clerk. He looked frankly ugly; ugly in temper as well as in features. He could see that they were not incoming guests, for they had no luggage; and it was too early for callers of any reputable type. He put them down as a breed suspicious, being unknown, of neither fish nor fowl variety. "*Well?*" he repeated urgently.

Barrison produced a card. "We would like to see Miss Legaye," he suggested pleasantly.

As he put down the slip of pasteboard on the desk counter, his quick eyes noted a bell boy standing at the news stand, taking over an armful of assorted morning papers. Obviously, the lad was just going up to leave them at the doors of the guests; they would have to work quickly, he and Tony, if they were to get ahead of them.

"Miss Legaye," repeated the clerk. "Miss Legaye. Are you guys dippy? Miss Legaye always leaves word that she ain't at home to no one till after twelve o'clock. Now beat it!"

Barrison sized up the clerk, and decided on his course.

"Say, brother," he murmured, with a confidential accent, "we don't mean to annoy Miss Legaye; we want to give her a boost. Get me? We're reporters, and we're looking for a first-class story. Say, take it from me, she'll be keen to see us if you'll just phone up!"

The slang won his case. The clerk looked at him with more respect.

"Say, you're talking almost like a human being!" he remarked. "Want me to phone up for you, eh?" He waited a perceptible space. "Times is hard," he declared, in an airy manner, "and phone calls is high. Did I hear you say anything?"

"Maybe not me," said Barrison, who had laid a dollar bill on the desk. "But I've known money to talk before now."

The clerk actually chuckled. "You're on," he said, pocketing the bill with a discreet look around the almost deserted office. "I'll phone up!"

He turned around a minute later to inform Barrison that Miss Legaye would see him at once.

A few minutes later they were knocking at the door of Kitty Legaye's apartment. Resting against the lintel were half a dozen morning papers; clearly she had ordered them ahead, in the expectation of criticisms of the first night. The indefatigable bell boy had been ahead of them, but there was still time to rectify that.

The boy who had piloted them had vanished. Barrison picked up the whole bundle, and gave them a vigorous swing down the corridor. This had barely been accomplished when the door opened, and an impeccably attired lady's maid asked them to please come in; Miss Legaye would see them in a moment.

Kitty's parlor was like Kitty herself, discreet, yet subtly daring; conventional, yet alluring. She had made short work of the regulation hotel furnishings, and replaced them with trifles of her own, which gave the place a dainty and audacious air calculated to pique the interest of almost anybody.

One of the modern dark chintzes had been chosen by the little lady for her curtains and furniture coverings; she also had dared to put cushions of cherry color and of black on the chaise longue, and futurist posters in vivid oranges and greens upon the innocuous drab wall paper. The extreme touches had been made delicately, without vulgarity. Barrison, who had rather good taste himself, smiled as he read in this butterflylike audacity a sort of key to little Miss Kitty's own personality.

She came in almost immediately, and, though Jim had never admired her, he was forced to admit to himself at that moment that she was very charming and quite appealing.

The creamy pallor which was always so effective an asset of hers seemed a bit etherealized this morning, whether by a sleepless night or the gray, rainy light. Her dark hair was pulled straight back from her small face, with a rather sweet absence of coquetry; or was it, instead, the very quintessence of coquetry, brought to a fine art? Her big brown eyes were bigger and brown-er than ever, and her slim, almost childish little figure—which looked so adorable always in its young-girl frocks before the footlights—looked incom-parably adorable in a straight, severely cut little white wrapper, like the robe of an early martyr.

She came forward to meet them quickly, but quite without embarrassment.

"Mr. Barrison!" she exclaimed, rather breathlessly. "What is it? Of course I said I would see you at once. I knew you wouldn't come without some good reason. What do you want of me?"

Her eyes were as clear as the brown pools in a spring brook, and Barrison felt suddenly ashamed of himself and—almost—wroth with Grace Temple-ton for putting him up to this.

"Miss Legaye," he said, with some hesitation, "I am already calling myself all sorts of names for having aroused you at this unearthly hour. And you were not well, too."

"Oh, that headache!" she said. "That is all gone now! I got to bed early, and had a really decent sleep for once, so I am in good shape this morning! But—what *did* you want to see me about?"

Just as Barrison was trying to find words in which to answer her properly, the maid spoke from the doorway:

"You told me to take in the papers, miss, but there's none there."

Kitty turned in astonishment. "Not there! But they always leave them at eight, and I particularly said that I wanted all of them this morning. That's funny! Never mind; you can go down to the stand and get them, and Mr. Barrison can tell me what I want to know first of all. Oh, Mr. Barrison, tell me about last night! Did it all go off as well as it seemed to be going when I left?" She looked with honest eagerness into his eyes.

Barrison felt most uncomfortable, but he forced himself to say steadily: "Have you really not heard anything about what happened last night, Miss Legaye?"

If it were possible to turn paler, she turned paler then; and her eyes seemed to darken, as though with dread; yet there was nothing in her look but what might come from honest fear of the unknown.

"Mr. Barrison! What is it that you are trying to make me think? What do you mean? Oh—*oh*!" She drew in her breath sharply. "Is that what it means? Is that what you came here for—to—tell me something? Is that it, Mr. Barri-son?"

Her eyes pleaded with him, looking earnestly out of her little white face. She looked a butterfly no longer; rather, a tired and frightened little girl. "Won't you tell me what it all means?" she begged.

"Miss Legaye," Jim said gently, "there was a tragedy last night at the theater after you left."

"A tragedy?"

"Yes; there was—a murder."

She stared at him, as though she did not yet understand. "A murder?"

"Miss Legaye, I see it is a shock to you, but you must hear it from some one; you might as well hear it from me. Mr. Mortimer was shot last night during the last act, and is dead."

She shrieked—a thin, high, deadly shriek, which rang long in the ears of the two men. Her face grew smaller, sharper; she beat the air with her hands. The maid ran to her.

News? Oh, Heaven, yes! There was no question of this being news to her; it was news that was coming close to killing her.

"Say that again!" she managed to say, in a slow, thick utterance that sounded immeasurably strange from her lips. "Alan Mortimer was murdered? You said that? You are sure of it?"

"Yes, Miss Legaye."

She flung up her hands wildly, and fainted dead away.

CHAPTER XVI
A SCARLET EVENING COAT

IT WAS A REAL faint. They had a good bit of difficulty in getting her out of it.

There wasn't much room in Jim Barrison's mind for anything except self-reproach. He *knew* that the tidings of Mortimer's murder had come upon Kitty Legaye like a stroke of lightning. She had no more been prepared for it than she would have been prepared for the end of the world. He had an idea that the end of the world would, as a general proposition, have affected her much less. Barrison was no new hand, and not too soft-hearted or gullible; and he knew that what he had looked upon that morning was sheer, absolute shock and grief, unlooked for, terrible, devastating.

Poor little Kitty, with all her frivolities, had bigness in her. As she struggled back into the gray world, she obviously tried to straighten up and steady herself. The terror was all the time at the back of her brown eyes, but she was doing her best to be game, to be, as she herself would have expressed it, "a good sport."

Of course, she wanted particulars, and he gave them to her, feeling like a pickpocket all the time. Papers were obtained, and she was induced to take coffee with brandy in it, and—at last—she broke down and cried, which was what every one had been praying for since the beginning.

Probably never in his clear-cut, well-established career had Jim Barrison experienced what he was experiencing now: The sense that he had brought unnecessary suffering upon an innocent person, and brought it in a peculiarly merciless and unsportsmanlike way. He felt savage when he thought of that "tip" of Miss Templeton's—or did he, really? He was obliged to confess to himself that, where she was concerned, he would be almost sure to discover approximately extenuating circumstances!

It was partly to soothe his own aching conscience that Jim forced himself to ask a few perfunctory questions.

"You don't mind?" he asked Kitty.

"Naturally I don't," she said, trying not to cry, and choking down coffee. "You've been awfully kind, Mr. Barrison. If there's anything I can do to help, please let me. You know"—she looked at him in a sudden, piteous way—"I had expected to marry Mr. Mortimer. Maybe you can guess what all this means to me? Will you tell me what you wanted to know?"

"For one thing," he said, "we want to establish as nearly as we can when the murderer—the murderess, as we think it was—entered the theater. Old Roberts says that he went out through the alley to the street to get you a taxi——"

"Dear old thing!" she whispered.

"Yes; he is a nice old sort. He made it very clear that it was only his devotion to you that induced him to leave his post. Well, it seems almost certain that some one passed him, and perhaps you, in the alley last night. You don't remember seeing even a shadow that might be suspicious?"

She shook her head thoughtfully.

"No, I don't," she said. "But I was in a hurry, and wasn't looking out for anything of that sort. Roberts knows I was in a hurry?" She spoke quickly.

"Oh, yes. He says you were in a hurry, and not feeling well. The point is, did you see anything at all on your way to the taxi?"

"Nothing. I was only thinking of getting home and to bed; it had been a horrid evening."

Now, of course, the obvious thing for Jim Barrison to do then was to take his leave. More, it was manifestly the only decent thing for him to do. He had proved conclusively that Kitty had not expected the news of Mortimer's murder; in addition, she had declared that she had noticed no one on her way out to the taxi the night before. On the face of it, there was nothing further to be found out here. And yet, after he had got to his feet and taken up his hat, he lingered. As a matter of fact, he never was able, in looking back afterward, to tell just what insane impulse made him blurt out suddenly:

"Miss Legaye, you were wearing a red wrap last night, weren't you? Something quite bright, scarlet?"

She looked up at him faintly surprised. "Why, yes," she answered, "you saw it yourself, just as I was going out."

Jim hesitated, and then said something still more crazy: "Would you—do you very much mind letting me see it—now?"

She stared at him in undisguised astonishment. "Certainly," she said, rather blankly. "Celine, will you bring my red evening coat, please?"

The maid did so at once; it flamed there in the gray light of that rainy morning like some monstrous scarlet poppy. Barrison lifted a shimmering, brilliant fold, and looked at it.

"It's a gorgeous color!" he said, rather irrelevantly.

"Scarlet!" whispered Kitty, in a strange tone. "And to think I was wearing *that* last night. I do not believe that I shall ever feel like wearing scarlet again! You are going, Mr. Barrison?"

"Yes; you have been very patient with me, and very forgiving for having been the bearer of such bad news. Good-by. I won't even try to express the sympathy——"

"Don't; I understand. Mr. Barrison, *why* did you want to see this coat?"

"It was just an impulse!" he declared quickly. "You forgive me for that, too?"

She bent her head without speaking, and the two men went away.

"Tony," said Jim Barrison, when they were in the street once more, facing the wet blast, "it's no lie to say that facts are misleading."

"It's no lie to say they very often mislead *you*!" retorted Tony, somewhat acidly. He felt the loss of sleep more and more, and was fretful. Also, he was hungry. "What wild-goose chase are you off on now?"

"None; I'm going round in circles."

"You said it!"

"It's a fact," continued Barrison, unheeding, "that the little woman back there was genuinely shocked and upset by hearing of Mortimer's death."

"Rather!"

"But it is also a fact—also a fact, Tony—that that evening coat of hers is damp this morning, and it didn't begin to rain till after midnight!"

CHAPTER XVII
BLIND TRAILS

"MIND YOU," BARRISON WENT on hastily, "there are a hundred explanations of a thing like that; it isn't, strictly speaking, evidence at all. Only—I couldn't help noticing! Now, Tony, I want you to go home and go to bed—see?"

"It's lucky you do!" said Tony.

"Shut up! Go to bed and sleep your fool head off; and then—get back there to the Golden Arms, and find out who saw Miss Legaye come in last night; what time it was, whether she seemed excited, and—*what she wore*! That last is the most important. Make up to the maid. You can bribe, torture, or make love to her; I don't care which. Only find out everything you can. Get me?"

Tony grunted, and departed.

Jim turned his face toward Forty-fourth Street. He knew that John Carlton usually breakfasted at the Lambs' Club, and he needed his help. Also, he thought tenderly of the prospect of a mixed grill. Barrison could get along with very little sleep, when he was on a case, but he had to have food. Carlton was at breakfast, devouring, with about equally divided attention, bacon and eggs and the morning papers. He welcomed Jim with much excitement and a flood of slang.

"Well, what do you know about this, Barrison? I can't seem to get a line on myself to-day. Am I the whole cheese, or am I an also ran? Do I stack up as the one best bet, or do I crawl into a hole and pull the hole in after me? Sit down!"

"Talk English!" suggested Barrison good-naturedly as he obeyed. "Order me some breakfast, first, and then tell me what you're talking about."

Carlton, having with difficulty been prevented from ordering a meal adequate to the needs of a regiment on march, condescended to translate his emotions.

"You see, it's this way," he explained, munching toast and marmalade. "That poor guy going out like that—I never liked him, but it was a rotten way to finish, and I'd like to broil whoever did it alive—leaves me, so to speak, guessing. My play is off, for the present anyway, and I've been spending my royalties already. On the other hand, I'm getting some simply priceless advertising! Everybody will be after me, I guess, and all the beautiful leading men will be thirsting to play the part in which poor Mortimer achieved eternal fame by getting killed. I may sound flippant, but I'm not; it's the only way I can express myself—except on paper! Now, where do I get off? Am I a racing car or a flivver?"

"You'll probably find out soon enough," Jim told him. "Meanwhile, I want your help."

"Nothing doing!" said Carlton energetically. "Meanwhile, I want yours! I can live just long enough for you to drink that cup of coffee without talking, but after that it's only a matter of seconds before I cash in, if you don't tell me everything that happened last night. Beastly of you and the governor not to let me back, so I could be in on what was doing."

Barrison told him what had happened. He was not too completely communicative, however; he liked the playwright, and had no reason to distrust him, but he knew that this case was likely to be a big one, and a hard one, and he had no mind to take outsiders into his confidence unless it was strictly necessary.

"And now," he said, "I've done my part, and, I hope, saved you from an early grave shared by the cat who died of curiosity. Come across, and do yours!"

Carlton grinned. "Talking slang so as to make yourself intelligible to my inferior intelligence? All right; fire away! What can I do for you?"

Barrison told him that he wanted to find out about a wild West show called by the name of its manager, Blinkey or Blankey.

Carlton scowled at him wonderingly. "Now, what sort of a game's that?" he demanded. "What has a wild West show to do with my perfectly good play——"

"Never mind. Can you find out for me?"

The writer shook his head.

"Not in a million years. I don't know anything about the profession except where it happens to hit me. Why don't you tackle the governor? He knows everything and everybody."

"I may yet. But it isn't anything that really concerns him. And I don't imagine he's very cheery this morning."

"I believe that little thing! It's beastly hard lines for him! Tell you what I'll do, Barrison. I'll give you a card to Ted Lucas. He's a decent sort of chap, on the dramatic department of the New York *Blaze*. If he can't help you, maybe there'll be some one in his office who can."

"Thanks. That's just what I want."

Armed with the card, Barrison said good-by and departed. He met two or three men whom he knew on his way out. One and all were talking about the murder. He was not known to have any connection with the case, so he escaped being held up for particulars, but he heard enough to show him that this was going to be the sensation of the whole theatrical world.

It was not yet ten o'clock, and Dukane would not be in his office, so he went downtown to hunt up Ted Lucas in the roaring offices of the *Blaze*.

He had to wait a bit, with the deafening clatter of typewriters, and the jangle of telephones beating about his ears. Then a keen-faced but very quiet young man rather foppishly dressed, and with sleek hair which looked as though it had been applied with a paint brush, appeared.

"I'm Lucas," he explained politely. "Wanted to see me?"

Barrison knew reporters pretty well, and this one was typical. The detective wasted as few words as possible, but stated what he was after. Lucas shook his head doubtfully.

"Never heard of any such show," he said. "I'll have a look at the files, though. My chief is rather a shark for keeping records of past performances. Will you look in a bit later—or phone?"

"I'll phone," said Barrison, preparing to leave. He had not expected any rapid results, yet he felt vaguely disappointed. Or was it because he was tired? "See here," he said impulsively. "You cover a lot of theatrical assignments, don't you?"

"Quite a lot," said the reporter indifferently, eying him.

"Isn't there anything playing here in town now with a—a wild West feature? Anything that includes a shooting stunt, or cowboy atmosphere, or—or that?"

Barrison could not help clinging to that faint clue concerning Mortimer's connection with the "daredevil" outfit, out West.

Ted Lucas considered. "Why, no," he said. "I don't know of any. You wouldn't mean a single act, like Ritz the Daredevil, would you?"

"Ritz the Daredevil!" Barrison leaped at the name. Of course, it might be nonsense, but there was something that looked like just the shadow of a coincidence. "Who is she?"

"Just a crack shot, a girl who plays at a bum vaudeville theater this week. I don't know why she calls herself a 'daredevil.' It isn't such a daring stunt to shoot at a target. But she's clever with a gun, I understand. I'm to 'cover' her act to-night."

Barrison thought quickly. It was only the ghost of a trail, but——

"You're going to see her to-night?"

"Yes. Going to see the show from the front and interview her afterward. She's through with her stunt, I hear, about nine thirty. It isn't a usual thing, but Coyne—who owns the theater—has a bit of a pull with us; advertising, you know; and we usually give one of his acts a write-up every week."

"Might I come along?"

"You? Sure thing! But I warn you, it'll be an awful thing! It's one of those continuous affairs. Well, have it your own way. If you'll meet me at the theater, I can get you in on my pass. Eight?"

"Eight it is."

Barrison waited for directions as to the whereabouts of Coyne's Music Hall, of which he had never heard, and took his departure. He went into a telephone booth to call up Lowry, but found that the inspector would not be at his office until the afternoon. Then he went uptown again, and, taking a deep breath and a big brace with it, went to call on Max Dukane.

He had no real reason for dreading an interview with him; the manager had always been most courteous to him. Yet he did feel a shade of apprehension. Something told him that the Dukane of yesterday would not be quite the Dukane of to-day. And it wasn't only the tragedy which had brought him so much financial loss which was to be considered. Ever since Willie Coster had intimated that Dukane had a secret reason for keeping dark the conditions under which he had come across Mortimer, Barrison had felt uneasy in regard to him. He had always recognized in the manager a man of immense power and authority. If he had a sufficient reason, he could guess that he would be immensely unscrupulous as well.

However, at a little after half past eleven o'clock, he presented himself at the great man's office.

This time, though there were half a dozen people ahead of him, he did not have to wait at all. The fact surprised him, but when he had been admitted to Dukane's presence, he understood it better. He had been thus speedily summoned in order to be the more speedily dismissed.

"Hello, Barrison," said Dukane crisply. "Anything I can do for you?"

He sat at his desk like an iron image; his face was hard and cold. He did not look so much angry as stern. It was clear that, in his own stony fashion, he had flung yesterday into the discard, and was not any too pleased to be reminded of it.

Barrison was not asked to sit down, so stood by the desk, feeling rather like a small boy reporting to his teacher.

"Yes, Mr. Dukane," he said quietly, "there is. I've come about the case."

"Case?"

"The murder of Alan Mortimer."

Dukane raised his heavy eyebrows. "I am not interested in it."

"Mr. Dukane, I can scarcely believe that. Mortimer was your star, under your management; I should imagine that the disaster to him must concern you very closely."

Dukane laid down a paper cutter which he had been holding in his hand.

"Concern me?" he said, in a hard, disagreeable tone. "Yes, it does concern me. It concerns me to the tune of several thousands of dollars. The part was especially worked up for him; there is no one available to take it at a moment's notice. But there my concern begins and ends. So far as his murderer goes——"

"Yes, that is what we are chiefly interested in."

"*I* am not interested in it. Mortimer was an investment, so far as I was concerned. It is an investment which has failed. I have other things to think of that seem to me more important—and more profitable."

"But you engaged me, professionally, to——"

"You will receive your check."

Barrison flushed indignantly. "Mr. Dukane! You cannot think I meant that. But if you were sufficiently interested to engage me——"

Dukane raised his hand and stopped him. "Barrison," he said, in short, clear-cut accents, "let us understand each other. I engaged you to keep Alan Mortimer alive. Alive, he was worth a good deal to me. Dead, he is worth nothing. I was perfectly willing to pay to protect my property; but having lost it, I wash my hands of the matter."

"Don't you really want to see his murderer brought to justice?"

"I really care nothing about it."

"Then you are not even willing to help the authorities?"

"Help?" The manager raised his head haughtily, and stared at him with cold eyes. "What have I to do with it? What should I have to say that could help?"

"You might tell us something about Mr. Mortimer's life—something that could point toward a possible enemy. You know as well as I do that when a man dies under such circumstances, it is necessary for the officers engaged on the case to know as much of his life and antecedents as possible. In this case, no one seems to know anything except you, Mr. Dukane. That's why I am obliged to come to you."

"I know nothing about his life, nor about his antecedents. I picked him up in a Western town, stranded, after his show had gone to pieces."

"What was the name of the show?"

"I haven't the faintest idea. Now, if you will be good enough to let me get on with my morning's business——"

"I shall certainly do so," said Barrison quietly, as he turned away. "But I must warn you, Mr. Dukane, that I believe you are making a mistake. The detective force will find out what they have to find out. If you have any reason——"

"Reason?"

"I say, if you have any reason for wanting them not to do so, you would do much better to forestall them, and give them your help frankly to begin with."

"Is that all?"

"That is quite all, Mr. Dukane."

"Very well, Barrison. As I say, you will receive your check in due time. Barrison——"

The detective turned at the door, and waited for him to go on. Dukane was sitting with his head somewhat bent; after a moment he lifted it, and said, in a gentler tone than he had used before during the interview:

"I have given you the impression of being a hard man. It is a truthful impression; I am a hard man. I should not be where I am to-day, had I not been hard, very hard. But if I have spoken to you with bitterness, you will remember, please, that I feel no bitterness toward you. I like you, on the contrary. But in my life there is no place for individual likes or dislikes. Long ago, I decided to play a great game for great stakes. I have won at that game; I shall continue to win. Nothing else counts with me; nothing! That is all. Good-by, Barrison!"

"Good-by, sir," the younger man said, and went out of the big, rich, inner office, where even the noise and bustle of the world came softly, lest anything disturb the imperious brain brooding and planning at the desk.

It was in a very sober mood that Barrison reached Miss Templeton's hotel at luncheon time, and sent up his card.

CHAPTER XVIII
MISS TEMPLETON AT HOME

"I THOUGHT YOU'D JUST as lief have lunch up here," said Miss Templeton.

Barrison looked at her as though he had never seen her before. Indeed, he was not sure that he ever had.

It is an experience not unknown to most of us, that of finding ourselves confronting some one or something long familiar, as we thought, but presented all at once in a new guise. From the first, Jim had felt in Miss Templeton a personality deeper and truer than would be superficially descried through her paint and powder and conspicuous dresses. But, so far, his idea of her had had to be more or less theoretical and instinctive; he had not had very much to go by.

To-day, and for the first time, he saw in the flesh the woman whom he had half unconsciously idealized in the spirit: a very sweet, rather shy woman, whose starry eyes and clear skin looked the more strikingly lovely for being, to-day, unassisted by artifice.

She wore a nunlike gray frock, and her splendid gold hair was simply arranged. It would be hard to imagine a greater contrast than that which she presented with the Woman in Purple of but a brief fortnight ago.

Her parlor was a further surprise. Unconsciously, he found himself remembering Kitty Legaye's dainty and bizarre apartment, and comparing the two. Who would have dreamed that it was in such surroundings as these that this woman would choose to live?

She had not, like Kitty, transformed her apartment with stuffs and ornamentations. Her individuality had somehow transfused itself through everything, superior to trappings or furnishings. She had left the room very much as it must have been when she took it. The curtains and the carpets were the same that the hotel manager had put there; but they seemed somehow of secondary importance. On that drab regulation background she had contrived to paint herself and what she lived for in colors that were, while subdued, unmistakable. No one could enter there without knowing that he was in the sanctum of a personality.

First and foremost, there were books; books on shelves, on the table, books everywhere. And they were not best sellers either, if one could judge by their plain heavy bindings.

"Italian history," she said, seeing him glance curiously at a title. "I take up wild fads from time to time, and read about nothing else until the subject is exhausted, or until I am! At present I spend my time in the company of the Medici!"

He thought that she was the last woman on earth whom he would expect to care for such things, but that was to be the least of his surprises. All her books sounded one persistent note, romance, adventure, a passionate love for and yearning after the beautiful, the thrilling, the emotional in life. There were books of folklore and legends, medieval tales and modern essays on strange, far lands more full of color and wonder than ours. There were translations from different tongues, there were volumes full of Eastern myths, and others of sea tales and stories of the vast prairies and the Barbary Coast. There was not a single popular novel among them all. Every one was a treasure box of romance.

The pictures which she had collected to adorn her rooms were equally self-revealing. They ranged from photographs and engravings to Japanese prints; more than one looked as though it had come from a colored supplement. Here, again, the message was invariably adventurous or romantic.

Miss Templeton smiled as she saw her guest's bewildered look.

"It's a queer assortment, isn't it?" she said. "But I can't stand the flat, polite-looking things that people pretend to admire. Things have to be alive, to *call* me, somehow!"

All at once, it seemed to Jim that he had the keynote to her character. It was vitality. She was superbly alive—with the vivid faults as well as the vivid advantages of intense life.

Luncheon was served at once, and it proved almost as cosmopolitan in its items as the rest of Miss Templeton's appurtenances. She had ordered soft-shell crabs to begin with, because she said that for the first twenty-five years of her life she had never had a chance to taste them, and now, since she could, she was making up for lost time, and ate them every day! With truly feminine logic, she had made her next course broiled ham and green corn, because she had been brought up on them in the Middle West. She had a new kind of salad she had recently heard of, solely because it *was* new; and she finished with chocolate ice cream for the reason, as she explained, that chocolate ice cream had always been her idea of a party, and when she wanted to feel very grand, she made a point of having it.

Barrison was no fool where women were concerned; he knew that she was purposely making herself attractive to him, and he knew that she was sufficiently fascinating to be dangerous. Her unexpectedness alone would make her interesting to a man of his type. But he could usually keep his head; he proposed to keep it now. So far as playing the game went, he was not altogether a bad hand at it himself, and Miss Templeton, he imagined, was not precisely a young or unsophisticated village maid. That there was danger merely made it the more exhilarating.

"Mr. Barrison," she said at last, "of course you are asking yourself what it is that I have to tell you—why, in short, I asked you to lunch to-day."

"I am asking myself nothing at the present moment," he returned promptly, "except why, by the favor of the gods, I should be playing in such extraordinary luck! But, of course, I'll be interested in anything you have to tell me."

"Yes," she said slowly. "I think you probably will be interested. You'll forgive me if I begin with a little—a very little—personal history? It won't be the 'story of my life,' don't be frightened! But it's essential to what I want to tell you afterward."

"Please tell me anything and everything you care to," he begged her, with the air of grave attention which a woman always delights to see in a man to whom she is speaking.

She sat, her chin resting on her clasped hands; her eyes abstracted, fixed on nothing tangible that he could see, as she spoke:

"You understand me a little better now, seeing me at home—in as much of a home as I can have—among the books and pictures that I love, don't you? Never mind; perhaps you don't. Though I don't think I'm very hard to understand. I'm just a woman who's always been hunting for something that——"

"The Blue Bird of Happiness?" he suggested gently. "You've read it, of course?"

"Naturally—and loved it. But—I don't imagine that *I* could ever find my Blue Bird at home, as they did. It would have to be in some very far place, I'm sure, only to be won after tremendous effort!"

"After all, that Blue Bird they found at home flew away as soon as it was found!" he reminded her. "I can see that you hear the call of adventure more clearly than most people. Have you always dreamed of the 'strange roads?' Or has it been a part of—growing up?"

"You were going to say 'growing older!'" she said, with a faint smile. "I think I've always been so. I seem always to have been struggling away from where I was—rotten, discontented nature, isn't it? Will you hand me those cigarettes, please?"

Barrison proffered his own case, and she took and lighted one with a grave, almost a dreamy air. "You see," she said, "I was brought up in a deadly little Illinois town. While I was still practically a baby, I got married. He was a vaudeville performer, and to me quite a glorious personage. The girls I knew thought so, too. He was better looking than any drummer who'd been there, and had better manners than the clerk at the drug store, who was the village beau."

She spoke calmly, without sentiment, yet she did not sound cynical; her manner was too simple for that.

"Well, I didn't find the Blue Bird *there*. I found nothing in that marriage with a glimmer of happiness in it, until I came in sight of the divorce court. That looked to me like the gate of heaven! Then I went into the movies."

"The movies! I never knew that."

"No, of course not. No one knows it. It's all right to advertise leaving the legitimate stage for the screen; but if you've come the other way, and graduated from the screen to the stage, you're not nearly so likely to tell the press man. Anyway, I was in an old-style picture company—I'm talking about six years ago—that was working on some blood-and-thunder short reels out in Arizona, when they hired a bunch of professional cow-punchers for some rough Western stuff in a feature picture. Alan Mortimer was one of them."

"Alan Mortimer!"

"Yes, or, rather, Morton. He changed his name later on." She looked at him. "Surely you must have guessed that I knew him before this engagement—this play? How did you suppose that we got to be so intimate in two weeks of rehearsals? *I* didn't spend the summer at Nantucket!"

"That's where Miss Legaye met him, isn't it?"

"Yes. She always goes down there, and Dukane wanted him to be there while Jack Carlton was—he was working on the play, you know. But I hadn't maneuvered and worked and planned for nothing. I'd got on in my profession, and played a few leading parts. I moved heaven and earth to get into his company—and I succeeded!"

"You mean—you wanted to see him again?"

Her eyes flashed suddenly. For a second she looked fierce and threatening, as she had looked that first day in the restaurant.

"Wanted? I had thought of nothing else for five—nearly six years! I used to be mad about him, you see. He made women feel like that."

"I know he did."

Barrison spoke naturally enough, but truth to tell, he was feeling a bit dazed. The Mortimer case was developing in a singular fashion. It was like one of those queer little Oriental toys where you open box inside box, to find in each case a smaller one awaiting you. He wondered whether he was ever to get to the end of this affair. The further you went in it, the more complicated it seemed to get. But she was speaking:

"I was very much in love with him. But I never had any illusions as to his real character. He was rather a blackguard, in more ways than one. It wasn't only that he treated women badly—or, anyway, lightly. He was crooked. I am very sure of that. He gambled, and the men in the company wouldn't play with him; they said he didn't play straight. There was one elderly man with a daughter, who was his particular crony; they were both supposed to be shady in a lot of ways—I mean the two men. So far as I know, the girl was all right. Evidently they stuck together, too; perhaps they had to, knowing too much about each other! But I saw the older man at the theater two or three times during rehearsals."

"What did he look like?" demanded Barrison, struck with a sudden idea.

"Oh, very respectable looking, like so many crooks! Elderly, as I say, and thin, and——"

"You surely don't mean Mortimer's old valet, Wrenn?"

She looked at him in a startled fashion.

"Why, yes, that's the name. I don't believe I should have remembered it if you hadn't reminded me. The man was Wrenn, I am sure."

Jim's pulse was pounding. Light at last, if only a glimmer! He was really finding out something about Mortimer's past, really coming upon things that might have led up, directly or indirectly, to his murder.

"Do you remember anything about the daughter?" he asked.

"Not very much. She rode for us in one or two scenes, but she was hard to use in the picture. I do remember that she was an awfully disagreeable sort of girl, and most unpopular. What I wanted to tell you particularly was that Mortimer had a crooked record behind him, and that at least one man near him—this Wrenn—knew it. That was one thing. The other——"

But Barrison could not help interrupting.

"Just a moment, if you don't mind, Miss Templeton! This is all tremendously interesting to me—more interesting than you can possibly guess! It's just possible that you've put me on the clew I've been looking for. Was there any man in that crowd called Blankey, or Blinkey, or anything like that?"

She shook her head wonderingly.

"Not that I know of," she said. "But Alan had several particular pals, he and Wrenn. One of them may have been called that. I don't know."

Jim was slightly disappointed, but, after all, he had gained a good deal already; he could afford to be philosophical and patient.

"And you don't remember anything about the girl at all?" he insisted. "Only that she was disagreeable, and could ride?"

"Wait a minute," said Miss Templeton thoughtfully; "I've some old snapshots tucked away. There ought to be some group with that girl in it."

Barrison smoked three cigarettes in frantic succession while she hunted. Finally, she put a little kodak photograph in his hand.

"There am I," she said, "rather in the background, dressed up as a beautiful village lass—do you see? And that's Alan. He was handsome, wasn't he?" Her voice was quite steady as she said it, but it had rather a minor ring. "And there—that girl over there in the shirtwaist and habit skirt, is Wrenn's daughter."

As Barrison looked, he felt as certain as though he had seen her with his own eyes, that she—Wrenn's daughter—was the woman who had been in Mortimer's dressing room the night before.

CHAPTER XIX
GLIMMERS IN THE DARKNESS

HE RAISED HIS EYES to find Miss Templeton regarding him from the other side of the table with a rather curious expression.

"I had no idea that you would be interested in the Wrenn girl," she said. "I thought that my information would point rather toward her father. Why are you interested in her?"

Barrison hesitated. Charming as he found this woman, he had no mind to confide in her just yet. He countered with another question, one which had, as a matter of fact, trembled on his lips ever since he had come into the room. It was an impertinent question, and he knew that she would have a perfect right to resent it. Yet there was an indefinable attitude about her—not familiarity, but something suggesting intimacy—when she spoke to him, that made him somewhat bolder than his good taste could justify.

"Miss Templeton," he said, "you have just told me that you cared so much for Alan Mortimer that you waited for six years to get in the same company with him. I know that only a few days ago you were still sufficiently interested in him to be——"

He really did not know how to put it, but she did.

"Jealous?" she suggested promptly, and without emotion. "Oh, yes, I was—in a way—insanely jealous. You see, it had become an obsession with me; I don't imagine I really loved him any longer, but I was being cheated of something I had worked for and sacrificed for. Probably, not being a woman, you wouldn't understand."

"Probably not," said Jim. "And—will you forgive me for adding this?—I understand even less your mood to-day. Last night you were deeply moved at the play; I saw that. Perhaps"—he paused; he did not know whether to speak of the revolver or not—"you were even on the verge of—some scene—some violent expression of emotion, some——"

She glanced at him, startled. "How did you know that? But, suppose it were true. Will you go on, if you please?"

"No; I am merely offending you."

"You don't—offend me." Her tone was singular. "I should really like you to go on. There was something else that you did not understand. What was it?"

"It is in the present tense," he answered. "It's something that I cannot understand now. Miss Templeton, you have done me the honor of asking me here to-day, and of talking to me with a certain measure of confidence. You have been most gracious and charming, a perfect hostess. I have enjoyed myself completely. And yet—last night, the man who has occupied your thoughts and, let us say, your hopes for years past—was tragically murdered."

She was silent for a second or two. "Is that what you don't understand?" she demanded abruptly.

"Yes. I cannot reconcile the two women I know to exist: The angry, passionate, jealous woman who looked—excuse me—as though she could have done murder herself, a short fortnight ago, and the woman who has been talking to me to-day about her fruitless quest for the Blue Bird of Happiness."

"I think that is rather stupid of you, then," she answered composedly. "Can't you see it's all part of the same thing? The quest for love—for the unattainable—but, Mr. Barrison, that is something else which puzzles you, which, in a way, jars on you. I can see it quite well. It is to you a strange and rather a horrible thing that I should be calm to-day, giving you lunch—and eating it, too!—talking of all sorts of things, while he, the man I used to be in love with, is lying dead. Isn't that it?"

"That is certainly part of it."

After a moment, she pushed back her chair and rose restlessly.

"No, don't get up!" she exclaimed, as he, too, rose. "Sit still, and let me prowl about as I choose. I am not used to expressing myself, Mr. Barrison, except in my actions. Words always bother me, and I never seem able to make myself clear in them. Let me see if I can make you see this thing, not as I do, but a little less confusedly. In the desert, a man sometimes follows a mirage for a long time; longs for it, prays for it, worships it from afar. He is dying of thirst, you see, and his feeling about it is so acute it is almost savage. The mirage isn't real, the water that he thinks he sees is just a cloud effect, but he wants it, and while he is hunting it, he is not entirely sane. One day he finds it is not real. All that everlasting journeying for nothing; all that thirst for something that never has existed! Men do strange things when they find out that the water they were traveling toward is nothing but a mirage. Some of them kill themselves. But suppose, just when that man was losing his reason with the disappointment and the weariness—suppose just then some traveler, some Good Samaritan, or—just a traveler like himself, or—some—never mind!" She choked whatever it was that she had meant to say. "Suppose, then, some one appears and offers him a real gourd of real water! Does he think much more about the mirage? He only wonders that he ever dreamed and suffered in search for it. But—it had taken the sight of the real clear water to make him see that the other was just a feverish dream."

She paused in her restless pacing up and down the room, and looked at him. "Do you understand better now?"

"No," said Barrison flatly. "It is very pretty, and, I suppose, symbolic, but I have not the least idea, if you will pardon me for saying so, what you are driving at."

"Think it over," said Miss Templeton, lighting another cigarette. "One more touch of symbolism for you. Suppose the—traveler—who showed him the real gourd of water should spill it, or drink it all himself, or—refuse to share it, after all? What do you think would be likely to happen then?"

"I should think the thirsty man would be quite likely to shoot him!" said Jim laughing a little.

She smiled at him. "Ah," she said, "you see you understand more than you pretend. Yes, that's just what might happen——Oh, by the by, Mr. Barrison, there was something else that I sent for you to say. You know I warned you in regard to Kitty Legaye?"

"Yes, but it is out of the question," said Barrison. "I am sure that Mortimer's murder was an overwhelming surprise to her."

"Maybe so," she said thoughtfully. "But I am sure that, when I rushed out of the theater last night in that darkness and confusion, I saw Miss Legaye's face at the window of a taxicab at the front of the house."

"At the front of the house! But that would be impossible!"

"I only tell you what I am certain I saw."

"Would you be prepared to swear that?"

She considered this a moment. "No," she admitted finally. "I would not be prepared to go quite as far as that. I felt very sure at the time, and I feel almost as sure now. But a glimpse like that is sometimes not much to go by. I only tell you for what it is worth. And now, Mr. Barrison, I have an engagement, and I am going to turn you out. You forgive me?"

"I am disposed to forgive you anything," said Jim, with formal gallantry, "after the help you have given me—to say nothing of the pleasure I have had!"

She made a faint little face at him. "That sounds like something on the stage!" she protested. "I wish you would think over my—my——"

"Allegory?" he suggested.

"I was going to say my confession. I am sure, the more carefully you remember it, the simpler it will become. Especially remember your own suggestion as to what would happen to the niggardly rescuer who might refuse to be a rescuer, after all!"

Barrison saw fit to ignore this. He shook hands cordially and convention-
ally.

"Good-by," he said. "And thanks."

"Good-by," she returned briefly.

As he went downstairs, his face was a shade hot. There were two reasons for
it. For one thing, Miss Templeton's attitude—the allegory of the mirage and
the gourd of water—what did she mean by it? Was it possible that she—that
she—Jim Barrison was not conceited about women, but he could hardly avoid
being impressed with a subtle flattery in her manner, a flattery dignified by
what certainly looked like rather touching sincerity. And on his part—well,
he was not yet prepared to tell himself baldly just what he did feel.

Several years ago, Barrison had imagined himself in love with a beautiful,
heartless girl who had baffled him in one of his big cases. She had gone
out of his life forever, and he had imagined himself henceforth immune. Yet
this woman, with her curious paradoxes of temperament, her extraordinary
frankness, and her strange reserves, her cold-blooded dismissal of a past
passion, and her emotional yearning for joy and the fullness of life—well, he
knew in his heart of hearts, whether he put it in words or not, that she thrilled
him as no woman in the world had ever thrilled him yet.

CHAPTER XX

CHECKING UP

"I KNOW that the Wrenn woman probably did it," said Barrison, speaking to Lowry in the inspector's office. "And I'm going to move heaven and earth to find her. But I've a hunch—a sort of theory—that those two women, Miss Templeton and Miss Legaye, know more than they've told us yet."

He tried to keep himself from feeling guilty when he spoke of Grace Templeton; certainly his own reasons for particular interest in her had no place in a police investigation, and yet he became subtly embarrassed whenever her name came up.

"Never," said Lowry, smoking his large, black, bad cigar, "never have theories. Find out the situation, and build your theories into that. You started off on the idea that these two women—Templeton and Legaye—were mixed up in the business somehow. You've been chasing 'round, worrying about them, to make that idea good. Now, I don't believe either of 'em knows a darned thing about it! They may both have been in love with the man, but nowadays actresses, with their futures ahead, don't often queer themselves that way. However, if there were any evidence against either of 'em, I'd go after it fast enough. But there isn't. In fact, there's conclusive evidence clearing them both. There's the pistol, for instance. Not one initial among the four belonging to the two women resembles an M."

"One moment, inspector!" broke in Barrison. "That isn't an M, it's a W."

"Discovered that, eh?" remarked the inspector imperturbably. "I wondered if you would. If you'll look at the pistol closely, though, my dear boy, you'll find that the angle at which it is engraved is a curious one. It might be either an M or a W. It depends on how you look at it. The letter is oddly shaped; looked at from different points, it makes just as good a W as it does an M, and vice versa. Well, the ladies in question have no more W's in their names than they have M's. Then, Miss Templeton could not have got behind the scenes in time."

"I imagine not," admitted Jim. "Of course, we are dealing in what was possible, not likely; the door was unguarded just then, and——"

"The door was unguarded after the shot, not before."

"If you believe the man Lynch. But—mind you, I suspect her no more than you, but—she was familiar with the theater."

"Familiar—hell! No one's familiar with any place in the pitch dark! And the other woman had gone home, hadn't she?"

"Miss Legaye had gone home, as it was generally supposed," said Jim, feeling obliged to register conscientiously every passing suspicion of his. "But Miss Templeton thinks she saw her near the front of the theater just after the tragedy."

"Well, you've only got that woman's word for *that*! Will she swear to it? No? I thought not! She's just talking through her hat, either to queer the other, or to make herself interesting to you! Say, Barrison, you're dippy on this thing! I always thought you were a pretty snappy detective for a young un! Now get rid of your theories, and your hunches and your intuitions and your suspicions, and check up! That's what I've been doing all day, and, take it from me, while it may be old-fashioned, it's the method that gets there nine times out of ten. Here goes!"

He took a sheet of paper and made notes, as he talked.

"Now that shot, according to the medical report, was fired at close range; very close range, indeed. The khaki of the man's uniform was quite a bit burned by it. The bullet entered under the right arm, so he must have had his arms lifted, either to take hold of Miss Merivale, as she said, or for some other reason. It entered the body below the right armpit, and made a clean drill through the right lung at a slightly upward angle. Then it lodged in an upper rib just under the right breast. That explains the big splotch of blood on the breast. It could have been fired from either of two ways."

He drew a rough diagram on the page before him, representing an imaginary, cylindrical man, two crosses, and a couple of dotted lines.

"So! If Miss Merivale did it," he explained, pencil in hand, "he'd have to be standing facing toward the front of the house, with his arm slightly raised, and his right side exposed to her aim."

"Isn't that an unlikely attitude, under the circumstances?"

"It is unlikely, but it is perfectly possible. It's only in songs that every little movement has a meaning all its own! Do you always have a good and logical reason for every motion you make? If you do, you're a freak! The great difficulty with most detectives is that they try to get a reason and a sequence for everything, as though they were putting a puzzle together or writing a play. In real life, half the things we do we do for no reason at all, or from sheer natural human contrariness! However, never mind that. Now, if the other woman—the woman we believe was in the theater last night—fired the shot, she only had to stand in close at the foot of the four-step entrance, and reach up. Even if she were a small woman, she would be able to place her bullet just about where it was found. It's a toss-up, Barrison. Either Miss Merivale fired that shot, or the unknown woman did."

"The unknown woman I don't consider unknown any longer. She is Wrenn's daughter, without a doubt."

"On Miss Templeton's testimony? Tut, tut, my dear Barrison!"

"But, surely, the unknown woman, if you insist on continuing to think her unknown, is the more likely bet of the two?"

Inspector Lowry pulled at his cigar, and wrinkled his heavy brows.

"Likely! I'm mortally afraid of those 'likely' clues! When a thing looks too blamed 'likely,' I get scared. Nature and life and crime don't work that way! Besides," drawled the inspector, "we've not got her, and we *have* got the other one! There's everything in possession!"

"But you aren't going to hold Miss Merivale on a mere——"

"Hold your horses, boy! We aren't holding her at all at present. She is as free as air, and will continue to be free for quite a while, anyway. But she's being watched, Barrison, my boy, she's being watched every minute. And she'll go on being watched."

Lowry relighted his defunct cigar.

"Incidentally," he added, "we've got a few fresh points on this. You'd be interested in hearing them, I suppose?"

"Interested!"

"Very well. For one thing, Mrs. Parry, the dresser at the theater, has given us rather an odd piece of evidence. She says that a messenger boy called at Miss Merivale's dressing room during the evening. She was not in the room at the time, but saw him knock, saw him admitted, and saw him go away."

"Nothing odd in that, surely—on a first night?"

"Nothing at all odd. Mrs. Parry also recalls that, when she went in to help Miss Merivale for the last act——"

"Miss Merivale had no change for the last act."

"No; so I understand. But she had gone back to her dressing room as usual for a few final touches. She had to alter her make-up slightly, hadn't she?"

"Yes; she had to be rather paler in the last act." Barrison was somewhat impressed by Lowry's thorough, even if archaic, way of getting his facts.

"Quite so," said the inspector equably. "Well, Mrs. Parry says that, as she entered the dressing room, she saw Miss Merivale walking up and down the room, evidently very angry. She had a note in her hand, and as she saw the woman, she tore it up in a lot of little pieces, and made an effort to become composed. Then she went hastily over to the dressing table, and caught up something that was lying there."

"Something! What?"

"Mrs. Parry does not know. She knows that it was a small object possibly as long as her hand. She does not vouch for its shape. She just saw it in the flash of an eye."

"And what is Miss Merivale supposed to have done with it?"

"Miss Merivale put it, very swiftly indeed, into the front of her white gown."

Barrison felt thunderstruck. That pretty, frank-eyed girl! Why, the thing was unbelievable! Impetuously he said:

"But, as you've impressed on me more than once, the testimony of a single person can't be conclusive. Suppose———"

"Suppose that testimony is borne out by that of others? Miss McAllister remembers Miss Merivale's fingering the buttons on the front of her blouse several times, in a nervous way. And two of the minor actors in that scene say that she kept her hand at her breast when it was not part of the business, as though she could not entirely forget something she carried there."

Lowry paused, as though to let these points sink into his hearer's intelligence. Then he continued:

"We found the torn scraps of the note, at least enough of them to be able to get quite a fair idea of what its purport had been." Lowry opened the drawer of his desk and took out a Manila envelope. From it he drew a sheet of paper upon which had been pasted a number of words, some of them in sequence and some of them detached and far apart. He pushed the paper across to Barrison.

"Have a look," he said laconically. Barrison read:

How madly—you—you accept—know I may hop—you pretend—needn't expect—scape, you beau—might just as—make up—rrender—to-ni———

"What do you make of it?" asked Lowry, after Barrison had stared at the cryptic mosaic of paper scraps for a moment or two.

The younger detective began to fill in and piece together. He evolved the logical complete letter:

> You know how madly I love you. If you accept the accompany-
> ing I know I may hope. Though you pretend, you needn't expect
> to escape, you beauty. You might just as well make up your mind
> to surrender the battle to-night.

Lowry read it and smiled.

"Quite good," he pronounced. "Here's another answer."

And he pushed another sheet toward Jim.

This one read—with the words of the recovered scraps underlined—as follows:

> No matter how determinedly, how madly you resist, you accept
> your fate. You know I may hope. You pretend courage, but you
> need not expect to escape, you beautiful fiend! You might just
> as well make up your mind to surrender to-night.

Barrison read, and then, with a slight shrug, pushed it back toward the older man.

"I see very little difference," he said.

"Really? Can't you see that one is a love letter, and one a threat?"

"If you choose to put in phrases like 'you beautiful fiend!'" said Barrison, raising his eyebrows.

Lowry chuckled. "Doesn't it sound kind of natural?" he queried. "Oh, well, maybe I'm behind the times! I just tried to make it natural. But seriously, Jim, there is a difference, and you'd better get on to it quick. That letter—which was from Mortimer; I've had the handwriting verified—might have been a threat to a woman whom he was dead set on getting, or a billet-doux to a girl he was sweet on, and who was acting shy. Isn't that right?"

Barrison frowned over the two epistles.

"You've something else up your sleeve," he declared, watching him closely. "I've a good mind to go and call on Miss Merivale myself."

"Do!" said Lowry, turning to his desk with the air of a man dismissing a lot of troublesome business, and glad of it. "You will find that she is too ill to see a soul; utterly prostrated since last night. Will that hold you for a while, you uppity young shrimp?"

CHAPTER XXI
TONY'S REPORT

BARRISON OFTEN DINED AT a chop house in the Thirties, near his own rooms. He repaired thither to-night, after having telephoned his whereabouts to Tony Clay's boarding house, with a message for that youth to come on to join him there if he could.

As he sat lingeringly over one of the meals he liked best, he endeavored to forget the problems which had stabbed at him relentlessly all day. He wished that it were only from a professional angle that the business worried him; to his own uttermost disgust, he found an enormous mass of personal worry connected with it. He would like, for instance, to have been able to eliminate Miss Templeton. Or—would he? He was alarmed to find his condition so critical that he was not absolutely sure.

He glanced up at last, uncertain whether with relief or disgust, to find Tony Clay wending his way toward him between tables.

"Hello!" he said, with a very fine show of enthusiastic welcome.

Tony bobbed an acknowledgment. When he was seated opposite Jim, he growled:

> *"How doth the little butterfly*
> *Improve each shining hour,*
> *By sending other folks to spy,*
> *And bring to him more power!*
>
> *"What pretty things he learns to do,*
> *What merry games he beats!*
> *He lets the other fellow stew,*
> *While he sits still and eats!"*

Barrison could not help laughing, as he greeted him:

"What do you suppose I've been doing? Sitting here ever since we parted? What are you going to eat, oh, faithful, good, and seemingly hungry servant?"

"I want all the ham and eggs there are in the place, and the ham cut thick, and the eggs fried on both sides!"

"You half-baked little ass!" remarked Jim affectionately. "Give your own order."

Tony ordered, with a vague yet spectacular carelessness which made Barrison roar.

"Not awake yet, Tony?" he queried, when his young friend had committed himself to mushrooms and guinea hen after the ham and eggs.

"Eh? Sure I'm awake! Say, you didn't give me a job at all, oh, no!"

"The point is, did you get it?"

"Get it? You bet your life I got it. But, Jim, your hunch about that Golden Arms business was punk. There's nothing doing there."

"No?" said Barrison. He tried to sound cool and casual, but it wasn't much of a success; he felt a bit flat about it all. "Go ahead, Tony; suppose you tell me about it, eh?"

Tony nodded, and straightened up at sight of the ham and eggs.

"Well; first off you wanted a line on the maid. I got that, all right. She was one of those musical-comedy sorts. I spotted her from the beginning, and I guess you did, too. She wasn't able to get away from her 'lady' much, but she was supposed to eat like anybody else, and——"

"Tony, if you tell me that you gave up your sleep to go and fix her at lunch, and that——"

"I don't, and I didn't tell you anything. But, as a matter of fact, I'd have bust if I hadn't got a chance on this thing, Jim; you know that. Maybe I seem a bit slow sometimes, but, take it from me, I'm there with the goods when the time comes! Anyway, the maid's story is perfectly straight, and I'm certain she's telling the truth. It seems that she isn't supposed to knock at Miss Legaye's door until half after eleven. She sleeps in a room on top of the house, connected by telephone, and only comes down at special times, or when she's phoned for. Last night, she didn't expect Miss Legaye in early, so didn't come downstairs to her door till about twenty minutes past eleven. It being a first night, she really didn't imagine Miss Legaye would be in much before midnight. But at eleven twenty Maria—that's the maid—came and knocked. She saw that the lights were turned up inside the room.

"Miss Legaye called out to her: 'Maria, don't bother about me to-night; I'm tired, and I'm going to bed right away. Come at about eight to-morrow, please.'

"Maria went up to bed then, and didn't come down again until eight, the hour she was expected. That was about fifteen minutes before you and I turned up this morning."

"Well?" demanded Barrison, not so much eagerly as savagely, for he was hot on what he thought to be a trail of some sort, even if not a criminal trail. "Well, what else does she say about when she came in to Miss Legaye's rooms this morning?"

"She says that she came to the door and knocked, as was always her rule, before using her key. She had a key, but was not expected by Miss Legaye to use it unless there was no answer. This time she didn't get any answer, so she opened the door, and went in.

"She went in to Miss Legaye's bedroom, and found her half awake and half asleep. She said she had had a bad night, and had had to take her sleeping medicine. She looked pale. Maria says that the thing that upset her, Maria, most was the sight of Miss Legaye's fine opera coat on a chair near the window, where the rain had made it all wet. She said she had barely hung it up, and made Miss Legaye comfortable, when we telephoned up."

Barrison thought a moment. "That sounds all right," he admitted. "Get ahead, Tony, to the rest of your investigation. For, of course, you must have got at some one else!"

"Yes," said Tony, as he munched fried ham; "I got at the night clerk of the Golden Arms."

"The night clerk? But he wasn't on duty?"

Tony buttered a piece of bread with a glance of scorn. "And would that make him inaccessible to *you*, you pluperfect sleuth?" he demanded caustically. "To me it merely meant that I would have to dig up his address and call on him when he was not on guard, so to speak. He is a very nice, pleasant youth. You would not get on with him at all; you would hurt his feelings. I have feelings of my own, so we were delighted with each other! You do neglect your opportunities, you know, Jim!"

"Did you find out when Miss Legaye got in last night?" asked Barrison, but Tony's answer was disappointing.

"I did not," he rejoined. "I found that my night clerk had not seen Miss Legaye at all last night."

Barrison jumped and stared at him. "Not seen her!" ejaculated he.

"No. She had not come through the office at all. But he says that she often avoids the crowd in the hotel office by going up to her apartment by the back way. He says she hates publicity."

"Oh!" Barrison was thinking. "Is there, then, no one who would have seen her, if she came in 'the back way,' and went up to her room?"

"I can't see how any one could have seen her. You see, Jim, it's this way. In the Golden Arms Hotel, there is a side door, which is kept open and unguarded until after eleven o'clock at night. Lots of people, women especially, who don't want to go through the crowded office at that hour, prefer to slip in that way. It's a regular thing; they all do it. As to the elevator boy who———"

"Yes, I was going to ask about him. Did he take her up?"

"No, he didn't. At that hour of the night, even an elevator boy sometimes nods. Anyway, he remembers the bell ringing for a long time while he was half asleep, and when he got to the lift there was no one there. The answer seems obvious."

"That she walked upstairs, having become tired of waiting?"

"I should say so. Especially as she lived only one floor up, and often ran up the flight to save time!"

Barrison thought of this as he drank black coffee. "And that is all you found out?" he demanded suddenly, raising his head.

"Not at all!" responded Tony cheerfully. "I found out that the first news the night clerk had had of Miss Legaye last night was a telephone message from her room at about eleven o'clock."

"A message? What was it?"

"She said that she had a frightful headache, and that she wanted one of the bell boys to go out to the drug store for her, and get a medicine bottle filled—stuff that she often took when she had trouble about sleeping."

"And then?"

"And then the boy went upstairs, and got the empty bottle from her. She was wearing a wrapper. He took the bottle out and had it filled. That's all. It establishes the fact that she was in, and undressed, at eleven."

Barrison called for the check and paid it; then he still knitted his brows over the thing that troubled him.

"Tony!" he said suddenly.

"Well?"

"*Could* she have gotten upstairs into that hotel without being seen? I can't believe it."

"Why not?"

"I thought there were maids or guards on every floor."

"Quite so," said Tony; "you remind me. There is a maid stationed on every floor of all decent hotels. There was one on every floor of this. But she is human, and therefore she is movable. This one, on Miss Legaye's floor, was on duty up to twenty minutes to eleven, and she was on duty after eleven had struck. In between she had been called in to settle some newcomer, an old lady who wanted eight hundred and seventy things to which she was not entitled. She was away less than half an hour, but it was during that time that Miss Legaye must have gone to her room."

Barrison still sat looking at his coffee cup in a troubled way, and Tony suddenly spoke:

"Jim, that's a cold trail, a dead one. See? Why do you keep tracking back to it? You know, and I know, that there's nothing doing at that end of the story. What keeps you nosing around it?"

"I can't tell you, Tony," said Barrison, low and not too certainly. "It isn't exactly evidence that keeps me following that trail. It's——"

"Say!" broke in his subordinate sharply. "Shall I tell you what it is? It's that woman—it's Miss Grace Templeton; that's what it is. You're dippy about her! And because she's tipped you that there's something queer about Miss Legaye, you believe it!"

"I thought you admired Miss Templeton yourself!" said Jim Barrison, rallying his forces.

Tony Clay surveyed him in surprise. "Admired her?" he exclaimed. "Of course I admire her! But that wouldn't prevent me from doing my bit on a case! I wouldn't let a thing like that interfere with me professionally!" He spoke most grandiloquently, with a swelling chest.

Jim Barrison looked at him a moment seriously; then his face broke into irrepressible smiles. "Wouldn't you?" he queried. "Tony, you'll be a great man one of these days!"

CHAPTER XXII
"RITA THE DAREDEVIL"

PROMPTLY AT EIGHT O'CLOCK, Barrison presented himself at the entrance to Coyne's Theater, where he had agreed to meet Teddy Lucas, of the *Blaze*.

The house was of the flagrantly cheap variety, to judge by the people then going in. On either side of the glaringly illuminated doorway were vivid lithographs of ladies with extremely pink cheeks and tights, and gorgeously yellow hair and jewelry; also, of prodigiously muscled acrobats, performing miraculous feats in impossible positions.

Barrison found his own eyes attracted, almost at once, by something which stood out, oasislike, among the more lurid and obvious sheets; a large frame containing three photographs, under the plainly printed title: "Rita the Daredevil! Late of the World-famous Blankley Daredevils!"

Then this *was* the girl who had been playing in the riding act with Mortimer when Dukane came upon him first. Now, if by any chance Jim could connect that girl with Wrenn's disagreeable daughter, whom Miss Templeton remembered! He was eager for a sight of her. Would that rather dim snapshot he had seen prove sufficient to identify her? He wondered! None of these pictures looked particularly like that nondescript smudge of a woman in the corner of the kodak picture which had been shown him that day.

He examined them with close interest. One was of Rita the Daredevil, sitting a vicious-looking, rearing broncho, with a nonchalant air, and huge, ornamental spurs; another was of Rita the Daredevil firing with a rifle at an apple held up by a fat man in evening clothes. The third was, presumably, a likeness of Rita the Daredevil herself, doing nothing in particular but scowl at the world from beneath a picturesque sombrero.

She certainly looked disagreeable enough to justify Grace Templeton's unpleasant recollection of her. Of a markedly Spanish type, with the faint Indian cast which is so prevalent in South America, she was in no sense beguiling or prepossessing. It would be hard to vision those glowering black eyes soft with any tender emotion; her mouth was as hard and as bitter in line as that of some fierce yet stoical young savage, brooding over a darkly glorious nightmare of revenge.

Fascinated, even while repelled, by the odd, forbidding face, Barrison started as he was roused from his momentary trance by the cool, rapid tones of Teddy Lucas:

"Awfully sorry if you've been waiting. I don't imagine we're late for our act, though. Have you a cigarette? We can smoke here. Righto! Come along!"

They went in and took the places reserved for them in a stage box. Jim was glad to be so close to the stage; he wanted to study this woman as minutely as he could. As they settled themselves, an attendant changed the cards giving the names of the acts. With a real thrill Barrison saw that they read:

"Rita the Daredevil."

"Good stuff," murmured Lucas critically. "They don't say what she does, nor what makes her a daredevil. They just say it, and wait for her to make good. Of course, she probably won't."

He took the evening newspaper from under his arm, and on the margin of the first page scribbled a short enigmatic note in pencil. On the stage was a small table decorated with a .44 rifle and several small weapons, a target painted in red and gold instead of black and white, and a large mirror. Almost immediately Rita the Daredevil made her entrance.

She was dressed in the regulation "cowgirl's" outfit—short skirt of khaki, sombrero, heavy leather belt, high-laced brown boots, embroidered gauntlets. As though to give a touch of daintiness to her costume, she wore a thin white shirtwaist, and a scarlet tie. Also, the buckle on her belt was of gold, and there was a golden ornament in the band of her broad felt hat.

Daintiness, however, seemed out of place. There was about the young woman an absence of feminine coquetry that set her apart from most vaudeville performers. Sometimes she forced a smile, and made a little bow to the house, but conciliatory measures were plainly foreign to this woman's temperament. She was there to do certain things; one would be safe to wager that she would do them well.

And she did. She was a marvelous shot, cool, and steady; and the men in her audience were genuinely enthusiastic. A good many of them could appreciate straight and clever shooting when they saw it.

She shot bull's-eyes, tossed glass balls, shot apples on the head of her meek partner, the smiling man of the photograph; she shot over her shoulder, looking in a mirror; she shot, after sighting carefully, with her eyes blindfolded; she shot with guns of every size and caliber. In everything she did was apparent the same crisp, grim efficiency. She did not do her work at all gayly, nor as if she enjoyed it. There was something resentful about her whole personality. Doubtless she grudged the entertainment she gave and would have preferred to earn her salary, if possible, by making herself unpleasant to people, instead of diverting them!

Barrison gave many glances to the man who so patiently and self-effacingly assisted her. He was, in spite of the professional smile, not a happy-looking man. There were moments when, for all his creases of flesh, he looked positively haggard, and his eyes were very tired. He was a man who for some reason lived under a shadow or a burden of some sort; and—this belief came suddenly to Barrison—she herself suffered from the same handicap. These two people were the victims either of a heavy trouble, a grievous disappointment, or a gnawing wrong. You could see the pinches and rakings of suffering in both faces.

The climax of Rita's act was now pending. The partner came down to the footlights, and explained that "The Daredevil, whose life had been one hourly challenge to such dangers as lesser mortals hold in justifiable dread," would now show the ladies and gentlemen how little she cared for common risks or common caution. It appeared that she wished any one who liked to come and examine the pistols she was going to use. It was necessary for the audience to understand that they were all loaded. Did any one care to examine them?

Yes; to Teddy Lucas' surprise, Barrison did. He leaned over the side of the box, and had the satisfaction not only of noting that they were all loaded, six chambers each, but that each one of the three that she intended to use was marked in precisely the same way as the one which was now locked up in his safe at home.

"I thought she did the stunt with four," said Ted, arching his eyebrows. "She was advertised to."

Another point. Until recently, she had done her trick with four pistols, all exactly alike. Where was the fourth? Jim knew where the fourth was. Naturally, there had not been time to have another made and marked in precisely the same way.

He handed back the weapons, saw them examined by several other curious people, and settled back to see what she was going to do with them.

The stunt itself turned out to be disappointing. It was a mere juggling trick, the old three-ball affair, done with loaded pistols; that was all. To be sure, there was a certain amount of risk about it, since even a clever shot cannot always be responsible for what will happen to a trigger when it is caught in the lightning manipulation of juggling. But it was not nearly so dangerous as it was advertised to be.

"Now, it's safe to assume," remarked Teddy languidly, in Barrison's ear, "that she never fired one of those things off yet, in that stunt, and never will!"

And then two things happened. It was difficult even for Jim Barrison's trained mind to tell him which had happened first. His eyes caught sight of some one in the box opposite, a gray-haired, dignified figure of middle height, not sitting, but standing with his look fixed sternly upon the stage. It was Max Dukane, the great manager, and Barrison, in a great flash of intuition, knew why he was there. He had come either to warn or threaten these people who knew him since the days when he had discovered Mortimer in the show known as Blankley's Daredevils.

And at the selfsame instant, it seemed, the pistols which Rita was tossing so composedly and surely, experienced a hitch in their methodical orbits. One, two, three, they rose and fell, and she caught them neatly each time, and sent them whirling as though they were tennis balls, instead of loaded guns. But something had happened. There was a faint cry, Barrison was near enough to hear it. And then a shot.

The detective's hair seemed to rise. It was so soon after that other tragedy! Was it possible? But nothing had happened, it seemed, except a flesh wound for Rita herself. She was holding her hand against her arm, and staring in front of her in a dazed and frightened way. Her partner was tearing away her sleeve to investigate, and the house was wildly excited. It was superb advertising, of course; only, Barrison knew that it was not advertising. She had been frightened by Dukane's sudden appearance, and even her sure hand had lost its cunning for a second.

He looked toward the other box sharply, at the very moment, as he thought, when Rita had sunk down wounded. But even so, he was too late. Dukane had gone.

"Shall we go behind now, and have a talk with her?" suggested Teddy Lucas, rising. "Really, that was quite well staged. Every one will be twice as ready to believe her a daredevil after they have seen her wounded. Ready?"

They made their way behind.

Barrison's blood was thrilling with that excitement of the chase which keeps a good detective alive on this earth, and without which one can scarcely imagine him contented.

CHAPTER XXIII
TWIXT THE CUP AND THE LIP

RITA RECEIVED THEM IN her dressing room, which was frankly a utilitarian apartment. Since she had to share it in turn with other performers, she had not much chance to impress her individuality upon it. And, for that matter, she was not the type of woman, probably, who would have thought it worth her while to take the trouble. She scorned frivolities.

When they saw her at close range, they were both struck by the fact that she was scarcely made up at all. Doubtless, if she had taken the trouble, she could have softened her face and expression, and made herself less hard and repellent. Not that she was ugly. She was not; her features were regular enough, and her black eyes quite splendid in their smoldering sort of way. If she had not bound up her hair so tightly, its masses and luster would have been a sensation; and her figure was good, in a lean, wiry style all its own.

The truth was that she was uncompromising, unyielding, ungraceful as she was ungracious.

If Rita had really experienced a shock during her act, she certainly had recovered from it, so far as the eyes of outsiders could determine.

After greeting them, she eyed her visitors coldly and sharply.

"Wanted to talk to me?" she demanded, in rather a metallic voice.

"Please, for the *Blaze*," said Teddy Lucas, in his most insinuating tone.

But Rita the Daredevil shook her head with a slight scowl.

"Waste of time," she stated. "We aren't playing here after next week, and——"

"I beg your pardon!" slid in Teddy smoothly but firmly. "You are not playing at this theater, but you have time at——"

"I tell you——" she began hotly. But another voice made itself heard. It was, as they were somewhat surprised to find, the voice of Rita's subservient partner, who had appeared just behind them, and who now confronted them with a curious little air of authority, in spite of his plump body and his very ancient evening dress.

"If you will excuse me for interrupting," he said courteously, and made them a bow which was quite proper and dignified. It was the bow of—what was it? Jim tried to think. Was it the bow of a head waiter, or a floorwalker, or—a ringmaster? That was it, a ringmaster. This man was used to the exacting proprieties of the circus. No one else could be so perfect! Instantly, Jim placed him as Blankley himself.

"If you will excuse me for interrupting," he repeated gently. "Our plans have changed. Vaudeville performers live, unfortunately, in a world of changes. We had expected to play in and around New York for some weeks; our expectations have not materialized. We leave New York to-night."

"To-night!" repeated Teddy Lucas, sitting up and opening his eyes. "Isn't that rather short notice?"

"It is," said the fat man, and Jim saw his hand shake as he raised it to wipe the perspiration from his forehead. But he was firm enough, for all that. "It is extremely sudden, but—it is—advisable."

"More advantageous time, I suppose?" said Teddy, watching him with seeming indifference.

"Yes, yes," said the fat man eagerly, and his hand shook more than ever. "More advantageous time! Meanwhile, if you care to interview Mrs. Blankley——"

Barrison pricked up his ears. Mrs. Blankley!

"She—I—we would be glad to be mentioned in your paper," went on the fat man hurriedly. "You could hardly give your space to a more scintillating—a more——"

"Nick," said Rita the Daredevil shortly, "I don't want to be interviewed. You arranged with Coyne for this gentleman to come, representing his paper, but I don't stand for it. You never can get it out of your head that we're not running our own show any longer, and that the public doesn't care a continental about us. You keep hanging on to the old stuff. You keep thinking that because you used to be a big noise in your own little gramophone, you're loud enough to take in Broadway nowadays. It doesn't get across, Nick. If these gentlemen want a story," and her voice was keen and bitter, "they'd better get after something else."

"Miss—er—I mean, Mrs. Blankley," said Teddy, "weren't you hurt, when that bullet exploded to-night?"

She changed color; oh, yes, she did change color. But she said with a swiftness that made Jim Barrison admire her the more: "That? Oh, that was just advertising! Didn't you guess?"

Teddy Lucas looked at her. "H'm!" he said, deliberating. "I confess I did think it was advertising at first, but——"

Rita looked strange; for a moment it seemed that she was going to strike the newspaper man. Then she let her heavy, dark eyes sink, and turned away with a muttered remark that none of them could catch.

It was Jim's moment; the only moment that had been put straight into his hands that night. He seized it boldly. The fat man was talking nervously and volubly to the reporter; there was a chance.

"Miss Wrenn," said Jim Barrison deliberately, "will you let me talk to you alone?"

He never forgot the look that came into those big black eyes, as she raised them then to meet his. He could not have told whether it was horror or hatred, but he was sure that it was one or the other. For a full half minute she stared at him so, her face white as chalk. Then she drew a deep breath, and took a step back.

"Since I must," she said, answering his request. "But I warn you, it will be to very little purpose—I know why you are here. Do you truly think that—this—this investigation—is worth your while?"

"I don't know that," he said steadily, but still in a voice that was audible to her alone. "I only know that it is necessary; that it is my duty. I know that you are the girl I am seeking. Your name is Wrenn. Is it not?"

"It is," she replied. "Marita Wrenn!"

Marita! So the initials were to be explained logically after all! M for Marita; W for Wrenn. The two engraved in that odd fashion which he could quite understand had been of her inspiration.

"Will you believe," he went on, steadying his voice, and keeping all excitement out of it, "that I am only trying to get at the facts? That I——"

"Marita!" came the voice of the fat man sharply. "This gentleman"—he indicated Lucas—"has asked us to take supper with him and his friend. We will go?"

"I should be delighted," she said, in the mechanical way, which one felt was her way of accepting all pleasures in life, however they came.

Blankley turned to them with his anxious little bow. "If you would pardon us——" he begged. "My wife must take off a little make-up, and then—may we join you at the stage door?"

Barrison hated to let the woman out of his sight, but he scarcely knew how to refuse so simple a request. He was here as Teddy Lucas' guest, and not in his professional capacity. So the two young men went out to the stage door to wait.

They waited until, with a short laugh, the reporter showed his watch. Almost sixty minutes had gone by.

"I don't know just your game, my dear fellow," he said, as he turned away. "But, for my part, I think you've been jolly well sold!"

"How about you?" said Barrison, raw about his part of it, and yearning to be disagreeable.

Lucas laughed. "I'm fixed all right," he said amiably. "I'm going to write a peach of a story about the shock which led to the canceling of the Blankley engagement!"

"What shock?" asked Barrison.

Lucas looked at him in polite scorn. "My dear friend," he said, in a tired voice, "didn't you see Dukane in the box to-night?"

Barrison jumped. "You mean you saw him?" he exclaimed.

Lucas sighed heavily. "Saw him?" he said. "My dear fellow, I'm a reporter!"

CHAPTER XXIV
WHAT SYBIL HAD HIDDEN

JIM BARRISON WAS DOG tired. He felt as though the past twenty-four hours had been twenty-four months; it scarcely seemed possible that the murder had been committed only the night before! Nevertheless, weary as he was he called up Lowry and told him of his evening's experience. The inspector made some cryptic grunts at the other end of the wire, and ended up with a curt "I'll see about it. Good night!"

Barrison smiled, but felt slightly annoyed as he hung up the receiver. "'I'll see about it!' As though he were Providence incarnate, and could wind up the moon and stars to go differently if he felt like it!"

He was past more than a fleeting flash of resentment, however, and lost no time in wending his way homeward and to bed. Tara made a dignified offering of Scotch and sandwiches, but he waved him away sleepily, and tumbled in.

So profound was the slumber into which he immediately fell, that the shrill ringing of the telephone hardly pierced his rest. If he heard it at all, it was only as a component part of his fitful dreams.

The voice which came to Tara over the wire was cool and crisp:

"Mr. Barrison, please."

Tara glanced compassionately toward the bedroom where his master was already in deep repose.

"No, sir!" he responded, politely but firmly.

"What do you mean—no? Has he gone to bed?"

"Yes—please." Tara was nothing if not deferential.

"Well, get him up. I want to speak to him."

"Honorably excuse," said Tara, with an instinctive bow to the instrument, "but—I *not!*"

"You won't call him?"

"Please—I not!"

The voice at the end of the wire cursed him gently, and then continued:

"Well, will you take a message?"

"Oh, yes, please—I thank!"

The Jap hastily seized pencil and paper, and, after making sundry hiero-glyphics in his own language, said good night humbly, hung up, and trans-lated what he had noted into English. In the morning, when he carried coffee in to a refreshed but still drowsy Barrison, the message which that gentleman read was as follows: "Hon. gent. paper man say if you please call. Import."

Barrison knew that this meant Teddy Lucas in all probability, but he also knew that it was too early to catch him at the newspaper office yet. He ate breakfast and hunted through the morning papers for matters of interest. In the *Blaze*, he found a picturesque little account of the spectacular exit of Mr. and Mrs. Blankley. It was toned down, however, a good deal, Dukane's name not being mentioned, and nothing more sensational being suggested than that "Rita the Daredevil" lost her nerve after the narrow escape which had left her in a state of collapse when the *Blaze* representative was admitted to her presence. Her husband had urged her discontinuance of the engagement, et cetera. Barrison could not entirely understand, but he knew that the ways of newspapers were strange and devious. Later he would call up Lucas and find out more about it.

It was at this point that his eye caught sight of another item on the page given over to dramatic news. It was starred in a half column, and was headed:

TRAGIC AND SENSATIONAL ROMANCE
OF MISS KITTY LEGAYE!
Popular Actress Announces Her Engagement
to Star Who Was Murdered.
(Interview by Maybelle Montagu.)

Miss Kitty Legaye, whose charm and talent have endeared her to thousands of the American public, is to-day that saddest of figures, a sorrowing woman bereft of the man who was to have been her husband. Alan Mortimer, whose terrible and myste-rious death has stirred the entire theatrical world and baffled police headquarters, has left behind him a woman whose white face bears the stamp of ineffaceable love and endless grief.

In deepest mourning, which enhanced her childlike loveliness, the exquisite little actress whose impersonations of young girls upon the stage have made her famous all over the continent consented to receive the representative of the New York *Blaze*. It was with a touching simplicity that she said:

"We had intended to postpone the announcement of our engagement until later, but he has been taken from me, and why keep silent any longer? It is, in a way, a comfort to let the world know that we were to have been married—that, at least, I have the right to mourn for him!"

Her sweet voice was choked with sobs, and in the eyes of even the seasoned interviewer there were tears.

Barrison shook his head, and smiled a wry, cynical smile.

"Not so prostrated that she can't make capital out of it!" he commented to himself. "Lost no time, I must say. However, it's no concern of mine."

Refreshed by his sound sleep, he rushed through the process of dressing like a whirlwind, and went off to try the doubtful experiment of another call upon Mr. Dukane.

But before he went up to the great man's office, he paused to take due thought. After all, was it the best thing to do? He considered, and before he had decided, the door of the elevator opened, and young Norman Crane came out. He looked fresh and wholesome as ever, but, Jim thought, a bit anxious. He greeted the detective cordially.

"Hello!" he said. "Beastly mess it all is, isn't it? Were you going up to see the old man? Because you won't. Not unless you've an awful drag at court! Every one in the world is waiting in the outer office, all the poor old 'Boots-and-Saddles' bunch, and everybody in town that's left over."

"I hadn't made up my mind whether I was going up or not," admitted Barrison. "Now I have, I think. I'll walk along with you, if you've no objection?"

"Rather not! I'm——" He hesitated. "I'm going to inquire for Sybil."

"How *is* Miss Merivale? I was sorry to hear that she was so ill."

"Who told you? Oh, it would be Lowry, of course! I can't get used to the idea of having Sybil watched and spied on by policemen. Beg pardon!" He flushed boyishly. "I don't mean to be offensive, Mr. Barrison, and you never strike me like that quite, but—you must know what I mean?"

"Naturally I do," said Jim, who liked the lad. "And, if you don't mind, I'll come with you when you go to inquire—not in a professional capacity!" he added hastily, seeing the glint of suspicion in the other's transparent eyes.

Crane laughed a little awkwardly. "I'd be very glad to have you," he said frankly, "and, for that matter, in your professional capacity, too! Mr. Barrison, am I right in thinking that—that man suspects Sybil?"

"Suspects is rather a plain term and rather a strong one. I don't think he absolutely suspects her; but there are things that will need a bit of clearing up."

"I thought so!" The young man's manner expressed a sort of angry triumph. "Now, Mr. Barrison, you must come. Sybil must talk to you, whether she feels like it or not! You know, the whole idea is too absurd——"

"I think it is absurd myself!" said Barrison kindly. "But you know it's just those ridiculous things that make such a lot of bother in the world! Miss Merivale, I'm convinced, is the last person in the world to have committed any sort of a crime."

"Heavens! I should say so!"

"And yet—what was it that she hid in her dress that night?"

Norman stopped and stared at him. "Why should you think she hid anything in her dress?" he demanded in unfeigned astonishment.

"I'll tell you by and by," said Barrison evasively. He saw that Crane was really surprised by this, and he was debating with himself just how far it was politic and wise to go in this direction.

In another few minutes they were at the boarding house where Sybil lived—a quiet house in the upper Forties, kept by a gentle, gray-haired woman who seemed of another day and generation, and who called Norman "my dear boy," with a soft Southern drawl.

Miss Merivale was better, she said; so much so, in fact, that she had had her removed into her own parlor at the front of the house, where she could have more cheerful surroundings and see her friends, the sweet lady added, smiling, if she felt strong enough. If the gentlemen would take the trouble to walk upstairs, she was sure they would do Miss Merivale good. She was better, but not so bright as one could wish.

The boarding-house keeper and Norman Crane ascended first, and shortly after the former came back to tell Barrison that they were expecting him, if he would go up.

"I thought," she added softly, "that they would want to see each other, and so I had her couch fixed in my place, where I can be in and out, so to speak. Not that I'd have the time," she added, gently humorous, "but it's the idea, you know! I'm from the So'th, sir, and I have my funny notions about the proprieties!"

Sybil, on the landlady's old-fashioned sofa, looked rather pathetically wan, but she made an effort to greet Jim with some animation and cordiality. It was plain that she was still very shaken and depressed, and that her fiancé was much worried about her.

She went at once to the matters that were in all their minds. It was characteristic of the girl that she did not shrink from approaching even the subjects responsible for her recent collapse. And she was very fair to look at, in her soft blue dressing gown lying back among the faded chintz cushions, with her ash-blond hair in two long braids upon her shoulders. Kitty Legaye should have seen her now!

"Mr. Barrison," she said at once, "it is awfully good of you to have called. Norman and I know that you are here as a friend, and not as an officer of the law, and we are both grateful. Mr. Barrison, you surely don't think I had anything to do with—with that horror the other night?"

"No, I don't," said Barrison, speaking as briefly and frankly as she was speaking herself.

"Well, will you tell me on what grounds they are—are watching me?"

"You are sure they are?" he said, to gain time.

"Sure! Of course, I am sure! Look at that man over there, reading the paper and occasionally glancing up at the sky to see if it is going to rain. Isn't he watching this house?"

Barrison smiled. "Probably he is," he admitted. He had noticed the man himself as he came in, but he had not imagined that the girl herself knew of her situation.

"Well," she insisted, and a faint spot of feverish color came into either cheek, "what is it that they expect to find out? What is it? I know that I was there, on the scene, but—but—surely that man would not have let me go if he had thought I had—done it!"

Barrison was convinced of her innocence; but he was also convinced that the wisest course would be to enlighten her as to the points wherein her position was open to question by the law. He had hesitated because his connection with the case, while unofficial, more or less tied his hands; but, after all, the inspector had given him leave to use his own judgment.

He spoke straightforwardly. "What did you hide in your dress, just before the last act, the night before last, Miss Merivale?"

She started upright on the couch, and looked at him with wide eyes of amazement. "How did you know that?" she asked blankly.

"But you didn't, did you, dear?" struck in Norman Crane, taking her hand in his. "What could you have put in your dress? It's absurd, as I told Mr. Barrison!"

She thought for a moment, and then said quietly: "I put into my dress something that I wanted to hide, chiefly from you, Norman. I knew that if you saw it, you would be angry."

Norman Crane looked as though she had struck him.

"You did hide something, then?" he exclaimed.

"I certainly did, and would again, under the same conditions. Only, I can't see how any one knew of the fact. Who was it, Mr. Barrison?"

"Your dresser, the woman Parry."

"Of course!" She nodded slowly. "She was always a meddlesome old thing! And I know that she was consumed with curiosity when I got the package and the note that night."

"The package and the note!" repeated Norman Crane. "Sybil, you are crazy! What are you talking about?"

"I know what the note was," put in Barrison, smiling at her reassuringly. "At least, I know part of it, and I was daring enough to make up the rest of it in Lowry's office last night!"

Sybil looked up at him with a flash of laughter in her eyes, though poor Crane was still dazed.

"And what did you make of it?" she asked, in a tone that tried for raillery and only achieved a certain piteous bravado.

"I made of it a sort of love letter, if you can call it so," said Barrison gently, "which might have accompanied a present, something which could be considered in the light of a test—no, that is not the word, a proof of——"

"A proof," she broke in passionately, "of my willingness to do something, and to be something that I could not do and could not be! And you made that out of it, with only those torn scraps to go by! Oh, you understand. I see that you do understand!"

She hid her face in her hands and cried. In a moment, however, she put aside her own emotion, and explained:

"He—Mr. Mortimer—had tried to make love to me many times; you both know that. Norman was furious with him, and I was always afraid that there would be trouble between them. Of my part of it—well, it is much harder to speak. Being men, perhaps you will not understand the sort of power of fascination that a man can have over a woman, even when she does not love him. I shall always believe that Alan Mortimer had some hypnotic power—however, that is not the point. Though I had always repulsed him, he could not help knowing that he had influence over me; a man always knows.

You see, I don't try to lie; I tell you the truth, even though it isn't a pleasant sort of truth to tell."

"I know it is most painful to tell," Barrison said, feeling indeed profoundly sorry for her, and most respectful of her courage in speaking as she did. Norman Crane said nothing.

"That night—the first night," Sybil went on, "Alan Mortimer made it especially—hard for me. He had chosen an ornament for me, a splendid jeweled thing, but I had refused it several times. That night, he sent it to me with a note, and told me that he expected me to wear it that evening, after the play was over."

"Have you got it now?" asked Barrison.

She reached out to a small table near by and took it from a hand bag. "I have never been separated from it," she said simply. "It is too valuable, and—until to-day—I did not know just what to do with it."

In another moment it lay before them—the case "as long as a hand," which Mrs. Parry had seen the girl hide in the front of her dress. In yet another instant the case was open, and the splendid piece of jewelry that was within flashed in the morning sunshine. It was a pendant of sapphires and diamonds, and it was the sort of thing that would be extremely becoming to Sybil Merivale.

Crane suppressed with difficulty a sound of rage as he saw it.

Barrison cut it off quickly by saying: "You told us you did not know what to do with it until to-day. Why to-day?"

"Because"—Sybil took up a morning paper, looked at a particular place, and dropped it again—"because to-day I know that Miss Legaye was engaged to him, and that, therefore, anything that he had, when he died, belongs to her. I am going to send the pendant to Miss Legaye."

She closed the case with an air of finality. "Isn't that what I ought to do?" she asked, half anxiously, looking from one to the other.

Norman Crane, who had been sitting moodily staring at the floor, suddenly lifted his head and bent to kiss her hand.

"My darling," he said honestly and generously, "I don't understand everything you've been talking about, but I understand that you're my dear girl—my fine girl—always. And—and whatever you say—must be right!"

"And you, Mr. Barrison?" she persisted, looking at him wistfully, as she left her hand in Norman's.

Jim rose to go, and, standing, smiled down upon her. "I think your notion is an inspiration!" he declared. "I would give something to see Miss Legaye when she gets that pendant!"

After which he departed, wondering how he was going to convince Lowry that the trail to Sybil was, professionally speaking, "cold."

CHAPTER XXV
NEW DEVELOPMENTS

HE TELEPHONED THE *BLAZE* office, and caught Teddy Lucas just as he was starting out on an assignment.

"Oh, it's you," said the reporter. "Wanted to tell you something about your friend Rita which might be useful in your business. I strolled round last night to the furnished rooming house where she and her husband hung out, and they never went home at all; just beat it to the train, I suppose. Their room was just as they'd left it, and full of junk. There was a shelf full of old photographs, and one of 'em was of two young girls, sisters I should say; at least, they were both dark. One's evidently Rita herself, as she may have looked ten years ago, and the other, unless I'm very much mistaken, is the lady that the sob sisters are interviewing this morning!"

"Not Kitty Legaye?"

"That's the one. Oh, and I poked about the files for you this morning. The Blankley Daredevils were a riding and shooting show that did small time in the East until a year ago. Then it bust up, and the company scattered. Blankley seems to have been a crook, for the reason for the smash-up was that he was arrested and sent to jail for six months! Quite a nice, snappy little story—what?"

"Are you going to write it?"

"Not my line. I've turned it over to a chap on the news staff!"

"I noticed that you didn't make much out of last night."

"My editor cut out most of it; thought I was giving Coyne's theater too much advertising. Well, that's all I had to tell."

"Where is that photograph?"

"I swiped it. Send it up?"

"Please! And I'm no end obliged."

"That's all right."

Barrison walked out of the booth more astonished than he had ever been in his life. In all the speculations he had made in his own mind concerning this twisted and unsatisfactory case, it had never occurred to him to connect those two women. Kitty Legaye and Marita Blankley! He recalled the two faces swiftly, and saw that there was a faint resemblance, though Rita's was far the harder and more mature. He would not swear that she was the older, though; little ladies like Kitty rarely looked their age. Kitty and Rita! The more he thought of it, the more astounding it seemed. Of course, the first thing to do was to locate Wrenn. But how? He wondered if Willie Coster could help him.

He got Willie's address easily enough from the theater, and went to call. He found him a little wan and puffy-eyed, but quite recovered, and amazingly cheerful for a man who has only been sober a few hours!

"Wrenn?" he repeated. "How should I know? He'd scarcely be staying on at Mortimer's hotel, I suppose?"

Barrison explained that Mortimer's rooms and effects were in the custody of the police, and that the old valet would not be allowed near them in any case.

"I don't believe that he's left town," Willie said, "and I'll tell you why. He wasn't at all well fixed for money. I don't believe Mortimer ever paid him any wages to speak of; whatever it was that held them together, it wasn't cash. He's touched me more than once, poor old beggar!"

"You! Why you?"

"I don't know," said Willie simply. "People always do!"

Good little fellow! Of course, people always did.

"And you think he'd come and borrow money from you, if he meant to leave town?"

"I'd not be surprised."

And, as a matter of fact, he did come that very day and for that very reason; and Willie, having ascertained his address, gave it to Barrison over the wire.

"I feel rather rotten about telling you, too," he added. "I don't know what you want him for, and the poor old guy is awfully cut up about something—scared blue, I should say. Say, Barrison, you don't suspect *him*, do you?"

"Lord, no! But I think he knows who did it."

Willie grunted uncomfortably. "Well, treat him decently," he urged.

"I'm not exactly an inquisitor in my methods, you know," Jim told him. "How much money did you lend him, Willie?"

"Only a ten spot," said Willie innocently.

Barrison laughed and said good-by.

Within the hour, he was at the address given him by Coster. It proved to be a shabby, dingy little lodging house east of Second Avenue, and the few men whom the young man met slouching in and out were as shabby and dingy as the place, and had, he thought, a furtive look. Sized up roughly, it had a drably disreputable appearance, as though connected with small, sordid crimes and the unpicturesque derelicts of the underworld.

In a dreary hall bedroom on the third floor, he finally found Wrenn.

The old man opened the door with evident caution in response to Barrison's knock, and when he saw the detective, his face became rigid with a terror which he did not even attempt to conceal. Mutely, he stood back and let the visitor enter, closing the door with trembling hands. Then, still speechless, he turned and faced him, his anguished eyes more eloquent than any words could have been. Jim was touched by the man's misery. He could guess something of what he must be suffering on his daughter's account.

"Don't look like that, Wrenn," he said kindly. "I've only come to have a talk with you."

The old man bent forward with sudden eagerness. "Then," he faltered, "you've not come to tell me—of—her arrest, sir?"

"No," said Barrison; "I don't even know where she is. Sit down, man; you look done up."

Wrenn sank onto the bed, and sat there, his wrinkled face working with emotion.

"I was afraid you'd arrested her, sir!" he managed to say, after a moment, in broken tones.

"You had been expecting that?"

He nodded. "I've known that the—the police were bound to find out some time that she'd been in the theater that night, and I knew what that would mean. She *would* come, though I tried so hard to prevent her! She *would* come!"

"Wrenn," said Barrison deliberately, "it's a pretty tough question to put to you, but—did she shoot Mortimer?"

Wrenn looked at him with haggard eyes. "Before God, Mr. Barrison," he said earnestly, "I don't know, I don't know! I didn't *see* her shoot him, but—I know she meant to."

"You know that!" exclaimed Barrison.

"I know that she had threatened him more than once, and—it was her pistol. You knew that, sir?"

"Yes, I knew that. Go on!"

"I'd better tell you the whole story, sir. I'm getting old, and it's weighed on me too long—too long! If you don't mind, sir, I'll go back to the beginning."

CHAPTER XXVI
WRENN'S STORY

"I WAS BORN IN the West," said Wrenn, "and I was fairly well educated, but while I was still in college—a small, fresh-water university—I got into bad company, and was expelled. My people disowned me after that, and I drifted into the sort of 'adventurous' life that attracts so many young men. I never really liked the idea of living dishonestly, but I didn't seem good for much else. I had not worked hard at college, and I had no particular ambitions, one way or another. I suppose I was lazy, and I know that I was very weak. Eventually I became what you, sir, would call a crook, though for a long time I tried to gloss it over and pretend it was just taking a chance or living by my wits, and the rest of it! Then I got more hardened, and admitted even to myself that I was no better than the rest of the crowd I went with—a cheat, a card sharper, a petty criminal. Twice I was in jail for short terms, and I don't think either experience improved me much.

"Then I married. She was a high-class Mexican girl—very beautiful. She was a Catholic, and had an idea of reforming me. So she did, for a short time, but the old wild longings came back. I'd settled down in a job as foreman on an Arizona ranch, and I was working hard and drawing good pay. We had two little girls, and things were going pretty well. Then my wife died, and I got reckless again.

"There was a tough bunch of cow-punchers in our outfit, and we got to gambling a lot, and pretty soon I found out that it was easier and more exciting to win when I played crooked than when I played straight. And there were others who felt the same way. We formed a sort of combination—a gang. And we did very well, indeed."

Barrison sat and stared at the mild, respectable old fellow, who so patently and typically looked the part of a decent, sober, and trusty servant, and tried to visualize him as a bold, bad man of the wicked West. But some things are past the powers of the human imagination. He thought, with a sort of grimly humorous awe, of the strange alchemy of time, and shook his head, giving the problem up, as have better and wiser men before him.

Wrenn went on with his story:

"My girls were brought up in a rough-and-tumble way, I'm afraid. It affected them differently. The older Caterina—she was named for her mother—never took kindly to it. She was selfish and headstrong—they both were, for that matter. But I think Marita had more heart. Not that I ever called out much affection in either of them!"

He bent his gray head for a moment.

"Anyway, I didn't give them much of a bringing up. Marita knocked about with the boys and learned to ride like a puncher herself. But Caterina—Kitty, we called her—hated the whole life, and when a rich prospector came along, she threw us over like a shot and went away with him. She was only just eighteen, but she was ambitious already. She wanted to get some pleasure out of life, as she had said twenty times a day since she could speak. I—I shall not mention her name, sir—the name which she is known by now, for—you would know it."

It was odd, the way he dropped so constantly into the respectful "sir," and all the air and manner of a servant. It was clear that his was one of those pliable natures that can be molded by life and conditions into almost any shape. His instinct of fatherhood, his late-awakened sense of conscience, responsibility and compunction, were struggling up painfully through the accumulated handicap of a lifetime of habit.

"I know her name," Barrison said quietly. "You mean Kitty Legaye, don't you?"

The start that Wrenn gave now betrayed an even livelier terror than had yet moved him.

"I didn't say it!" he gasped in fright and agitation. "I have never said it—never once, through all these years! She always made us swear we would tell nobody. I don't know what she would do if she thought I had spoken! She was so ashamed of us—and I can hardly wonder at that, sir. She has done so well herself! Oh, sir, if ever it comes up, you—you'll see that she knows that it wasn't I who told?"

"I certainly will," said the detective, pitying—though with a little contempt—this father's abject fear of his unnatural daughter's displeasure. "As a matter of fact, I found it out by accident. I only told you that I knew just now to show you that you have nothing to conceal about her. Nor," he added, entirely upon impulse, "about Mr. Dukane!"

This time Wrenn's jaw dropped, in the intensity of his astonishment.

"You—you know about—him—too!" he muttered breathlessly. "Is there anything you—do not know?"

"Several things, else I should not be here now," rejoined Jim, with an inner thrill of elation over the success of his half-random shot. "Suppose you go on with your story, and then I shall know more."

The other sighed deeply, and proceeded:

"Since you know so much, sir, there is no sense in my hiding anything. Not that I think I should have hidden anything, in any case. As I told you, I am an old man, and all this has been hard to bear. But you don't want me to tell about my feelings, sir; you want the story.

"When Kitty had been gone a year or more, and Marita was about seventeen, Nicholas Blankley came to the town where we lived. It was a little Arizona settlement, where I ran a saloon and gambling place. Blankley was one of us—I mean he was a natural-born crook, but he wasn't a bad sort of fellow at that, if you know what I mean, sir. He was a good sport, and square with his pals, which is more than can be said for most of us! He was in the theatrical line, and had worked on all sorts of jobs of that kind—advance man, stage manager, all sorts of things. He was interested in Rita from the first—saw her possibilities as a 'cowgirl,' and was fond of her, too—for she was young and fresh in those days, and the daring, reckless sort that got men. Nick got the daredevil name from her; that's what he used to call her.

"His idea was to start a sort of wild-West show, on the cheap; get some down-and-outers who could ride and shoot and who wouldn't want much pay, and do short jumps at low prices. We would have to carry the horses, but no scenery, and no props to speak of, and we could use a big tent like the small circus people. It looked like a good venture, and I was tired of staying in one place. Marita was wild about it from the first. So I sold out my business, and we started. We made a success of it, though nothing very big, and kept at it fifteen years! Fifteen years! It seems impossible that it could have been as long as that, but it was. In that time Marita married Nick, and we ran across Alan Morton—I might as well go on calling him Mortimer, though.

"There's no use pretending that we were running our outfit strictly on the straight. We weren't. We were out to get what we could out of the public, and we didn't care much how we did it. But we didn't do anything very bad; I, for one, was getting careful as time went on, and Nick had a notion of reforming after he married Rita. We did run a gambling business in connection with the show, and we did cheat a bit, and we did take in any sort of thug or gunman or escaped convict who had ever learned to ride, and Nick got away with a very good thing in phony change at one place. Very neat, indeed, it was, and he never had any trouble with it, either."

Wrenn spoke of this with a sort of pride which made Barrison shake his head again. He was the queerest felon with whom the detective had ever come in contact.

"But as I say," resumed Wrenn, "we got along all right, and did no great harm for all those years. Then we struck Mortimer. He was a bad one—just a plain bad one, from the very first."

"And I always thought you were so fond of him!" ejaculated the detective.

"But I was, sir," said the old man at once. "I was very fond of him, indeed! He was a—a very lovable person, sir, when he cared to be."

Barrison, again rendered speechless, simply stared at him for a moment or two.

"Go on!" he managed to articulate, after a bit.

"Well, sir, it was this way. Mortimer's blood was younger than ours, and he was more venturesome, more energetic, more daring."

"Like your daughter."

"Yes, sir," said the ex-gambler, rather sadly. "Like her. There was a time when I was afraid that she was getting too fond of him—he had such a way with women! Wherever he went there was trouble, as you might say. He helped the show—put new life into it, and he could ride—oh, well, no one ever rode better than he did. And you know how handsome he was?"

Strangely enough, the old man's voice choked a bit just there.

"I don't know why I always felt just the way I did about him," he went on quietly. "He was often very rough and careless in his ways, but—but I was as fond of him as if he'd been my own son—and that, sir, is the gospel truth.

"Mortimer had a scheme to branch out bigger, and get a sort of organized company together, with capital, and a circus arena somewhere with the right sort of scenery and music, and that sort of thing. Mr. Dukane had seen our show once, and had taken an interest in it—at least, had taken an interest in the lad—and Mortimer wrote to him for a loan to back the new plan."

"Wrote Dukane—for a loan?" repeated Jim, in admiration.

"Yes, he did. I felt just as surprised as you, sir, when he told me what he had done. And—to this day, I'm not sure whether it was just plain, pure nerve on his part, or whether he—he—had in mind what the result might be."

"Result?"

"Yes." For the first time the old scapegrace's utterance was slow and troubled—hardly audible. He would not meet Barrison's eyes. What he said now seemed to be dragged up from the depths of his sinful and unwilling soul.

"You know—you must know, sir," he said, in those new and halting accents, "since you know so much—about the deal with Dukane?"

"I know something," said Jim, truthfully, but very cautiously—his heart was beating hard. "I know that there was a deal at all events."

"It—it doesn't sound very well—put into words, does it, sir?" Poor old Wrenn's tone was tired and appealing. "But there! I said I was going to make a clean breast of it, and I might as well. Dukane and Mortimer fixed it up between themselves——"

"Dukane and Mortimer only?" interrupted Barrison, with a sudden intuition.

Wrenn's poor, weak, tragic eyes met his piteously, shifted, and fell.

"Dukane and Mortimer and—I—fixed it up, sir," he confessed humbly. "We were to double-cross Nick Blankley, and Dukane was to star Mortimer."

"He must have had a pretty high opinion of him!" exclaimed Jim Barrison wonderingly, for the great manager, while a shrewd gambler, was no plunger.

"He knew that he had the makings of a favorite, sir; any one could see it. Mr. Dukane wanted him the way the owner of a racing stable wants a fine horse. He knew there was money in him if he was put out right. And Dukane was the man to do that. Anyway, that was the idea. They—I mean we—were to get Blankley out of the way, and Dukane would take care of us afterward."

"How do you mean get him out of the way?"

"Oh, not kill him, sir!" Wrenn's tone was virtuously shocked. "You wouldn't think that, surely? It was just my way of putting it, as it were. No; he'd done a number of shady things, Nick Blankley had, and——"

"So had you!" interpolated Jim Barrison, rather cruelly.

"Oh, yes, sir! But we had—if you'll pardon the expression—got away with it."

There it was, the point of view of the born criminal. If you weren't found out, it was all right! Jim looked at the wretched creature before him, and mused on man as God made him.

"Well?" he demanded, somewhat impatiently.

"Mortimer told Dukane something that Blankley had done; it wasn't very much—just a fraud."

"And Dukane lent himself to this!"

"He's a business man, sir. He suggested it, I believe. At least, Mortimer said so."

No wonder the manager did not care to talk about it!

"Anyway," continued Wrenn, "it was on Mortimer's testimony that Blankley went to jail."

"For six months."

"You know that, sir? But it was eight months. He got pardon for good behavior. We"—he stumbled over this—"we hadn't expected it yet a while."

"Great Scott!" said Barrison, looking at him. "And you tell all this! You mean that you double-crossed—betrayed your pal, your partner—got him out of the way, so that you could be free of him while you got rich in the new venture?"

"It—it comes to that, sir; I told you it didn't sound well when you put in into words. But it's the truth, and I don't care any longer who knows it. I'm tired. And, anyway, I think it's more Dukane's fault than ours."

Barrison thought so, too, but he said nothing, only waited in silence.

"I came as Mortimer's valet because there wasn't much of anything else that I could do, and I swore I'd stick to him, and—and he liked me, and wanted me round him. And I did stick to him! I was fond of him, and I took care of him as well as I knew how. No one could have looked out for him better—no one, sir!"

"I believe that. It's queer; but, no matter, I believe it! What were you to get out of it?"

"When he made his hit, I was to have ten thousand dollars."

"And what did your daughter—the one married to Blankley, whom you had sent to jail—what did she say about this pleasant little arrangement?"

Wrenn's head drooped once more.

"Marita was always hard to manage, sir," he said, in a faint voice. "She turned against me—her own father, and——"

"I should think she might!"

"And she turned against Mortimer, and against Mr. Dukane, who offered her money. She said she would wait for Nick to come out of prison, and would spend the rest of her life in getting even!"

"Well, I sympathize with her!" said Barrison sincerely. So that was the meaning of the tragic and haggard lines about her mouth and the weary look in her eyes.

"Well, Wrenn," he went on quietly, "I don't know just how the blame is to be divided in all this, but I imagine you've had almost your share of suffering. And Mortimer is done for. Dukane will get his eventually. I shall be sorry personally if your daughter Marita has to pay the penalty for the death of a rotter like the man who died the other night. I wish you could tell me something about her visit which would make her case look a little better."

Then Wrenn broke down, and, burying his head in his hands, cried like a child. He might have been a crook, a weakling, neglectful of his children through all the days of his life, but he was suffering now. His gaunt old body quivered under the storm of grief that swept him. In that abasement and sorrow it was even possible for Barrison to forget the despicable things he had just admitted. He was now merely an old man, bitterly punished not only for the sins of his youth, but those of his age.

"That's what I keep saying," he panted at last, lifting his swollen eyes to the younger man's pitying gaze. "I keep asking myself if there isn't something that'll clear her. Though we've been apart so long, and I was always a bad father to her, and a false friend to her husband, it will kill me altogether if I find that she is guilty of murder!"

"She wrote those letters—the ones threatening Mortimer?"

"Yes."

"And she took advantage of the time permitted her by the hours of her act at Coyne's to come to the theater that night?"

"Yes, sir. Let me tell you just how it was. She slipped in while Roberts was out getting the taxi for Kitty." He spoke his daughter's name shyly and with embarrassment. "She came straight into the dressing room—though why no one saw her I can't see! She was dressed just as she had come from the theater, in a khaki skirt and a white waist. And she pulled a pistol out of her dress as she came in. I knew the pistol, because it was always a fad of hers, in all her stunts, to carry guns like that—very small, and very much decorated, and with a letter that might be either an M or a W, according as you looked at it.

"The moment she and Mortimer saw each other they flew out like two wild cats. I'd always tried to keep this from happening, because I knew that they were both past controlling when their blood was up, and they both had a lot to fight for."

"Both!" repeated Barrison. "I can't see that. Your daughter had something to fight for, because of the wrong done to her husband, and incidentally to herself. But where was Mortimer's grievance?"

"Well, sir," said Wrenn slowly, as though he were seriously trying to express something rather beyond the intelligence of his hearer, "you see—maybe it hasn't struck you, sir, but, if you've risked a great deal on a thing, and find that something is going to interfere with it, after all, at the last moment, you—well, sir, you are apt to lose your head over it. Aren't you?"

Barrison laughed a trifle grimly.

"Crooked logic," he remarked, "but excellent—for the crooked kind! So you sympathize with Mortimer in his annoyance at seeing your daughter?"

"I don't sympathize, sir. In a way, I may say I understand it. But when she pulled out that gun, I fell into a sweat of fear, sir, for I knew that she was afraid of nothing, and that if she'd said she'd kill him——"

"Never mind how you felt! Tell me what happened!"

Wrenn wiped his forehead. "She went for Mortimer, and he got to her first, and caught hold of her arms. He was very strong, but she struggled like a demon, and every minute I expected one of two things to happen, the pistol to go off or some one to hear and knock at the door. After, I suppose, two or three minutes like that, I pulled her away from him—her waist was torn in the struggle, you remember."

"I remember."

"And I managed to get her out of the door, begging her to make a run for the stage entrance and to get away if possible without being seen. It was nearly dark then, you see—not the regular dark scene, but all the lights were being lowered, because there was to be so little light on the stage."

There was silence for a moment, then Wrenn went on again: "I've wondered, you know, sir, several times, whether she and Kitty met that night. I've—I've been afraid of it, I confess, because I don't believe my daughter Kitty would feel much sisterly affection for Rita. She might even give it away if she had seen her."

Barrison sat plunged in deep thought for at least two minutes, while the shaken and troubled old man watched him very anxiously indeed. At last he spoke, not ungently:

"Wrenn, will you give me your word that you will not leave this place, this address, until I see you again?"

He supposed that he was rather mad in asking the word of a self-confessed crook like Wrenn, but he thought he had got to the end of his tether. At any rate, the old man lifted his head with quite an influx of pride, as he answered:

"Yes, Mr. Barrison!"

Jim departed, with just one determination in his brain—to pay Kitty Legaye a second call as fast as a taxi would take him to the Golden Arms!

CHAPTER XXVII
AN INCRIMINATING LETTER

KITTY LOOKED VERY PRETTY and quite pathetic in her smartly simple mourning. She saw Barrison at once, and received him with a subdued cordiality that was the perfection of good taste under the circumstances.

"What is it?" she said, in a low voice. There was no artificiality about her now; she was disturbed, apprehensive. "I know it's something. Please tell me."

"Yes, there is something," he said. "It's about—your sister."

He could hear her draw in her breath.

"My sister!" she whispered. "Marita! How did you know anything about her?"

"I don't think we need go into an account of that," Jim said steadily. "As it happens, I do know quite a good deal about her. I know, for instance, that she was in the theater only a little while before Alan Mortimer was murdered."

"You know that!" she exclaimed, in unfeigned surprise. "I thought——"

Then she checked herself, but it was too late; she saw at once what she had admitted.

"I knew it," said Barrison, watching her. "The question is—how did you know it, Miss Legaye?"

She dropped her eyes and was silent until he felt obliged to insist:

"I am afraid I must ask you to tell me about it, though I can easily suppose it isn't very pleasant for you."

"Pleasant!" she flashed out at him then. "Think what a position I am in! To lose him—*like that*—and then—to find my own sister mixed up in it!"

"You think she was mixed up in it, then?"

"How on earth do I know?" she cried excitedly. "I—I—oh, Mr. Barrison, you aren't brutal, like most detectives; you are a gentleman! Won't you make it a little easier for me? My sister and I were never very fond of each other, but I can't be the one to implicate her now. I can't!"

"It may seem very dreadful to you, of course, Miss Legaye. But—how can you keep silent? She is already under suspicion. I don't see how you can avoid telling everything you know."

"I thought—I never dreamed—that it would come to this!" she said miserably. "I thought no one knew of her being there except myself and—and my father." She seemed to wince as she said the word; Jim remembered that Wrenn had said she was always ashamed of him. "He did not give you this information?"

"He only corroborated what we already knew. Now, please, Miss Legaye, for all our sakes, even for your sister's, tell me what you know."

"For my sister's?" she repeated.

"I don't know what you have to tell; but, seriously, one of the reasons why I have come to you is that I can't help hoping that you can supply some tiny link of evidence which will help to clear her. If you saw her leave the theater, for instance——"

She shook her head, with an air of deep depression.

"I did not see her leave the theater," she said quietly. "I did not see her at all."

"Did not see her! Then how——"

"Wait, Mr. Barrison, and I will tell you. I will tell you just exactly what happened, and you must believe me, for it is the truth. I did not see my sister, but—*I heard her voice!*"

Now that she had made up her mind to speak, the words came in a rush, as though she could not talk fast enough, as though she were feverish to get the ordeal over with.

"When I left you to go home, I had to pass his—Alan's—door, as you know. Just as I reached it, I heard voices inside—not loud, or I suppose they would have been stopped by some one, for the whole stage was supposed to be quiet while the act was on. But there was rather a noisy scene going on then—the bandits quarreling among themselves over the wine, you remember—and, anyway, the voices inside the dressing room could only be heard by some one who was standing very close to the door. I stopped for a moment, instinctively at first, and then—I heard my sister's voice, panting and excited!"

All this tallied with Wrenn's story. "Could you hear what she said?" asked Barrison.

"Only a word or two."

"What words?"

She flashed him a glance of deep appeal, then went hurriedly on:

"I heard her say 'Coward and cad,' and—and 'You ought to be shot, and you know it!' That's all."

All! It was quite enough. Barrison looked at her with faint pity, though he had felt at first that she was not sincere. She had a way of disarming him by unexpected evidence of true feeling just when he expected her to play-act. He could see that she was finding this pretty hard to tell.

"What did you do, Miss Legaye?"

"Do—I? Nothing. What was there for me to do? I went home."

"Didn't it occur to you to try to see your sister, to interfere in what seemed to be such a very violent quarrel?"

She shook her head vehemently.

"No, it did not. Why should it? My sister and I had nothing in common. I had not seen her for many years; I—I did not want to see her. For the rest—I knew that she hated Alan Mortimer, and if she was talking to him at all, it seemed quite natural that she should talk to him like that."

"You did not feel afraid, then—did not look on those chance phrases you heard as—well, a threat?"

She shuddered. "Oh, no; how could I? I thought she was just angry and excited. She always had a frightful temper. How could I guess that she had—anything else—in her mind?"

"So you went straight home, without waiting?"

"Yes." She bent her head, and added, in a low, troubled tone: "You will think me very selfish, very much a coward, Mr. Barrison, but—those angry voices made me want to get away as fast as possible. I hate scenes and quarrels and unpleasantness of all kinds. I was thankful to get out of the theater, and to know that I had not had to meet Marita, especially in the mood she was in then."

"I see," said Barrison, not without sympathy. "And is that all—really and absolutely all—that you know about the matter?"

Kitty hesitated, and then she lifted her head and faced him bravely.

"No," she said clearly, "it is not all. If you will wait a moment, I have something I ought to show you."

She rose and went to a desk, returning with an envelope. She sat down again and took a letter from this envelope, which she first read herself slowly and with a curious air of deliberation. Then she held it out to Barrison.

"I am going to trust you," she said, meeting his eyes proudly, "not to make use of this unless you have to. Wait, before you read it! When I knew of the horrible thing that had happened at the theater that night, I thought of my sister. I—I am afraid it is scarcely enough to say that I suspected her. I remembered the angry words I had heard her say inside the dressing room. I knew her ungovernable rages and the bitterness she had for Alan. And I knew that she was a wonderful shot, and that she had never got out of the habit of going armed. I—well, I felt very sure what had happened."

She was breathing quickly, and speaking in a hoarse, strained tone.

"I knew that there was more than a chance that some one else knew of her presence, and—I could not bear to have her arrested. I won't pretend that it was all sisterly affection, but I think it was that, too, in a way. I couldn't forget that, after all, we were of the same blood, and had been children and young girls together. I—I sent her money; I had seen in the paper that she and her husband were playing in New York, and I sent it to their theater, and with it I sent a note, begging her to lose no time in getting out of town. Was it—do you think it was very wrong?" she asked him rather piteously.

"It was at all events very natural," Jim answered, a little surprised and touched by what she had told him. "And may I read this now?"

"Yes, read it. It is Marita's answer to me. She accepted the money and sent me this letter."

With an odd movement of weariness and sorrow, she turned and laid her hands upon the back of her chair, and her face upon them.

The note was in the same scrawling hand that had made all the threats against Mortimer, that he knew to be that of Marita Blankley. And it ran thus:

Kitty: I am glad that you have some feeling as a sister left in you. I did not suppose that the day would ever come when it would be *you* who would help me get out of trouble! I dare say at that it was only your hatred of having our names linked together, or having any one know you knew me even! Of course I was a fool to go to the theater last night. I might have known what would happen. Now I am going to try to forget it all. I shall live only for my husband, and we shall get out of town as soon as possible! I can trust *you* not to talk, I know! There was never much love lost between us, Kitty.
Your sister,

Marita.

Barrison sat very still after reading this. At last he noticed that Kitty had lifted her head and was watching him with an anxious face.

"Well?" she demanded.

"You told me not to use this unless it were necessary," said Barrison very gravely. "It is necessary now, Miss Legaye. I must take it to headquarters at once!"

She gave a little cry.

"Oh, I was afraid—I was afraid!" she exclaimed. "You think it—it looks bad for her?"

"I think," said Jim Barrison, "that it is practically conclusive evidence!"

CHAPTER XXVIII
A STRANGE SUMMONS

IT WAS BARELY AN hour later, and Lowry and Barrison sat together in the inspector's office. Before them lay the letter which Kitty Legaye had given Jim, side by side with the threatening letter which had come to the Mirror Theater. The handwriting, as was to be foreseen, was identical. There, too, lay the photograph "swiped" by the reporter Lucas, showing the two young faces, so easily recognized now as the likenesses of Rita Blankley and Kitty. There was the pistol with its odd, non-committal initial, which had been identified as Rita's.

A telegram was handed to Lowry, and, after reading it, he passed it to Jim. It was signed with an initial only, obviously one of the inspector's regular men, and came from Indianapolis. It read:

Got your friends. All coming back on next train. G.

"The Blankleys?" asked Barrison.

"Sure. They'll be here to-morrow, and then I guess the case'll be over."

Just as Barrison was leaving the office, the inspector said casually:

"By the bye, Jim—if you want to take a look at the place where the Blankleys lived, here's the address on a card. I'd like you to go round there and have a look. You're the sort of fellow who gets on with people better than the regular officers. Will you?"

"Rather!"

Jim went off with his card, wondering just what the inspector meant. "The sort of fellow who gets on with people!" That sounded as though there were people on the premises whom the inspector had failed to pump satisfactorily. He decided to "take a look" without delay.

It turned out to be quite the usual type of furnished rooming house, kept by a faded, whining woman, with hair and skin all the same color.

It seemed that she had a boy—thirteen he was, though he looked younger. He went to school mostly, but he was a good deal more useful when he stayed away. "And what was the good of schooling to the likes of him?" said she.

Barrison refrained from shaking her till her teeth rattled, and soothingly extracted the rest.

Freddy, who appeared to be a sharp youngster from what she said, could always turn a pretty penny by acting as messenger boy for the "ladies and gents" in the house. Some of them were actors; more of them were not. It was fairly evident that the place was largely patronized by denizens of the shady side of society. Before Jim was done with the woman, he had ascertained that Freddy had more than once acted as messenger for the Blankleys, for whom, by the bye, she had a sincere respect. She said they were "always refined in their ways," and paid cash.

Barrison remembered that Roberts, the stage doorkeeper, had reported that the threatening letters had been delivered by a street urchin. He asked to see Freddy, but he was at school—for a wonder. His mother appeared to resent the fact, and to look upon it as so many hours wasted.

She promised that the evening would find him free to talk to the gentleman as much as the gentleman desired. Barrison had given her a dollar to start with, and promised another after he had conferred with Freddy.

When he left, he had an unsatisfied instinct that he had somehow missed something Lowry had expected him to get. The unseen Freddy was in his mind as he went uptown—in his mind to such an extent that he spoke of him to Tony Clay when he met him on Broadway and accepted that youth's urgent pleading to go to a place he knew of where they could get a good drink. The boy was in his mind when, on coming out of the café, they found themselves stormbound by crosstown traffic and looking in at the windows of Kitty Legaye's taxicab.

Her charming, white-skinned face framed in its short black veil and black ruff, lighted to intense interest as she caught sight of them.

"Have you any news?" she cried, in carefully subdued excitement.

Barrison could not bring himself to tell her that the police had caught up with her sister, and that she was on her way back to face her accusers. Kitty saw his hesitation, and thought it might be because Clay was present.

"Let me give you a lift!" she said impulsively.

Barrison accepted, after a second's cogitation. "Go on to my rooms, Tony," he said. "I'll be there shortly."

He got into the machine with Miss Legaye, and said to her gravely, as they began to move again:

"Tell me, please, Miss Legaye, you had no intercourse with your sister since she came to New York—I mean until you sent her the money, and she answered you?"

"None!" she said quickly and frankly.

"Did your letter come by mail or by a messenger boy?"

She started, and looked at him in surprise. "By mail," she replied. "Why?"

"Perfect nonsense," he said, really feeling that the impulse which had made him speak was an idle one. "I've found a boy who did a lot of errands for her, and I wondered if you could identify him, that's all."

She shook her head; though it was getting dusk, he could see her dark eyes staring at him.

"I don't know anything about that," she said. "What sort of a boy, and what do you expect to prove by him?"

"He's merely a witness," Barrison hastened to explain. "You see, the—the letter you let me have corresponds exactly in writing to the letters that came to Mortimer, threatening him. We think this is the boy who carried Mrs. Blankley's messages while she was in New York. That's all. You see, though it's a small link, it is one that we can't entirely overlook."

"Have you seen him?" she asked.

"No; I am to see him to-night," said Barrison. "And—Miss Legaye, I must tell you"—he hesitated, for he was a kind-hearted fellow—"I ought to warn you that you may have an unpleasant ordeal ahead of you. Your sister and her husband are—coming back to New York."

She was silent for half a minute.

"Thank you," she said. "You have been very good to—warn me. I don't think you will ever know how glad I am to have met you this afternoon, Mr. Barrison."

He did not pretend to understand her. As they had gone several blocks, he said good night with more warmth and consideration than he had ever expected to feel for Kitty Legaye, and, alighting from the taxi, made his way directly to his rooms.

He found Willie Coster awaiting him there, with his hair standing on end, and an expression of blank and rather appalled astonishment on his mild countenance.

"Say!" he cried, as Jim entered. "I went to call on the gov'nor this afternoon, and—he's sailed for London to put on three or four plays! And I'm out of a job! Now, what do you think of that?"

Barrison stood still in the center of the room and nodded his head slowly. So Dukane had heard the warnings in the air, and had slipped away! Well, it was only a matter of time! They had nothing criminal against him, but—the story would not make a pleasant one, as noised abroad about the greatest theatrical manager of America. Eventually, it would come out. However, meanwhile he had gone. He was sorry for Willie; sorry for the hundreds of actors and other employees who would suffer. It looked from what Willie had to tell that Dukane's exit had been a complete and clean-cut one. He had closed up his office, put his road companies in subordinate hands, and—cleared out.

"And I—who have been with him all these years—don't even get a company!" complained poor Willie.

Barrison remembered what Dukane had said to him about not being able to afford to consider any man personally. For some reason he had chosen to forget Willie Coster, and, true to form, he had forgotten him!

Tony Clay came in then. It was half past seven, nearly an hour later, when Tara reminded them politely of dinner.

"We'll go out somewhere," said Jim, rising and stretching himself. "You two shall be my guests. I feel that this case is practically over, and when I'm through with a case I feel like Willie after a first night—I want to relax. I don't want—at least not necessarily—to get drunk, but I do want to——"

Oddly enough, it was Tony Clay who interrupted him in a queer, abrupt sort of voice. He sounded like a man who hated to speak, but who was driven to it in spite of himself.

"Look here, you fellows," he said, "don't let's go out for dinner to-night."

"Why not?" demanded Barrison, in astonishment. "I thought you were always on the first call for a feed, Tony!"

"Oh, well, maybe I am. And—I know you think me an awful duffer in lots of ways, Jim, but—I have a hunch that perhaps——"

"That what?" demanded Jim, as he paused.

"That something is going to happen!" declared Tony defiantly. "Now call me a fool if you like! I shan't mind a bit, because I dare say I am one. But that's my hunch, and I'm going to stick to it. I don't know whether it's something good or something darned bad, but—if something doesn't turn up before another hour's out, I miss my guess!"

They laughed at him, but they stayed.

"Tony," said Barrison, after the lights were lighted and Tara had gone to prepare dinner, "you have something more than a hunch to go on. What is it? Out with it!"

"Well," said Tony unwillingly, "maybe I have something, but it's too vague for me to explain, yet. Only—I'd be just as pleased if we three stuck together to-night. That's all."

The boy spoke earnestly, and Barrison looked at him in real wonder.

"Tony," he said, "if you really know anything——"

The bell rang, and Tara brought in a telegram.

Barrison tore it open and read:

> Am in danger. Come to me, Ferrati's road house, two miles beyond Claremont, before nine. Come, for Heaven's sake, and mine.
>
> G. T.

Barrison gazed at the words in dazed stillness for a moment; then seized his hat.

"Stop, Jim!" cried Tony urgently. "You must tell us—you must tell me—what is the matter?"

Barrison shook his head as he dashed to the door.

"I can't tell any one anything!" he cried, as he went. "I am needed. Isn't that enough for any man?"

He was gone, and the door had slammed after him.

Tony quickly picked up the telegram which had fluttered to the floor. "Didn't I warn him?" he muttered.

CHAPTER XXIX
THROUGH THE NIGHT

ON—ON THROUGH THE BLUE dusk of the September evening.

Now that he found himself actually in the touring car that he had so impetuously engaged, Jim Barrison found his chaotic thoughts settling into some sort of approximate order, if not of repose. He began to analyze himself and this strange ride through the night.

He knew that suddenly he had forgotten the habit and the prompting of years; the caution that usually made him project himself into a possible future and meet it intelligently; the restraint and sensible skepticism which had always made him consider risks and appraise them, even while being quite as willing to take them as any other brave man. He knew that he had in a single moment forgotten all the training and the custom of his mature lifetime, because a woman had asked him to come to her!

A woman? That would not have been enough, he knew, in any other case. He was as chivalrous and as plucky as most men—a gallant gentleman in all ways; but his discretion would have aided his valor in any ordinary enterprise. As it was—he had been deaf and blind to any and all promptings save those that pounded in his ardent pulse. And all because a woman had sent for him! A woman? Say, rather, the woman! The one woman in the world who could so move him, change him, separate him from himself!

For the first time, but with characteristic honesty and thoroughness, Jim Barrison acknowledged to his own heart that he loved Grace Templeton.

He loved her, and he was going to her. The fact that she wanted him was enough. It was strange—some day when he was sane, perhaps, he would see how strange.

The chauffeur slowed up and turned to say over his shoulder:

"I guess it's here, sir. There's a sign that says Fer—something, and that's a road house in there, all right! Shall I drive in, sir?"

"Yes; go ahead."

The big car crept in slowly around the curving drive toward the low row of not too brilliant lights, for this road house was set far back from prying eyes. There were a few trees in front, too, which further enhanced the illusion of privacy. Barrison could not help noticing that, unlike most road houses, this one seemed bare of patrons for the nonce. There was not another automobile to be seen anywhere about.

He had heard of Ferrati's before. It was one of those discreet little out-of-town places, far away from the main road, hidden by trees, vines, and shrubbery, and known only to a certain selection among the elect. Whatever its true character, it masqueraded as modestly as a courtesan behind a cap and veil. Proper to the last degree was Ferrati's; any one could go there. The tone was scrupulously correct—if you frequented its main rooms. And the authorities saw nothing wrong with it. Ferrati himself saw to that!

But there were stories—Barrison had heard a few of them—which suggested that the resort, like some people, had a side not generally known to the public. It was even said that it was a headquarters for a certain blackmailing concern much wanted by the police; that all manner of underworld celebrities could be sure of a haven there in off hours, and that the bartender was nearly as skillful at knock-out drops as he was at mixed drinks.

How, Jim asked himself, had Grace Templeton ever got into these surroundings? Of course he sensed something queer about it all, and he could not help wondering despairingly whether that unquenchable thirst for adventure to which she had borne witness had been the means of bringing her inadvertently into such an unsavory neighborhood.

He did not dismiss the car, but told the man to wait, and, running up the short flight of steps at the front door, asked the rather seedy-looking maître d'hôtel, or whatever he was, for Miss Templeton.

The man did not seem to understand him, but a second individual, who was clearly his superior in position, made his appearance, and greeted Barrison politely and with some air of authority.

"Is your name Ferrati?"

"Giovanni Ferrati, if the signor pleases." He bowed, but Barrison had the impression that the man was watching him. He was dark and foreign looking, with a face like a rat.

"The signor wished——"

"I am to meet Miss Templeton here," said Barrison shortly.

The rat-faced one's expression cleared from a dubious look to delighted relief. So far as he was able, he beamed upon the newcomer.

"Ah, that is well! If the signor would come this way——"

Jim followed where he led, with an unaccountable sense of distrust and discomfort gaining place in his breast. For the first time, a genuine doubt assailed him. Suppose it were a trick, a trap? Nothing since he had first entered this "joint," as he savagely termed it to himself, had put him in any way at his ease. And at last he was conscious of a well-developed instinct of suspicion. It was not only what he had known before—that Grace was in trouble; it was a conviction that the whole situation was an impossible one—false, danger-ous, utterly unlike what he had been expecting. Suppose—he hardly dared to put his thoughts into words. He only knew that he found his environment singularly menacing. He could not tell what it was that was in the air, but it was something wicked and deadly. He wished that he had waited long enough to verify that telegram! If Grace Templeton had *not* sent it——

"This way, signor, if you please!" said the rat-faced man called Ferrati.

At the end of a dim and unsavory corridor, he turned the knob of a door.

"The lady awaits you, signor!" he said, with a remarkably unpleasant smile.

The room within was highly lighted, as Jim Barrison could see, even through the small space where it was held open by Ferrati. He walked in promptly.

On the instant, the lights were switched out—at the very second of his entrance. He could see nothing now; it was pitch dark.

Mingled with his rage was a perfectly human mental comment: "You idiot; it serves you right!"

For of course he was in a trap—a nice, neat trap, such as any baby might have walked into!

The door closed behind him quickly, and something straightway clicked.

He was locked into this mysterious room in this strange and murderous resort, and the darkness about him was that of the grave.

CHAPTER XXX
THE WHISPER IN THE DARK

DARKNESS IS A VERY strange thing. It is probably as strong and mysterious an agent when it comes to transmuting—and to deceiving—as anything on this earth. Nothing known to man is the same in the dark as at another time, and under the light.

It seemed to Jim Barrison that a series of pictures were being painted upon that cruel, that unfeeling, darkness. He had never, perhaps, been so close to himself before. The possibilities of human pain had certainly never been so apparent to the eyes of his mind. For suddenly, and with terrible clearness, he recalled his conversation with Grace Templeton, and seemed again to hear her say:

"Suppose the traveler who showed him the real gourd of water should refuse to share it, after all? What do you think would be likely to happen then?"

And once more he could hear himself reply:

"I should think the thirsty man would be quite likely to shoot him!"

And then—then—what was it she had said, with that enigmatical smile of hers?

"Yes, that's just what might happen!"

Yes, that's just what might happen! She had said that. How much had she meant by it, and how much had she meant it? He did not know. But, though he was not willing to apply it too closely as a key to his present position, he could not bring it to mind without a strange chill. For, if there were women of that kind, he was sure that she—lovely and idealistic as she was—was one of them.

He stood still, perfectly still, straining his ears, since it would have been utterly vain to have strained his eyes. For a time he even heard nothing. Yet he was poignantly conscious of another presence there—whose?

He was afraid to permit himself much in the way of conjecture; that sharp and taunting memory was still too fresh with him. He would rather a thousand times over that he had been tricked and trapped by some desperate criminal determined to torture him to death than that *she* should have thus deliberately led him here, should have thus cruelly traded upon her certain knowledge of his interest in her! The thing would not bear thinking of; it could not be!

He scarcely breathed as he stood there, motionless, waiting for that other's first movement. He was so tensely alert that it seemed strange to him that the other could even breathe without his hearing it. He wished for a revolver, and cursed himself for the precipitancy which had carried him off without it.

And then he heard—what he had dreaded most of all to hear—the faint, almost imperceptible rustle of a woman's dress!

It was the veriest ghost of a rustle, as though the very lightest and thinnest of fabrics had been stirred as delicately as possible.

But—it *was* a woman, then!

"Who is it?" he demanded, and his voice to his own ears seemed to resound like an experimental shout in one of the world's famous echoing caverns.

And the answer came in a whisper—a woman's whisper:

"Hush!"

Then there was a long, blank, awful silence, and then the rustle once again. And again that sibilant breath voiced:

"Can you tell where I am standing?"

"Who are you?" Barrison repeated, though dropping his own voice somewhat.

"Please don't speak so loud!" He could barely hear the words. "I am Grace Templeton—surely you know?"

"Why are you whispering?"

"Because we may be overheard. Because there is danger, very great danger!"

"Danger—from whom?"

"Come closer, please! I am so afraid they will hear! Can't you place me at all? If you are still at the door—are you?"

"Yes."

"Then come forward to the right, only a few steps, and then wait."

Now it has already been pointed out in these pages that the dark is paramountly deceptive. Barrison could not accurately locate the woman who was whispering to him; neither could he entirely identify the voice itself. If you will try the experiment of asking a number of different people to assemble in pitch darkness and each whisper the same thing, you will probably find that it is painfully easy to mistake your bitterest enemy for your very nearest and dearest friend. Jim Barrison had no soul thrill, nor any other sort of evidence, to assure him that the woman in the dark room was Grace Templeton; on the other hand, there was nothing to prove her any one else.

And yet—and yet—he had a curious, creeping feeling of dread and suspicion. He did not trust this unknown, unidentified, whispering voice in the darkness.

It came again then, like the very darkness itself made audible; insistent, soft, yet indefinitely sinister:

"Come! Come here to me! Only a few steps forward and just a little to the right."

Barrison took one single step forward, and then stopped suddenly.

He did not know what stopped him. He only knew that he *was* stopped, as effectually and as imperatively as if some one in supreme authority had put out a stern, restraining hand before him.

And then, all at once, something happened—one of those tiny things that sometimes carry such huge results on their filmy wings. The whisper came again, more urgently this time:

"Aren't you going to come to me, when I'm in danger?"

When people are born in the West, they carry certain things away from it with them, and it matters not how long they are gone nor in what far parts they choose to roam, they never get rid of those special gifts of their native soil. One is the slightly emphasized "r" of ordinary speech. No Easterner can correctly mimic it; no Westerner can ever get away from it except when painstakingly acting, and endeavoring to forget that to which he was born. The two r's in the one brief sentence were of the nature to brand any one as a Westerner. And Barrison knew that Grace Templeton had never spoken with the ghost of such an accent in her life. Who was it whom he had heard speak recently who did accentuate her r's like that? Marita did! And one other—though much more delicately and——

He remembered, with a throb of excited pleasure on dismissing a hideous suspicion from his mind, and on entering normally into the joys of chance and danger, that he had one weapon which might turn out to be exceedingly useful in his present predicament. He had come away without his gun, but he had with him the tiny pocket lamp, the electric torch of small dimensions but great power, which had been the joy of his life ever since it had been given him. Like all nice men, he was a child in his infatuated love of new toys!

He drew the little cylinder from his coat pocket cautiously, and, with the same exultant feeling that an aviator doubtless knows when he drops a bomb on a munitions factory, he flashed it.

The result was surprising.

Straight in front of him was a square, black hole in the floor. If he had taken that step forward and to the right which she had urged, he would have gone headlong to practically certain death. The human brain, being quicker than anything else in the universe, reminded him that there had been some unexplained disappearances in this neighborhood. But he was now chiefly concerned in finding out who the woman was. Before he could flash his light in her face she had flung herself upon him.

There was no more pretense about her. She was grimly, fiercely determined to force him toward that wicked, black hole into eternity. Not a single word did she utter; she did not even call for assistance, though, since the people in this house were her friends or tools, she might well have done so. She seemed consumed by one single, burning desire: to thrust him with her own hands into the pit.

Never had Jim struggled against such ferocity of purpose. She was like a demon rather than a woman, in the way she writhed between his hands, and forced her limited strength against his trained muscles in the bold and frantic effort to annihilate him. And, in that dense blackness, it was a toss-up as to who would win. The woman herself might easily have gone headlong into the very trap she had planned for him. But she did not seem to think or to care for that; her whole force of being was centered, it seemed, in the one sole purpose of his destruction.

At that furious, struggling moment, Barrison became convinced of an odd thing. He was perfectly certain, against all the testimony of all the world, that the woman who fought him so murderously was not only the woman who had planned his own death that night, but also the criminal for whom they were so assiduously seeking. He was sure that his hands at that very minute grasped the person who had killed Alan Mortimer.

It seemed to last forever, that silent, breathless struggle in the dark. But finally he got her hands pinioned behind her in one of his, and deliberately, though with a beating heart, raised his electric torch and flashed it full in her face.

Mutinous, defiant, almost mad with rage for the moment, the dark eyes of Kitty Legaye blazed back at him.

CHAPTER XXXI
TONY DOES HIS BIT

THINGS HAPPENED VERY RAPIDLY in Jim Barrison's rooms after he had made his hasty departure. Tony Clay stood for a moment, holding the telegram in his hand; and then, tossing it to Willie Coster, he made a jump for the telephone. There he called Spring 3100, and, getting his number, demanded Inspector Lowry in a voice that might have been the president's for authority, and a Bloomingdale inmate's for agitation.

"Now, now," came the deep, official tones from the other end of the wire; "hold your horses, my friend! Is it an accident or a murder?"

"It's probably both," stormed Tony.

He had the inspector on the wire, and was pouring out his tale, trying his best to keep himself coherent with the ever-present picture in his brain of Jim in trouble. Tony was not one of the most inspired of detectives, but he was as good a friend as ever a man had, and he loved Jim.

It happened that Lowry had a weakness for Jim himself. Also, the story told by Tony was, though wild, certainly one to make any police official sit up and take notice. Ferrati's, as has already been suggested, was not looked upon favorably by the police.

He told Tony Clay that he would come up to Ferrati's himself with a couple of men.

"And we'll stop for you," he said, meaning to be most kind and condescending.

Tony retorted hotly: "I'm leaving for Ferrati's now! I can't wait for the police department to wake up!"

He hung up viciously and turned to face Willie Coster, also Tara, who, though less demonstrative than these Occidentals, was clearly about as anxious as either of them.

"Tara, get a taxi!" said Tony briefly.

"Immediate, honorable sir!"

Tara's alacrity was rather pathetic. Willie Coster looked after him with a kindly nod.

"D'you know," he remarked, in a low tone, "that Jap is just as keen to help Barrison as we are. You'll find when we start out after him he won't let himself be left behind."

Tony turned to scowl at him in bewilderment.

"When 'we' start out after him!" he repeated. "You aren't expecting to spring anything of that sort, are you?"

Willie Coster looked at him a moment only. Then his small, pinched face blazed suddenly into fiery red.

"Say," he snapped, "do you think you're the only he-man on the premises? And do you suppose that no one else is capable of a friendly feeling for Barrison, and a natural wish to help him out of a mess, except just your blessed self? Because, if that's what you think, you forget it—quick!"

Tony felt abject, and would have apologized, too, but a snorting arose in the street below them, and Tara announced the taxi which, in some inscrutable way, he had maneuvered there in more than record time.

Tony recalled what Willie Coster had said.

"Tara," he said abruptly, "you are fond of Mr. Barrison, I know."

"Yes, sir," Tara said.

"We think Mr. Barrison is in danger. We are going to see what we can do for him. Now remember, there isn't a reason in the world why you should come too, only——"

The Jap spoke in his elaborately polite way:

"Honorably pardon, sir! There is reason."

"But——" Tony was beginning, but he never finished. He saw the reason too plainly. Tara, like himself and like Willie, was too fond of Barrison to stay away. That was reason enough.

"All right, Tara, you come along!" he said, turning away. And his voice might have been a bit husky.

"Where, first?" said Coster, as they entered the taxicab. And there were three of them, too!

Tony gave the name of the hotel where Miss Templeton lived, which was not so far away. Once there, he left his companions in the taxi and went up alone to interview the lady. In his hand, tightly crumpled with the vehemence of his intense feeling, he kept the telegram which had come for Jim Barrison, signed with her initials.

He penciled a note to Miss Templeton which made her send for him as soon as she received it.

They knew each other, but she was so excited that she did hardly more than acknowledge his hasty bow.

"Mr. Clay," she exclaimed, "what does it all mean? I know you would not have sent me this message without a reason! You say: 'Mr. Barrison is in grave danger because of you. Will you help me to save him?'" She confronted Tony with pale cheeks and wide eyes. "Now, Mr. Clay, you know that such a thing is impossible! How could Mr. Barrison be in danger on my account without my knowing it? And I swear to you that I can think of nothing in all the world which could subject him to danger—because of me! Nevertheless, I cannot let a thing like this go—no woman could! If there is danger to Mr. Barrison, I should know it! If it is, in some way, connected with me, I should know it all the more, and care about it all the more! What is it?" Suddenly she dropped the rather haughty air which she had assumed and clasped her hands like a frightened child. "Oh, Mr. Clay, you know that I would do anything to help him! What is it? What is it?"

By way of answer, Tony handed her the telegram.

After she had read it, she held it in rigid fingers for a moment; it seemed they were not able to drop it. She looked at Tony Clay.

"And, receiving this," she murmured faintly, "he—went?"

"He went," answered the young man, "so fast that we could not stop him; though I, for one, suspected something shady, and had warned him he must be on his guard."

It is probable that in all his life Tony Clay never understood the look that flamed in the woman's face before him now. In that strange combination of emotions was pain and fear, but there was also joy and triumph.

"So he cared like that!" she murmured.

And then, before Tony Clay could even be sure that she had uttered the words, she had changed again to a practical and utilitarian person. She seized a long raincoat from the back of a chair and said immediately:

"I am ready. Shall we go?"

Tony glowered at her. Another one? Aloud he remarked:

"If you will merely testify that you did not send that telegram——"

She looked as though she would have liked to slap him in her exasperation.

"Of course I didn't!" she raged. "But what has that to do with this situation? I thought you said he was—in danger?"

"I am afraid he is. Very well, ma'am; if you must come, you must. We have rather a larger crowd than I had expected at first."

It was impossible for him to avoid an injured tone.

However they felt about it, Miss Templeton went with them. When the light of passing street lamps fell upon her face, it had the look of an avenging angel.

On the way, she insisted that Tony should tell them what had made him suspicious as to danger awaiting Barrison that night. And after a little hesitation he told—this:

"You know Jim had put me onto the Legaye end of the case—had suggested my talking to the maid, and all that. Well, I did it, and, as a matter of fact, I got in deeper than I expected to." He looked at each of them defiantly, but no one seemed disposed to sit in judgment, so he continued: "Maria—she's quite a nice girl, too, and don't let anybody forget it—told me to-day that her lady was terrifically upset about something."

"When was that?" demanded Coster.

"Late in the afternoon, just before I came to dinner—to the dinner that didn't come off. Jim and I parted when he took a ride in Miss Legaye's taxi, and he left me to come on to join him alone."

"Did you come straight on?"

"Yes," said Tony, "I did. But something happened on the way, and that has given me the clue to—to—what's taking us out here."

"Well, tell it, for Heaven's sake!"

"Well, it seems," said Tony unwillingly, yet with the evident realization that he was doing the right thing, "it seems that Miss Legaye was in the habit of going shopping with her maid—Maria—and of dropping her when she was tired—I mean when Miss Legaye was tired, not Maria—and leaving her to come on with packages and so on. She had done that to-day. Just after she and Jim Barrison had gone on, I met Maria, and I stayed with her, too"—defiantly—"until after the time I should have been at Jim's rooms!"

"Not very long, was it?"

"Not more than half an hour, I'm sure."

"And in that time, what could have happened that——"

"Nothing happened. Nothing could have happened. It was only that—that——" Tony swallowed hard, and then went on courageously: "She asked me when her mistress had gone home, and I told her just a few minutes before. Then she said she must telephone her, if we were to have a moment together. She said that she could easily make out an excuse. And, though I had no—no particular interest in Maria," faltered poor Tony unhappily, "I couldn't see what I could do to get out of that! And—and she did telephone, and when she came back from telephoning," he said, speaking carefully, and evidently trying his best to make the thing sound as commonplace as possible, "she told me that her mistress had just come in, and that she was so excited she could scarcely speak, and she wanted Maria at once, and that she had told Maria that if ever she had cared anything about her, she must be prepared to stand by her now—and to hurry—hurry—hurry—hurry! That's what poor Maria kept repeating to herself. And that's what I had in my mind when I went into Jim's rooms, for it was the last thing in my mind.

"I was afraid then and there of Miss Legaye's doing something—queer—but before I had a chance to tell Jim what I thought—that message came, and he was off!"

Almost directly they were at Ferrati's and confronting Ferrati himself, who looked alarmed at the sight of these visitors.

It required small astuteness to see that his party was an unexpected one, and that the unexpectedness was only rivaled by the lack of welcome.

Finding that ordinary and moderately courteous inquiries were only met with extreme haziness of perception, Tony saw that he would have to push his way in.

He glanced over his shoulder and saw that Willie Coster expected the same result; also that Tara looked mildly pleased. Doubtless he was pondering enjoyably upon jujutsu and what it could accomplish. Considered collectively, the party was not one to be ignored.

As though to put an exclamation point after the sound sense of the rest, Miss Templeton, who had been extremely quiet through it all, suddenly drew out a revolver from the pocket of her raincoat. Tony thrilled, for it was the one that he had seen her buy.

"Before we fight our way in," she said amiably enough, "suppose we try just walking in? I don't believe that these poor creatures will make much trouble."

She smiled, not too pleasantly, at the poor creatures.

But they did!

They made so much trouble that it took the lot of them fifteen minutes to get to that dark inner room where Jim Barrison was imprisoned. By that time Lowry and three good men had arrived in a racing car, and by the same time, Tony Clay had been put out of business by two of Ferrati's "huskies."

"Never mind about me!" he had implored them. "Get Jim out!"

They did. And they found Jim blinking at them out of that awesome darkness, holding Kitty in an iron grip. He was rather white, but he tried to smile.

"Suppose you take her?" was his first utterance. "She's one handful."

Kitty, once in the hands of the officers, shrugged her shoulders and changed her tune.

"What a lot of fools you are!" she exclaimed contemptuously. "You had the clue in your hands a dozen times over! It was only to-day that this fellow got onto it, though, and so"—again she shrugged her shoulders—"I had to finish him, if I could, hadn't I?"

CHAPTER XXXII
THE LOST CLUE

FERRATI WAS THE SELFSAME man who had first induced Kitty to run away from her home, her father, and her sister. As she had progressed, she had grown away from him and his evil influences; but, as often happens in a situation of this sort, when she found herself in trouble of a criminal nature, she had gravitated most naturally back to the man who, she was sure, could help her out of her problem.

Face to face with each other in the inspector's own office, neither Kitty nor Ferrati had the nerve to hold out; between them, as a matter of fact, they cleared up sundry police mysteries which had worried the heads and irritated the underlings for months past.

The trap set for Jim Barrison elucidated a good many mysteries and showed the way in which several rich men had disappeared from the face of the earth. The trapdoor was not in any sense a secret one; it had been seen by half a dozen policemen during the energetic investigations of Ferrati and his establishment which had gone on from time to time ever since it had become generally known that men who subsequently disappeared had been "last seen dining at Ferrati's." But the explanation had been so simple and there had been so little attempt, seemingly, at subterfuge or evasion, that the law had been put off the scent so far as that trapdoor was concerned.

The room in which it was situated was a kind of pantry, and directly under it was a part of the cellar. Like many restaurant keepers, he had bought an old country house and made it over into a resort. Thrifty Italian that he was, he had made as few and as inexpensive alterations as possible in the actual structure of the building, and had found it cheaper to put in a trapdoor and a ladder than to build a complete staircase reaching to his cellar. This was the explanation that he gave the police, and it was probably true, and was assuredly logical.

What became apparent now, however, was that the trapdoor had served other ends than that of legitimate café service. What could be easier than to inveigle a man into the room and get rid of him through the cellar door? As for the disposal of the body, that, too, was quaintly provided for and covered by

Ferrati's business. Every morning, just at dawn, the restaurant garbage was carted away. It was not difficult to carry other and more ghastly things away at the same time; and the road is lonely at that hour. A couple of discreet henchmen could quite easily drop something over the cliffs in the direction of the river. But, after all, this was a secondary matter for the moment.

The great thing was that they knew now who had fired the seventh shot. It only remained to find out how it had been done, for even after Kitty had admitted it, the thing seemed impossible from the facts which they had securely established.

She did not in the least mind telling them about it. She told her story with simplicity and directness. In her curious, calculating little head there was not the slightest trace of regret or remorse for what she had done. Barrison, watching her, remembered his talk with Wrenn, and seemed to descry in the daughter the same strange bias he had noted in the father; the same profound selfishness, the same complete absence of conscience where her own wrongdoing was concerned. It also appeared clear that only one person had ever sincerely touched the heart of either of them, and that was the man who was dead.

There was one thing that Kitty did truly grieve for, and that was Mortimer's death. Whether it was because she had loved him, or because in losing him, she had lost the chance of marrying and so squaring her somewhat twisted and clouded past, would never be known to any one but herself. That she did grieve, however odd it might appear, was certain.

The detectives exchanged glances of wonder as they realized how simple the case had been from the very first, once given the clue. As for the clue itself, Barrison had had it once, but had lost it. It was, as he had at one time suspected, that red evening coat. It had left the theater exactly when it was supposed to have left; only—it was not Kitty who had worn it!

It was the morning after the episode at Ferrati's, and Lowry was holding an informal inquiry. None of them who were present would ever forget it—nor the enchanting picture which the self-confessed murderess presented as she sat there with a poise that her situation could not impair, looking exquisite in the swathing black which she wore for the man whom she had herself killed!

Inspector Lowry was, for once in his life, totally at a loss, absolutely nonplused. To Barrison, and the other men who knew him well, his blank amazement in the face of the phenomenon represented by Kitty Legaye was, to say the least of it, entertaining.

At last he remarked, still staring at her as though hypnotized: "It is a most remarkable case! Miss Legaye, if you feel the loss of this man so deeply—and

I am convinced that you do, in spite of the paradox it presents—why, if you don't mind, did you shoot him?"

She flashed him a scornful glance. "Shoot him!" she repeated vehemently. "You surely don't suppose for one moment that I meant to shoot him?"

"But——" the inspector was beginning.

"Shoot *him*!" she rushed on, with a different emphasis. "Of course I didn't! It is the sorrow of my life that it turned out in that horrible manner. No; it was that Merivale woman whom I meant to shoot! He was making love to her, and I couldn't stand it! I aimed at her, but—but—I suppose he was closer to her than I thought, and—it happened!"

She bit her lips and clenched her small hands. They could all see that it was only with the greatest difficulty and by the most tremendous effort that she was able to control the frenzy of her rage and despair over that fatal mischance.

"At that, I hadn't planned to kill even her," she went on, after a moment or two. "Not then, at any rate. But when the opportunity came, sent straight from heaven as it seemed," said this astounding, moralless woman most earnestly, "I simply could not help it."

"Suppose you tell us what actually happened."

"Why not, now? What I told him"—she looked at Jim Barrison—"was all quite true up to the point where I stopped at Alan's door and heard my sister's voice. The rest, of course, was different. What I really did then was to wait, listening to the struggle and quarrel inside until I could make out that my—my father was succeeding in separating them. The door opened and Marita almost staggered out, with her waist all torn and her hair half down. She looked dreadful, and I was so afraid some one would see her.

"At the same second I saw the pistol lying just inside the door. Alan said: 'Shut that door!' Neither he nor my father had seen me. I bent down quickly and, reaching in, picked up the pistol. The next second my father had shut the door very quietly and quickly, for no lights were to be shown in the theater.

"I still had no real intention of using the thing that night. I just picked it up, acting on an impulse. Besides, I didn't think that my sister was in any state to handle it then; so I kept it, and did not give it to her. Then I pulled off my evening coat and made Marita put it on."

"One moment, with Inspector Lowry's permission," Barrison interrupted. "All that must have taken time, Miss Legaye, and there were people all around you. I myself was only a short distance away."

"You were standing up stage," she informed him tranquilly, "and the stairway going to the second tier of dressing rooms masked Alan's door from where you were. As for the time, it took scarcely a minute; it happened like lightning. Such things take time to tell about, but not to do."

"And in giving your sister your wrap, you were trying to shield her, and were moved by sisterly affection?" suggested the inspector sympathetically.

"Indeed I was not!" snapped Kitty resentfully. "I never had the least affection for my sister! I was moved by the fear of a lot of talk and scandal. I wanted to get her out of the theater, and out of my life entirely, and the quickest way I could think of was to give her my coat and send her home in my taxi."

"Why did you not go with her?"

"Haven't I told you I wanted to get rid of her? I didn't think of anything but that for a moment, and then—then something else came over me, after she had gone."

Her tone had changed. It was plain that she was no longer merely narrating something; she was living it again. She was again stirred by what had stirred her on that fateful night; no eloquence in the world could have made her hearers so vividly see what she saw, nor so gravely appreciate what she had felt, as the expression which she now wore—a terrible, introspective expression, the look of one who lives the past over again.

"Sybil Merivale was waiting for him at the top of the little flight of steps, and—I had the pistol still in my hand. Even then I was not perfectly determined on killing her. I hated her and I feared her, but I had not planned anything yet. There was a dark scarf over my arm; I slipped that over my head so that it shaded my face from any chance light, and I slipped across the few feet of distance and stood just below her, close by the steps.

"Then Alan came out of his room. There was no light, for he had had them put out, of course, according to Dukane's directions, for the dark scene which was almost on. I stood so near that I could have touched him as he went up two steps and stopped, and laughed under his breath and spoke to her."

Again she fought for self-control, and again she won it, though her face looked older and harder when she began to speak once more.

"He was trying to make love to her, and she would have nothing to do with him."

"Didn't that make you hate her less?" queried Lowry, being merely a man.

"It made me hate her more! She was throwing aside something which I would have risked anything to get! I went mad for the moment. Then the shots began, and it was pitch dark. I—I found myself lifting my hand slowly, and pointing it. I knew just where she was standing. It seemed to me I could scarcely miss. When I had heard what I thought was the fifth shot, I fired. I suppose I was excited and confused, and counted wrong. I meant my shot to come at the same time as the last shot; that would have given me a longer time to get away. As it was, she screamed, and I was sure I had hit her. And I was very glad!

"But I had no time to make sure. There was commotion and confusion, and I had to get away. I did not dare to go out through the stage entrance where there was a light. I knew my way to the communicating door, and I took a chance that the lights would not go up until I was through it. I brushed past the man who was supposed to guard it, in the dark, but I suppose he was too excited to notice. I got through and ran down past the boxes to the front of the house. People were already beginning to come out, and there was a lot of confusion. I had my dark scarf over my head, so I easily passed for one of the women in the audience who had turned faint and wanted air. I walked quietly out of the lobby and hailed a taxi. That's all."

"What did you do then?"

"I went home—to my hotel. I didn't go in by the front way, but through the side entrance, and slipped into my room without meeting any one. I sent out for some chloral, for I knew I could not sleep without it, but I would not let my maid see me, for she would have noticed that I was without my coat."

"And the coat?"

"Marita sent it back to me in the morning before Maria came to the door. I put it on a chair by the window so that it would seem to have been rained on that way. When the boy brought it, it was pouring outside, and the wet had soaked through the paper wrapping."

There was a short silence. The mystery was solved. It was curious to think that this small, black-clad figure was the criminal. Yet—when one looked deep into Kitty's eyes, one might discern something of her Mexican mother's temperament and her time-serving father's selfishness which could explain her part in this tragedy.

"And did you still believe that it was Miss Merivale that you had killed?" asked Inspector Lowry.

"Yes; I believed it until that man"—again indicating Jim—"came to me in the morning and told me of Alan's death. It was a frightful shock."

"I should imagine that it might have been," remarked the inspector thoughtfully. "And when did you decide that it was—er—advisable—to get rid of him?" pointing to Barrison.

"Yesterday afternoon, when he told me that you were bringing my sister back, and that he was going to have an interview in a short time with the boy who had done her errands. I knew then that he would soon learn too much. It was that boy who brought me the red coat the morning after Alan's death, and I did not want him to talk."

"But surely you did not think that investigations would stop just because you had got Mr. Barrison out of the way?"

She shook her head. "I didn't reason about it very clearly," she said. "I had been under a good deal of strain, you must remember. All I thought of was that he was on my track, and that the sooner I put him where he couldn't harm me, the better for me. So far as any one else was concerned, I suppose, if I thought of them at all, I thought that it was worth a chance. I've got out of some pretty tight places before now; I'm always inclined to hope till the last moment."

"I am afraid, Miss Legaye," said the inspector seriously, "that you have come to that last moment now."

She glanced at him, and she had never looked more charming. "Sure?" she said, in her prettiest, most ingénue way. "I haven't been before a jury yet, you know, and—and men usually like me!"

The inspector was red with indignation. But more than one of the men present suppressed a chuckle at his rage and Kitty's composure.

"Why," asked Jim, "did you sign Miss Templeton's name to that decoy telegram of yours?"

Kitty shrugged her shoulders. "I certainly couldn't sign my own, could I?" she rejoined calmly. "And she'd been suspected at the beginning. She seemed a good one to pick."

There was not much more to clear up, but Barrison was on the point of putting one more question when an officer came in and whispered to the inspector.

"Bring them in," he said at once.

The new arrivals were the Blankleys, accompanied by the detective who had found them in Indianapolis. They looked frightened, but Lowry quickly relieved their minds and assured them that they would only be required as witnesses.

The meeting between the sisters was curious. Seeing them together for the first time, Barrison saw the resemblance plainly, though Rita looked more Mexican than Kitty, and was, he knew, far the better woman of the two.

"Well, Kit?" said she quietly, almost compassionately, but Kitty looked straight in front of her, and neither then nor at any other time deigned to recognize her existence.

Barrison prompting the inspector, the latter turned to Marita and held out the letter which Jim had turned over to him the day before, the note which both he and the younger man had accepted as conclusive evidence of her guilt.

"Did you write this, Mrs. Blankley?" he asked.

She glanced down the page and nodded. "Certainly," she responded; "when I returned the coat Kitty had lent me."

When they read it over, they found that its wording was innocent enough. It was only Kitty's evil ingenuity which had twisted it deliberately.

"Did you really hate me as much as all that, Kit?" asked Marita, almost in wonder, but Kitty said never a word, and did not even look in her direction.

A little later, Jim Barrison was bidding Inspector Lowry good-by.

"The inquest is to-day," remarked the inspector, who was smoking very hard and looking very bland and satisfied. "And we won't have to have any 'person or persons unknown' verdict this time! Found the murderer inside of forty-eight hours! We didn't do so badly, eh, my boy?"

Barrison dropped his eyes to hide an involuntary twinkle at the "we."

"Splendid, sir!" he declared cordially. "Good-by! I'm off to make a few extra inquiries—of a strictly personal nature."

CHAPTER XXXIII
THE FALSE GODS GO

"WELL?" DEMANDED MISS TEMPLETON, at whose apartment Jim Barrison presented himself in record time after leaving headquarters. "And is the case now closed?"

"Not quite," said Barrison, putting down his hat and stick deliberately and standing facing her.

She was standing, too; and, as she was a tall woman, her eyes were not so very much below his own. She was, he thought, most splendidly beautiful as she stood there gravely looking at him.

"Not quite," he repeated, in a voice he had never before permitted himself to use in speaking to her. "I want to ask a few more questions, please?"

She nodded, still watching him in that deep, intent fashion.

"First," pursued Jim, trying to speak steadily and to keep to the unimportant things, even while his heart was throbbing violently, "why did you always suspect Kitty Legaye?"

"Because I had an instinct against her; also because I was sure that she knew that man Wrenn. I could tell by the way that they looked at each other that they were not strangers, though I never knew them to speak to each other. And, you see, I knew that he was connected with Alan Mortimer's old life. The suspicion seemed to slip in naturally."

"And at any time—at any time, mind you—did you have it in your mind to kill Mortimer yourself?"

"Never!" she returned at once, and firmly.

He paused a moment, looking full into the clearest eyes that ever a woman had.

"Grace," he said, calling her so for the first time, "why did you buy that revolver?"

She colored painfully, but her eyes met his as truthfully as before. "Ah, you knew that!" she said. "I had hoped that you did not. However, what can it matter now? I am very much changed since the day I bought that revolver. You know that, I think?"

"I know it," he acknowledged gently.

"I was terribly hurt, terribly outraged, terribly disappointed. You must always remember that I am a woman of wild emotions. I felt myself flung aside—not only in love, but in my profession. I had lost my part, and I had lost the man who, after all, I had believed I loved."

"And did *you* want to kill Sybil Merivale, too?"

She stared at him in astonishment. "Kill Sybil Merivale!" she repeated. "Why on earth should I? I had nothing against the girl, except that I believe I was a little jealous of her youth and freshness just at first. No; I had made up my mind to kill myself."

"Yourself!"

"Yes. Didn't you guess? I had an idea that you did, and that that was one reason for your keeping so near me all that evening in the box. I had the insane impulse to kill myself then and there, and spoil Alan's first night!" She laughed a little, though shakily, at the recollection. "It was ridiculous, melodramatic, anything you like, but women have done such things, and—and I'm afraid I am rather that sort. I meant to do it, anyway."

"And—why didn't you? You had the revolver; I felt it in your bag on the back of the chair. Why didn't you?"

He had not known that a woman's eyes could hold so much light.

"You know," she said softly and soberly. "You were there. You had come into my life. The false gods go when the gods arrive!"

There was a long stillness between them, in which neither of them stirred, nor took their eyes away.

"You—love me?" Jim said, in a queer voice.

"Yes."

When he let her leave his arms, it was only that he might look again into her eyes and touch that wonderful golden hair, now loose and soft about her face.

"It—it isn't dyed!" she said hastily. "I did make up, but my hair was always that color—truly!"

"Oh, my dear, my dear!" he laughed, though with tears and tenderness behind the laughter. "What do I care whether it is dyed or not? It's just a part of you."

A little later a whimsical idea came to him.

"You know," he said, "the inspector said to me yesterday that in drawing in our nets we sometimes found that we had captured some birds that we had never expected. I didn't know how right he was, for—we two seem to have caught the Blue Bird of Happiness, after all!"

"And I am sure," said Grace Templeton solemnly, "that no one ever really caught it before!"

www.ingramcontent.com/pod-product-compliance
Lightning Source LLC
Chambersburg PA
CBHW011445170626
46816CB00008B/2531